The Jäger Journal

By John A. Anderson III

To Sandy —
my wife, and the love of my life,

and in memory of Susan Pitto,
my sister,
who fought the good fight
and lay hold on eternal life.

Acknowledgments

This is my first foray into the world of novels, and I must extend my thanks to the family and friends who have helped and encouraged me every step of the journey. To my editor and friend, Pat Clemens, I say thanks for all you have done in editing and encouraging. You are truly a wordsmith of the first degree and have rendered invaluable assistance with grammar, punctuation, vocabulary, and general plot development and refinement. You inspired me to keep forging onward, chapter by chapter. To Will Kelly, thank you for the time and talent you have invested in the striking art work for the cover of *The Jäger Journal*. To Bradley and Kathleen, my children, thanks so much for your interest in the project from the beginning and your expertise through the end to get the book to publication. To my sons Nathaniel and Wallace, I greatly appreciate the ideas and insight on various weapons from different time periods. To my daughter Marian, you took my picture for the book and put me in the best light. To the rest of my sons and daughter and daughters-in-law, John, Jonna, Daniel, Melodie, Michael, and Deborah, I am grateful you kept cheering your dad on to finish this novel. To my parents, Colonel and Mrs. John Anderson Jr., thanks for giving me a love for reading and an excellent education. To my office staff and countless patients from my office who were genuinely excited to hear about this evening and weekend project of their family doc, thanks for your encouragement. To Peter Sherrouse and Lyle Vihon, I appreciate the help with the details of cyber security for the plot. Sincere thanks to you and many others that provided bits of detail information. Thanks to Jordan Kelly for editing assistance. And finally, to my wife, Sandy, my only lover and my very best friend, I thank you for blessing me beyond measure every day.

Contents

Cast of Characters

Harrison family

Jack Harrison- contractor, father of five, husband of Jean, high school educated. Age 53.

Jean Harrison- wife of Jack, mother of five, college graduate with a nursing degree from University of Georgia. Age 51.

Stuart Harrison- eldest son of Jack and Jean, former Air Force parajumper, high school coach and math teacher, walk on football player in college at Valdosta State University , married to Leigh, 2 children. Lives in Stone Mountain, Georgia. Age 30.

Annette Harrison- architect with Holland and Hatton Architects, single. Lives in Charlotte, North Carolina. Age 28.

Michelle Harrison Black- part-time accountant with Chick Fil-A, married, no children. Lives in Atlanta suburb. Husband Zach Black, electrician. Age 27

Glen Harrison- tax attorney, widowed. Wife died by drowning in a swimming accident. Lives and works in Manhattan, New York. Age 24.

Jim Harrison- youngest child of the Harrisons, journalism student in Barcelona, Spain, friend of Greta Rose. Age 20.

Mosby- family dog, male, golden retriever.

Mohawk- family cat, black and gray, male Maine Coon.

Axis

Benito Mussolini- leader of Fascist Italy.

Adolph Hitler- leader of Nazi Germany.

Heinrich Pfeister- sergeant, German paratroopers (Fallschirmjäger), author of *The Jäger Journal*.

Hauptsturmfuhrer Otto Skorzeny- SS captain, part of the raid to free Mussolini.

General der Fallschirmtruppe Kurt Student- commander of Fliegerkorps XI, parachute unit.

Leutnant zur See- Kurt Niemiller, coast watcher for the German Kriegsmarine.

Major Dietrich Meier- commander of Operation Ulric to free Hitler.

Leutnant Johann Kruger- deputy commander of U-1020.

Oberleutnant Otto Eberlein- commander of U-1020.

Tower Intelligence and Security Agency

T.J. Davidson- CEO, high school friend of Jack Harrison.

Ashley Nordstrom- receptionist.

Blake Carter- operative, German linguist.

Jake Ewell- computer/IT specialist, nicknamed "The Snake", retired Army.

Reynaldo Cintron- operative, specialist in sweeping buildings and vehicles for electronic bugs.

Frederick Michaels- operative, specialist in hostage rescue, package retrieval, client protection, suspect surveillance, former Marine.

American Scout Unit

Lt. John Owen- commander of American scout squad, 28th Reconnaissance Troop. Age 22.

Sgt. Shiloh Chadwell- Cherokee scout. Age 25.

Cpl. Mel Sweringen- cowboy from Texas. Age 20.

Pvt. Pete House-jack of all trades. Age 19.

Pvt. Walter King- of German descent, from Montana. Age 19.

Pvt. Rocco Pitto- from Cleveland, Ohio. Age 21.

Pvt. Chuck Cameron- life of the party. Age 19.

Balder Chemical

David Braun- CEO of Balder Chemical.

Eric Riddell- head of assassination team.

Mitchell Fluke- team member.

Curtis Ballinger- team member, back up for telephone man, artist.

Thomas Kopf- team member, driver of tanker truck.

Walter Dyson- team member.

Zygmunt Swift- team member, sniper.

Federal Bureau of Investigation

Special Agent Braxton Roby- agent at the Atlanta field office.

Special Agent Andrew Papadakis- Roby's partner.

IT Specialist Regina Rhodes- previous employement with Kaspersky Labs in Woburn, Massachusetts.

Others

Greta Rose- Austrian student in Barcelona, friend of Jim Harrison, great granddaughter of Heinrich Pfeister. Age 20.

Elena Rose- Greta's mother.

Marta Rose- Greta's younger sister.

Sgt. Gabriel Washington- drill sergeant with the US Army Field Artillery School, Ft. Sill, Oklahoma, divorced, combat veteran of Operation Iraqi Freedom.

Chandra Rahman- US Capitol grounds maintenance unit, former US Army.

Airica- operative for Norse Industries.

.

Prologue

The square windows of the subway train flashed by the solitary figure standing only inches from the edge of the concrete platform. Air, drafted by the flying cars, swept across the man's solemn face. Train B711T of the northeast-bound Hibiya line abruptly stopped and the automatic doors whooshed open. Dozens of passengers spilled out of the subway cars onto the platform and flowed toward their individual destinations. Twenty-seven-year-old Toru Toyoda looked at the mass of humanity moving past him but saw no one. He pushed his way toward the door of the first car and entered, clutching a copy of the *Hochi Shimbun* newspaper under his left arm and tightly grasping his black umbrella with his right hand. He sat down in a seat adjacent to the door. No one noticed him.

The young man was brilliant. He had graduated with honors from the University of Tokyo with a degree in applied physics. He had gone on to complete a master's degree and had begun doctoral studies. Today, March 20, 1995, he would apply physics and chemistry in a horrific plot to bring down the government of Japan.

As the doors closed again, the sleek silver train accelerated away from Naka-Meguro Station and plunged into the darkness of the subway tunnel. The seat next to the budding physicist was occupied by a well-dressed man in his thirties who was absorbed in a sports tabloid. Toyoda slowly scanned the car. Everyone was stone-faced, engrossed in their own thoughts and cares or riveted to their own newspaper or magazine. The whirr of the racing subway car was a group hypnotic. There was no conversation in the crowded compartment.

Four other conspirators were similarly situated on four other subway lines, each with his own copy of a newspaper and each with his own umbrella. Toyoda rested the sharpened end of his umbrella on the rubberized floor of the car in front of his seat. The tip had been carefully honed to a fine, piercing point. Now Toyoda leisurely placed his newspaper wrapped bundle on the floor beside his seat and off to the side of the door. Hidden within the *Hochi Shimbun* were two plastic bags containing a total of 900 milliliters of a deadly liquid.

The conspirator glanced up at the lighted subway line guide on the ceiling of the car. Beads of perspiration glistened on his forehead. As the train pulled into Ebisu Station, he quickly used his umbrella to stab multiple punctures in the plastic packets inside the newspaper and got off the train. He had been on the subway car for two minutes.

A clear liquid oozed from the newspaper bundle and spread onto the floor of the car. Oblivious of the insidious danger, new passengers entered the subway train. The mechanical jaws of the car sealed the compartment shut, and the train careened down its rails. For a few moments, nothing seemed to happen. But the odorless, colorless Sarin liquid was evaporating, and the vapor was filling the unsuspecting car. By the time the train reached its third stop, most passengers were sweating profusely and their eyes were watering uncontrollably. Several began vomiting and gasping for air. Two women fell to the floor and began to convulse violently. Passengers desperately opened the windows of the car seeking relief. But no relief came, and the entire car was now engulfed in a flood of fear and panic even as the train raced headlong to its next appointed stop.

As the train pulled into Kamiyacho Station, station attendants quickly evacuated the first car of all its passengers and arranged transport for several victims to local hospitals. Incredibly, the subway train, with a now empty first car, continued on its prescribed route for one more stop where, finally, it was completely evacuated.

Five separate, simultaneous attacks were made that day on the portion of the Tokyo subway system which serviced the districts of Kasumigaseki and Nagatcho, home to the majority of Japanese government agencies. The nerve gas strikes killed twelve and seriously injured fifty. Almost four thousand others experienced temporary symptoms, a thousand of whom were hospitalized. Experts postulated that this frightening, concerted terrorist attack would have had far greater tragic consequences but for the fact that the form of Sarin liquid produced by the Aum Shinrikyo cult was of low-grade quality and was poorly dispersed.

1 The Call

The phone on the nightstand rang several times. Jean Harrison poked her sleeping husband. "Are you going to answer that?"

Her husband grunted, "Huh?"

"The phone?"

"Oh, yeah," he answered. Jack Harrison rolled over and picked up the black phone. The small digital alarm clock glowed blue with the local time- 3:15 am.

"Hello," he said with his best try at an alert voice.

"Dad?"

"Jim? What's up? You alright?"

"I got trouble here. Need your help."

"What you got?"

Jim's voice was tense. "I don't know exactly what's happened. I went for my morning run about 6:30 as usual. I pretty much have a fixed routine, you know, probably not a good thing. Anyway, when I got back to my apartment, the door was unlocked. Thought it was strange. I eased open the door and looked in. My apartment was a total mess. To make a long story short, I've been robbed. All my stuff's been ransacked, and all my electronics are gone. Fortunately, I had my cell phone on me. I'm not sure what to do. All I can tell you is, I'm frothing mad."

"Have you called the Barcelona police?"

"Yes," Jim answered, not very encouraging. "They just left a few minutes ago, but they weren't much help. They suspect it's a group of local thieves operating out of the El Raval district. I'm not so sure."

"Why not?" his dad asked.

"Well, you remember the girl Greta I've mentioned?"

"Yes," his dad said with curiosity.

"I thought I'd just check in with her while I was waiting for the police. But she didn't answer her cell phone, and she didn't return my text."

"O.K. So maybe she just left her phone at her apartment, or her battery's dead," Jack said, trying to be reassuring. "It'd be very unlikely that petty thieves would also be into kidnapping."

"Yeah, you're probably right. I guess I'm just stressed. This whole scene just blows me away. I mean, I've never had anything like this happen before."

"Look, we're here for you. Take some time to straighten up your things, make an inventory of everything that's missing, and then go over and check on your friend. Call us back in say, three hours."

*****

6:30 am Eastern Time Jack Harrison's phone rang again. This time he was up and having his morning coffee. He sat in the kitchen reading his Bible. "Hello."

"It's me," Jim said.

"Did you reach your friend?"

"No, and we've got bigger problems. I went over to her apartment, and hers has been hit too. It looked just like mine - a train wreck."

"I suppose the police have been by again?" Jack asked.

"Yeah, and another big zero. They said that multiple break-ins are not uncommon. They advised me, as best as I can understand Catalan, to stay calm and leave it to them to investigate. I have this real uneasy feeling in my gut."

Jack paused for a moment. "Alright, let's think through this. All we know for sure is there have been two break-ins and Greta is not answering her phone. Have you been to the school to look for her?"

"No, but that's where I'm headed now. I'll get back to you as soon as I find her, or not," Jim said.

"Good. I'll be waiting on your call. Use my cell number next time as I'll be at work. And, Jim,"

"Yes, sir," Jim answered.

"Stay alert. Remember, situational awareness."

"Right," Jim responded remembering the training his older brother had shared with him from his military experience. "And thanks."

"We love you," his mom chimed in before her son hung up. "We've had you on speaker so I could hear what's going on."

"Love you too, Mom!"

*****

Jack Harrison's construction business was small but thriving. His customers trusted him, and his only advertisement was by word of mouth. If you wanted a home that was well built, Jack Harrison was your go-to guy. The family home was in a rural area just north of Macon, Georgia, and his office was in a shop he had built on the property. Business overhead was low, so his bids were very competitive.

At 12:40 his cell phone rang. He was in his shop going over a list of bathroom fixtures submitted by a subcontractor for a home he had under construction.

"Dad?"

"Yeah, Jim. How's it goin'?" Jack answered.

"Not good." His son's tone was darker now. "I can't find Greta anywhere. No one at the school has seen her. I don't have any of her relatives' phone numbers. I know her Mom and little sister live in Austria, but I don't know how to reach 'em."

Jack paused a moment thinking. "Where in Austria?"

"Oberndorf, near Salzburg in western Austria," Jim answered. "But I don't know her mom's first name or address either. I guess she'd have the same last name, Rose."

"Well, how big is Oberndorf?"

"Not very. Maybe I could get the number off the internet. I'll give it a shot. I really can't think of anything else to try. This whole scene stinks!" Jim aired his frustration.

"Alright. Are your summer session classes over?" Jack inquired.

"Yes."

"Then, if you can't get any leads on Greta, I think you should come back here. We can work on this together with more resources available. And you'll be safe here until we sort out what's goin' on."

2 The Heat

Jim Harrison looked weary. As he stepped off the escalator from the arriving flights area at Hartsfield-Jackson International Airport in Atlanta, he saw his father watching for him. A small crowd was waiting for arriving passengers. Jack Harrison stood patiently near the back of the group. Jim slowly weaved through the crowd, and son and father embraced. "Welcome home," Jack said.

"Good to be back."

"How was the flight?"

"Long, *too* long. I'm beat," Jim said as they walked down the hallway.

"Baggage claim?" Jack inquired.

"No, I just have my carry on. I'm learning to travel light," Jim remarked.

"Good. Let's get to the car and get you home to a shower and clean sheets."

"Sounds good to me, Dad. Thanks for coming this late to pick me up."

"Wouldn't have missed it."

The two Harrisons walked out of the terminal and into the hot Atlanta night. The air was humid and heavy.

Driving away from the airport, the Harrisons turned on to the interstate leading south. The dashboard clock showed 11:15 pm.

Jack fumbled behind the passenger seat and handed Jim a small brown paper bag. "Your mom insisted on sending these."

Jim smiled and pulled out a bottled water and a zip lock baggie with a stack of homemade chocolate chip cookies. "Ahh! She's always taking care of us. You want one?"

"No thanks, I already sampled several," Jack confessed.

Changing subjects, Jim asked, "Why are you driving Mom's Lexus instead of your truck?"

"She asked me to drive it tonight to check it out. She said the air conditioner isn't working right. I think the compressor is cycling, but it probably needs a recharge of refrigerant. I guess we'll just ride with the windows down if that's ok with you."

"Sure," Jim answered.

"Did you ever find a phone number for Greta's family?" Jack asked.

"Yeah, and I called several times but never got an answer."

"Strange," Jack mused.

"Yeah, it is. And I'm worried she's in deep trouble. It felt like I abandoned her by leaving Barcelona."

"It's tough. But you'd done all you could there. She may not even be in Barcelona."

"That's what I'm afraid of... And why? Why would anybody want to hurt her?" Jim asked with a tone of anger.

"I don't know," his father answered.

The hot night air rushed into the car through the open windows as the pair drove on through the night.

"We'll start building a plan to find her first thing in the morning. We *will* find her." Jack's voice was calm, and resolved. Jim knew his father meant exactly what he said.

After driving a few miles, Jack exited the interstate and pulled into a quick mart/gas station to fill up. "This won't take but a minute. You need anything?" Jack asked.

"No I'm fine, just fine." Jim closed his eyes and relaxed in the passenger seat while his dad got out of the shiny black Lexus.

As Jack pumped the gas, he noticed a silver Mercedes SLK 350 roll in to the fueling island adjacent to him. Two tall brunettes stepped out of the luxury car. The tails of the driver's white blouse were tied in a knot revealing a bare midriff above her abbreviated version of denim hot pants. She wore elevated red stiletto heels that clopped as she walked around the front of the car to swipe her card at the gas pump. Her companion had on a loose fitting tan top, and her matching miniskirt was as short as was still legal in the state of Georgia. She accessorized with gold bracelets and bling-bling gold earrings. Her black stiletto heels echoed off the pavement as she quick-stepped toward the entrance of the convenience mart.

Jack hastily turned his back grabbing the windshield squeegee from its slot on the gas island. He furiously began to clean the not-so-dirty windshield. Startled by the squeaking sound on the glass in front of him, Jim opened his eyes to see soapy water flying in all directions. As soon as the pump shut off, Jack replaced the nozzle and spun the gas cap onto the filler tube. He immediately got back in the car and started the engine. His son was about to speak when he heard, "Excuse me."

The voice sounded like honey over gravel. "Can you tell me how to get to the Sheraton?" the Mercedes driver asked, each syllable enunciated deliberately. As Jack cleared his throat, the woman placed her left hand on the roof and rested her right hand on the still open window, stroking her red fingernails on the door fabric.

Looking straight ahead, Jack responded, "Get back on the interstate and get off at the Sullivan Road exit. The hotel is a quarter mile down the road on the right."

Leaning down the brunette lowered her voice and asked, "Would you like to take me there?"

In a forced whisper Jack responded, "No, I wouldn't!" Simultaneously, he pulled up hard on the power window control with his left ring finger and mashed on the accelerator. The Lexus literally jumped out of the gas station as the tires squealed.

With a wide grin playing on his face, Jim smirked, "Nicely done, Dad."

"Son, there's a time to stand and a time to run...er...drive!"

Glancing through the rear window, Jim could still see the woman standing with her right hand on her hip and her left hand suspended in midair as if resting on an invisible roof.

Jack Harrison never looked back.

3 The Gym

Doc's Gym was situated in a strip mall off I-75 north of Macon. The usual clientele pumped iron and ran the treadmills in the early morning from 5:30 until 7:30 or after work from about 4:00 in the afternoon until 8:00 in the evening. Although "Doc" kept the doors accessible and the lights on 24 hours a day, business definitely slacked off after 10:00 at night. Doc's place was snugly wedged between two other locally owned businesses. To one side of the gym was The Silver Chalice, a fusion of coffee shop and bookstore. Doc loved old books and found himself spending almost as much time in the bookstore as he did in his own establishment. On the other side was El Gordo, a purveyor of delicious Mexican fare with no illusions of caloric or fat restriction.

Men and women of all ages frequented the gym and felt secure knowing security cameras kept vigil on the patrons. Entry was by coded key pad or swipe card and for active members only.

When "Doc" finally sold his family medicine practice to a young physician from Savannah, he decided to pursue his vision for community-wide fitness. He had *treated* disease his entire medical career. But, entering his second career, he decided to push everyone he knew to embrace *prevention* of illness. He set the example and was in great shape, looking 10 years younger than his seven chronological decades.

The Harrisons had an annual membership, and Jim took advantage of the family pass nightly during his first week back home. He was still having trouble adjusting his internal clock to Eastern Daylight Time and found himself napping some during the day and going to bed an hour or two after midnight. He had tried some melatonin from the local health food store without success.

Carrying a backpack with his workout gear, Jim entered the fitness center and headed for the locker room. The gym was empty except for one nerdy-looking character on a treadmill near the end of the room farthest from the entrance. From his frail build, Jim concluded the man must not have been into an exercise program for very long.

Inside the empty locker room, Jim changed from his slacks and shirt into Air Force Falcon gym shorts and tee shirt. His big brother, knowing his status as a rabid Air Force Academy fan, had delighted him with Air Force gear for Christmas two years in a row. He folded his street clothes and put his wallet, keys, and cell phone with them on the top shelf inside one of the black metal lockers. He set his slightly scuffed Rockports on the bottom shelf with his backpack on top of them. He closed the locker door and spun the tumbler on his combination lock.

Back in the exercise area, Jim stepped up on a treadmill and started a slow jog. Within a minute, he advanced to a brisk run. Sweat began to bead on his forehead as he noticed an advertisement for Lipton Iced Tea on the widescreen TV suspended from the ceiling in front of him. *That would taste great right now.* At the same moment, out of the corner of his eye, he noticed a tall brunette enter the gym, her hair pulled into a ponytail. Dressed in a black jogging suit, she moved to a

Nautilus machine and set her small backpack on a bench. Her figure was supple, well fit. *She's in good shape*, Jim mused. He snapped his attention back to the Fox News channel now in front of him. *No time for distractions.*

Jim ran for a few more minutes and thought about the iced tea. He slowed the pace on the treadmill down to a jog. As he slowed to a walk, he saw a burly man in his late 20s enter the gym and stride over to the Nautilus machine. He wore a maroon polo shirt, black slacks, and street shoes. *He is obviously not at the gym for exercise,* Jim thought.

The brunette woman in black tried to ignore the interloper, continuing to lift a 30-pound bar repetitively with her back to the machine. The man spoke harshly to the woman, although Jim couldn't make out the words. Jim tried to ignore the scene unfolding at the Nautilus. When the creep in street clothes grabbed the girl by her pony tail and pulled her face toward his, Jim decided he'd had enough. He jumped off the treadmill and walked towards the confrontation. Flipping open his cell phone, he spoke directly to the thug, "You wanna leave, or you want me to call up the cops."

The man in the polo shirt turned slowly, releasing his grip on the ponytail. Facing Jim, he spat out, "And what business is our business of yours?"

"When a creep accosts a lady in public, it becomes my business. You want this guy to leave you alone, ma'am?" he asked the brunette, who appeared visibly shaken.

"Yes, but… I don't want any trouble for you."

"No trouble, Ma'am. He was just leaving, weren't you friend?" Jim said with an almost pleasant tone.

The muscular, heavy lunged for Jim, who spun left, allowing the big man to rush by in front of him. The man missed Jim completely. Striking him hard at the base of the neck with a hammer fist, Jim dropped him in his tracks. He stared down at his assailant and rubbed his now mildly aching hand. "Hope I didn't injure him too bad," he said to the brunette. "How do you know him?"

"Ex-boyfriend. He wouldn't take 'goodbye' for an answer," she said, slightly embarrassed.

"So did you used to come here together?" Jim asked.

"Yeah. I guess he used my passcode to get in tonight," the woman said with an edge to her voice. Looking Jim in the eyes she said, "Thank you so much for your help. What now?"

"Oh, he's coming around. I'll give 'im the same options. He leaves, or I call the cops," Jim answered.

The big man sat up, rubbed his neck, and looked at Jim. "She ain't worth it, bud. She's just a ..."

"Shut your filthy mouth and get out of here, NOW!!!" Jim demanded.

Scrambling to his feet, the offender shuffled toward the door. Only once did he shoot a venomous look over his retreating shoulder at the brunette. He exited the gym and slammed the door behind him.

"Well, I guess I've had enough exercise tonight. Are you okay?" Jim asked the woman.

"Yes, thank you so much. He's such a jerk. I don't know what I ever saw in him," she said almost to herself.

"Yeah, me either," Jim agreed, still rubbing his right hand. "Never could figure why a beautiful woman would want to hang out with a goon like him." The brunette smiled slightly, but didn't blush. For some reason he couldn't explain, Jim hadn't expected this woman to blush. "See ya later." Jim excused himself and headed for the locker.

"Bye," a light smile played on her lips as she returned to her reps on the weight machine.

Jim changed quickly, put his gym clothes in his blue backpack, passed through the exercise area, and headed toward the exit. Fox News still blared from the four TV sets hanging from the ceiling. They broadcast an item about a train derailment in southern India. The gym was now empty of patrons. Jim had half anticipated speaking to the brunette as he left but concluded she probably was self- conscious and embarrassed over the episode. Stepping into the muggy Georgia night, Jim looked out and surveyed the nearly empty parking lot.

"Heh, you thirsty?" a soft voice startled him.

Jim turned and looked behind and to his left. The brunette had a large drink cup in each hand and a winning smile on her face. "Sweet tea or regular?"

"Uh, regular," he answered, amused that his mind had been read. "Thanks. How did you know?"

"Lucky guess." She handed Jim the large cup. "You earned it. You mind walking me to my car? I just don't want to have to face Carl again by myself."

"No problem. Which one is yours?" Jim responded, taking a big swig of the ice cold tea.

"The red BMW," she said pointing to the far end of the lot.

"Nice! Where'd you get tea this time of night?" he asked as they walked across the parking lot toward the sports car.

"At the taco shop next door. They're open all night. Can I give you a ride somewhere?"

Taking another long drink of tea, Jim tried to focus his thinking. *Fast car, nice brunette… be careful.* As hard as he tried, his thoughts kept getting foggy. As they reached the BMW, Jim stumbled and put a hand out toward the car to catch himself. And just then, everything went black.

4 The Interrogation

Jim raised himself up to his hands and knees. It was dark and damp. He could hear the slow drip of water somewhere. *Where am I?* he thought. He carefully looked over the room. A layer of green –brown slime covered the floor. *Well, not exactly home sweet home. At least it's not a scorching hot corrugated hut in the Sahara or some freezing cold cell in Siberia.* He stood and checked his pockets and clothing: no wallet, no belt, no watch, and no jewelry. All of his buttons had been removed as well. He stepped to the nearest wall. Placing his now brownish palm on the cool, wet surface, he pushed hard. *Solid.* He quickly moved down the wall to the corner and then around the rest of the dark room. There was no window and only a solid metal-hinged door in the center of one wall. The door had a single sliding peep slit two-thirds of the way up. A fine coating of rust covered the door as if it had been sprayed onto it. The only light in the room was a dim reflected light coming from a square hole in the center of the ceiling. His eyes had fully adjusted to the darkness. The room had no chair, table, or bunk. The only thing in the chamber was a rough wooden bucket. There was no foul stench, just the musty odor of mildew. Jim slowly concluded he was confined in a cell which had not been used in a very long time.

He stood quiet, breathing, thinking, praying. He began to pace slowly around the cell for three reasons: to keep his muscles loose, to keep a rough track of time, and to think clearly. He always did his best thinking while walking. The rhythm of his legs focused the rhythm of his thoughts. He continued to walk for what he estimated was an hour and a half. He wasn't terribly discouraged, just focused. God had gotten him out of tough spots before.

He suddenly stopped and listened. He could faintly hear several sets of footsteps. They moved steadily closer and then stopped outside his cell door. A key turned, groaning in the aged lock. The door swung in on its hinges loudly, protesting a need for the oilcan. Three men entered, the first two armed with MP-5K Heckler and Koch machine pistols and the last with a Glock 9-mm which he had holstered on his right hip. Jim was standing in the middle of the cell and quickly took mental inventory of what physical details were available- black boots, black BDUs, black Under Armour shirts, black shooter gloves, and very tight-fitting black hoods. *Fashion and diversity are certainly not their strong suit.* Heckler and Koch pointed their guns at Jim's chest and Glock pulled three zip ties- black, of course- from a BDU pocket and secured both of Jim's hands behind his back. The men were quick, firm, silent. Obviously professional, they wasted no motion.

Jim was pushed out into the hallway and down a brightly lit corridor, his eyes smarting from the abrupt change in candlepower. He followed Glock with Heckler and Koch encouraging him from behind. At the end of the corridor, the leader unlocked and opened a heavy, gray metal door and led the party through. He relocked the door and proceeded up two flights of gray metal stairs with his entourage trailing close behind. The only sounds were the footsteps of the four men heading for what three of them believed was an important destination. *So far, meaningful conversation is just not on the agenda.*

The leader opened the door at the top of the stairs, and the men entered another corridor. They turned immediately right into a clean, brightly lit room measuring approximately 15 by 20 feet equipped like a small medical clinic. An exam table was situated in the center of the room. Heckler and Koch seated Jim roughly on the table. Heckler pulled a combat knife from his boot and cut the tie holding Jim's hands. The leader stepped over to a green metal cabinet on one wall of the room. He removed the screw cap from a brown glass bottle of tablets and took out two. Pulling a paper cup from a dispenser, he filled it with water from the tap at a sink to the left of the cabinet. Turning, he handed the two tablets and cup of water to Jim.

"No thanks, I don't really have a headache."

The leader placed the muzzle of his pistol against Jim's head.

"On second thought, maybe I do feel a little pain coming on," Jim smiled. He put the two tablets in his mouth and swallowed a gulp of water. The leader motioned for Jim to open his mouth. He did so, and the leader placed a wooden tongue depressor under Jim's tongue finding the two tablets he had hidden there. The gun went to the head again. "Can't blame a guy for tryin'." He swallowed more water, and this time the pills went down. "See, I feel fine."

The leader motioned for Jim to lie supine on the exam table. Jim complied. He closed his eyes. Neither fight nor flight was an option. But in his heart of hearts, as dark as his situation looked, he realized he was not alone.

Jim had had a strong faith ever since he had come to the end of himself just before his graduation from high school. He had been a rebel of sorts for two years in his teens. His self-indulgent choices had dragged the entire family through emotional torment. He regretted that. But, his senior year, he had found God. Or, rather, he finally surrendered to the God who had been pursuing him all along. Two things had been instrumental in his redemption. The most important was the relentless, selfless love of his mother and father. The second had been his reading of *Mere Christianity* by C.S. Lewis. His older brother, Stuart, had challenged him, no, dared him, to read it. He had at last concluded that the life he saw in his parents and siblings was the life he wanted for himself. And, he knew, it was a life that resulted from right choices. In just two wild years, he had made a string of poor choices long enough to last a life time.

Jim came to consciousness as if out of a deep sleep. He first noticed a tight feeling on both wrists. His arms were locked down. No way could he move them. He was on his back. His legs were locked down tight as well. He felt a sudden pressure in his chest as air rushed in, but it made him cough. Only, he couldn't cough. He tried to inhale deeply. He heard a whoosh and felt the pressure in his chest again. He opened his eyes. *What is this?* He could see nothing. Everything was a total blur. He could only perceive light. He tried to speak. *No go.*

"Mr. Harrison, please do not struggle, it only makes it more difficult for you. Let me explain. You have had your trachea intubated. You are on a ventilator. We are using an advanced interrogation technique. It is a significant refinement of methods currently used by national intelligence, military, and counterterrorism services. We have placed an endotracheal tube in your windpipe. We now control your very breath. You have had mydriatic drops placed in both eyes. They blur your vision for a time so that you cannot see. That is only temporary. We want to ask you a series of questions. If you are cooperative and helpful, you will be released. If not, it will be a long and unpleasant affair. If you work with us, we can make this all go away."

Jim closed his eyes and prayed, "Dear Lord, please help me…" He continued to breathe slowly and deeply as an unnatural calm seemed to sweep over him.

Questions raced through his mind, "Ok, what can I give them that won't compromise my family? What do they want? How bad do they want it? How long can I hang on?" He was about to find out.

A crisp, lightly accented voice, different from the first, began to instruct him. "You now have buttons placed in each hand. The right button is 'yes', the left is 'no'. Just think of our little session as a special kind of '20 questions'. Alright, let us begin."

"Are you American?"

Jim did not move. *Let's make them work for this a little bit.*

"Mr. Harrison, time is precious. Let's not waste yours or mine. Let me demonstrate what we can do to you." For a moment, Jim noticed no change. Then, he tried to inhale and nothing happened. He tried a more vigorous pull. Nothing! He began to feel the terror of smothering to death. *I can't breathe!* He jerked violently with his arms and legs! The ties dug into his skin. His lungs were screaming for air. He tried again and again to inhale. He desperately tried to sit up, but his chest was secured to the table. He knew now he was going to die.

Finally, he squeezed the button in his right hand. Immediately he felt a surge of air rush into his lungs, and he panted rapidly in and out for several more breaths. He had his life back. But, he knew, he had lost.

"Are your parents alive?"

Right button.

"Do you have siblings?"

Right button.
Do any of your siblings work for the US military?
Left button.
Have you or they ever worked for the US military?
Right button.
Did any of your immediate relatives serve in World War II?
Left button.
Did either of your parents go to college?
Right button.
Father?
Left button.
Mother?
Right button.
Were any members of your immediate family born in a foreign country?
Left button.
Have you ever visited France?
Right button.
Germany?
Left button.
Austria?
Left button.
Russia?
Left button.
Israel?
Left button.
Mexico?
Right button.
Italy?
Right button.
South America?
Left button.

The interrogation went on and on. There seemed to be no theme or direction to the line of questioning- just random facts about Jim and his family. Jim continued to breathe. Only once did he give a deliberately false answer, and the ordeal of near-suffocation was repeated. *They know all the answers anyway,* he realized.

A pause in the interrogation came as Jim heard two voices conversing in a language he did not understand or recognize. Then the interrogator continued, "Mr. Harrison, that is all for now. One thing I wish to indelibly burn into your mind. You must forget you ever knew Greta Rose, and you must forget about her journal. And I assure you… our people are everywhere. "

Jim felt his heart pound as he grasped the thought that somehow his tormentors were connected to Greta's disappearance. Simultaneously, he felt a sting in his left forearm and then a burning inside. And then, everything went black again.

5 The Return

A searing pain burned in Jim's left forearm. He remained motionless and fought to sustain a pattern of slow steady breathing. He determined not to allow his captors to realize he was conscious. The fire in his forearm remained constant. "*It must be an IV line that's infiltrated into the skin,*" he decided. The sedative was no longer dripping into his vein but instead was slowly oozing into the loose subcutaneous tissue of his dorsal forearm with almost none of its intended effect. "*Well, even these guys make mistakes,*" he realized.

He continued to lie still, to breathe slowly and deeply, feigning peaceful sleep. His head was cloaked in a black hood and his arms restrained as before. But his hearing was acute and his mind becoming sharper by the minute. By the soft rumble he heard and felt, accompanied by a very gentle occasional rocking, he concluded they were flying in a small corporate jet. He listened quietly for some time and could barely discern the low tones of voices several feet away. He recognized the language as German but could not understand what was being said.

In what he estimated was about a half hour, Jim began to feel a pressure change in his ears and guessed they were beginning to descend. A whoosh sound followed by a dull thud signified that the aircraft landing gear had been lowered. Within minutes, the jet had landed and taxied to a stop. As the engines whined down, Jim's arms were released and he was jerked roughly onto a stretcher by two pairs of large hands. He strained to notice as many details as possible as he was quickly transferred to a vehicle waiting on the tarmac with its engine running. He was placed upright in a seat, securely strapped in, and his wrists were bound together in front of him. His IV bag was checked and hung from a clothes hook above him and to his right. No one bothered to check the IV site. "*Sloppy; these boys are slipping.*"

Jim allowed his head to drop forward, as he continued playing the role of unconscious captive. Someone noticed and used the power control to recline the seat back. Jim was grateful. Even in the cloth hood, he sensed ambient darkness and the lack of radiant heat. "*Nighttime*," he thought. The air was very dry, and there was a light breeze. He could hear the sounds of assorted vehicles and aircraft at what he judged was a relatively busy metropolitan airport. Which city, country, or even continent he was on, he could not determine.

The vehicle sped off into the night. Jim could not guess where they were headed. Sensing that his life might depend on alertness, he struggled to stay keenly observant of details while appearing to be comatose. They pulled on to what he assumed must be a major highway, and he guessed they would be driving for a while.

There was almost no conversation in the vehicle. No radio was ever turned on, but a spirited interpretation of Wagner's *March of the Meistersingers* wafted from the vehicle's CD player. By road noise, vibration, and general "feel", Jim thought he must be in a fairly large van. He could occasionally hear the men around him make small shifts in body position, and by these and other sounds, he counted three captors —

one in the seat to his left, apparently another in the seat directly in front of him, and the driver to the front and left.

When they exited the major highway, Jim estimated that they had been driving for approximately two hours. The road was now smooth and seemed very straight. And there was barely any traffic. Jim concluded they must be way out in the middle of nowhere indeed. A disturbing thought crept into his mind. His abductors were getting him far away from civilization so they could kill him and dump his body. The idea didn't particularly frighten him as much as it made him angry. He began to search mentally for some sort of escape plan. A desperate explosive jump out of their grasp, commandeering one of the guns he was sure they had, seemed like the only plausible solution. Even the chance of this succeeding seemed remote, as his wrists were bound tightly together in front of him with the ubiquitous zip ties and his head remained shrouded in his black hood.

Suddenly, the van pulled off the road and came to an abrupt stop. Jim heard the flick of a switch blade to his left. Before he grasped exactly what was happening, his zip ties were cut and his hands released. He let his arms fall to his sides, concluding that if his abductors had genuine plans to kill him, they wouldn't be releasing his hands. A few words were exchanged between the driver and the man with the knife — harsh, guttural words, quickly spoken. Jim's IV was deftly removed and a bandage placed over the now swollen site. His male nurse either did not recognize the swelling in the forearm as a sign of infiltration, or he did not wish to acknowledge it to his possibly unforgiving friends. Jim was unstrapped from his seat and unceremoniously deposited prone on the shoulder of the road. His captors snatched off his hood, and, continuing to assume he would sleep for an hour or more, rushed back to their seats in the van. The driver started the engine, but one of his companions returned to Jim and rapidly poured a large bottle of liquid over his head and back. The cold fluid sent a shiver across Jim's skin, but he remained motionless. The strong aroma now drenching his body told him he had been treated with a fifth of cheap gin. After the executor of this dousing joined his companions in the van and the three sped away, Jim whispered an earnest prayer of thanks for his survival.

Jim stayed motionless as the roar of the departing van engine quickly faded. He opened his eyes and rolled over. An inky black canopy pierced with brilliant stars stared back at him. He sat up, dusted off, and then stood beside the empty road. The sky seemed perfectly bright compared to the total darkness of the ground around him. He slowly took in a 360-degree scan of the horizon and noted not a single human source of light. There were no trees, no buildings, no mountains. He was absolutely in the middle of nowhere.

From his earliest days Jim had been taught to pray, think, and act. This he now did and immediately began to gather data. He assessed his bodily state — he was exhausted, he was dirty, he was thirsty, and he was hungry. On the other hand, he had no serious injuries, and he was mentally alert. His left forearm continued to burn. There was moderate swelling. But he had full range of motion of wrist, elbow, and shoulder. His legs worked and his eyes and ears were keen. His shirt was soaking wet and sticky, but he decided this was a minor inconvenience. He was grateful to have shoes and socks intact. His slacks tended to slip on account of the theft of all his buttons and belt. Deciding that he could make better time if both hands were free, he removed his shirt and rolled it into a kind of short rope. He tied this around his waist securing his pants as best he could.

Locating Ursa Major and then Polaris, he determined north. The road he had been dumped by was a recently repaved asphalt and ran roughly northwest to southeast. For no particular reason other than walking toward the coming sunrise, he started walking east. He hoped he could hitch a ride toward some kind of civilization.

In about half an hour, Jim noticed a set of vehicle lights approaching. His spirits jumped. But his enthusiasm faded as the lights came and went despite his vigorous gesturing. He mused that this shouldn't have been unexpected, as, given his appearance, *he* probably wouldn't have picked himself up either. Over the next two hours, a sedan and two farm pickups passed. All three declined to stop for Jim — or even slow down. One new piece of information did emerge, though. Three of the four vehicles that passed him had New Mexico plates. He concluded with confidence that he was in the USA.

Jim's thirst was becoming acute. He was frustrated that, as he topped each successive rise of the highway, the terrestrial darkness remained unbroken. There was not a sign of water. But he resolved to keep moving; he eventually had to come to some kind of man-made structure.

Shortly, the first hint of pink began to kiss the horizon. He could just begin to make out the gently rolling but flat terrain. Jim Harrison smelled and looked awful, but the sunrise he walked toward was fresh and clean. Morning had unpacked its multicolored red and orange blanket and was slowly unfolding it before him. Strangely, he thought it was one of the most beautiful dawns he had ever witnessed.

Occasionally checking the highway behind him, Jim noticed another car in the distance headed his way. He decided to try once more to hail a ride. He untied his shirt rope, unwound it, and slipped it on. It still reeked with the smell of alcohol but at least it covered his bare torso. He wanted to give his very best first impression to the oncoming driver. Putting on his most winsome smile, he tried to figure what stance to assume in order to present the least threating persona. With growing hope he watched as the blue Nissan Sentra approached, but resignation returned as the sedan whizzed by. The tinted windows prevented any eye contact with the driver. But about 200 yards past him, the car skidded to a stop. The white backup lights came on and the Nissan began to back up towards Jim. He was cautiously hopeful. He slowly approached the driver's side but kept a respectful distance as the power window came down.

"Man, you are a MESS!" the driver noted.

"Yeah, you are definitely on to something there," Jim replied. "You wouldn't happen to have some water, would you?"

"Sure," the driver answered reaching into the passenger seat where he had a small cooler perched.

As Jim eagerly took the bottled water offered him, he surveyed his rescuer. He noted he was a muscular black man in his late twenties, and he was wearing digital camouflage ACU's. "You're Army!"

"Man, you're sharp for this time of the morning."

"Where are we?"

"What?"

"I said, 'Where are we?', and what day is it?"

Taking his own survey of the situation as Jim downed the water, the soldier commented, "So, you're in the middle of nowhere, you don't know where you are or what day it is , and you've been on some kind of wild drunk?"

Jim looked incredulous. "I'm not drunk; I'm as sober as you are. And if I told you how I got here, you probably wouldn't believe me."

"Right, I wouldn't believe you; but it'd probably be an entertaining story. Any chance you know your name?"

"Yeah, Harrison, Jim Harrison."

"Well, that's progress. So are you gonna stand there all morning or are you gettin' in?" the soldier asked.

"Right, thanks a lot, and thanks for the water!" Jim hurried around the Nissan and got in. "By the way, you got a name?"

"Yeah, but don't tell me you can't read either." Pointing to his Army nametag he replied, "It's Washington, Gabriel Washington."

"You're kidding me, right?"

"No, it's Gabriel, like the angel. But you can call me Washington."

"Where you headed?"

"I'm going back to Ft. Sill, Oklahoma. I teach at the Army Field Artillery School. Been on leave for a week. Went out to Denver to see my grandmother. She's eighty –five years old and still the best cook in the whole state!"

The conversation remained superficial. Jim was hesitant to share any details of his harrowing experience. And apparently the GI had had enough life experience to recognize when someone wanted to leave a topic alone. When Washington's phone finally showed they had cell coverage, he allowed Jim to call home. It was 6:30 am.

6 The Homecoming

"Jim, where are you? Are you ok?" Jack shouted into the phone.

"Yes, I'm fine. I'm just outside Clayton, New Mexico."

"New Mexico? What on earth are you doing there? Jim, you've got to know we've been worried spitless about you. Where've you been the last four days?"

"I've got a new friend with me who's helping me out. His name is Sergeant Gabriel Washington. He's active duty Army stationed at Ft. Sill, Oklahoma. He was kind enough to pick me up while I was hitch-hiking on a remote highway. I don't have any money or wallet, no cell phone, no identification. My clothes are a wreck. I need you to either wire me some money or come and get me."

"We'll do both. Are you sure you're ok?"

"Yeah, I'm fine."

"What happened, and how did you get all the way out to New Mexico? Why didn't you call sooner?"

"Dad, it's a really complicated story, but I'm not in any danger now. I just need a shower, some food, and about 12 hours of sleep in that order. And we're getting ready to take care of all of those needs."

"Great, can I speak to your friend?"

"Sure, I'll hand him the phone."

"Hello," the soldier said.

"Sergeant Washington, this is Jack Harrison. I'm Jim's dad. I want to thank you for how you've taken care of my son."

"Yes, sir. Glad to do it. And don't you worry about him, sir. I've got a couple of days before I have to report for duty back at post. We're going to get him fed and cleaned up and put to bed."

"Great. And Sergeant, whatever expenses you incur on his account, I'll cover. Just take care of him till we get there. And thanks again."

"Yes, sir."

"Can I speak to Jim again?"

"Yes, sir. And, sir… I wasn't so sure about him when I picked him up; but after talking with him for a while, I believe you've got a good boy here."

"Thank you, Sergeant."

"Jim, are you sure you're safe?

"Dad, I'm ok, but I think it'd be best if we catch up when you get here. I'll explain what I know then. OK? I'll call again when we find a room in Clayton."

"Alright. Be safe. And Jim, we love ya, son."

"You too, Dad."

The Days Inn of Clayton, New Mexico, was small but clean and comfortable. The front desk clerk proudly informed Sgt. Washington it was the height of Clayton's busy season, but he still had rooms available. Sgt. Washington booked a room for the two of them. "Is there a clothing store around here?" he asked the clerk.

"Sure," the young man replied with a smile. "Jake's Outfitters is just down the road. They don't have the largest selection in the world, but if you're into western wear, you'll be ok."

"Thanks," he said, taking the room key.

"And by the way, I gave you our military discount on the room!"

"Appreciate it."

The two men found their room on the first floor and entered it, the sergeant carrying his shaving kit and Jim carrying nothing. Washington stretched out his 6 foot 2 inch frame on one of the two double beds in the small room. He clasped his hands behind his head and looked at Jim. "I guess you think it's crazy that I'd share a room with a complete stranger with no I.D., no money, and obviously in a heap of trouble a long way from home. Well, let me just put it out on the table."

Jim sat down in the single desk chair in the room wondering where the conversation was headed. "I don't know you from Adam's house cat, but… there's some things the good Lord just leads me to do. I don't always understand 'em, but I do my best to follow. And He's never led me wrong. I just know helping you is the right thing to do." The soldier's gaze drifted to the ceiling and some place way beyond. "Everybody needs help… sometime."

For a moment, the room was quiet, and then Washington's serious tone was gone. Throwing one of the bed pillows at Jim he smiled and said, "Man, you smell worse than something the cats drug in. Scratch that—no self-respecting cat would drag you in."

"Come on, Washington. Don't hold back; tell me how you really feel."

"OK, well, tell me what sizes you wear and I'll scoot down to the store and get you some new gear to wear while you take a shower, a long shower. Then we'll go find us a place to get some chow. Deal?"

"Right, and Washington?"

"Yeah?"

"I want you to know how much I appreciate what you're doing for me!"

"Look, this may sound corny to you, but my grandmother taught me a long time ago that I must do for others what I'd want done for me. If I looked as bad as you do, I'd definitely want some help."

An hour later, Sgt. Washington put his key in the room door and opened it. The room looked empty. For a split second his pulse bounded, but he was immediately reassured as he saw light emerging from under the bathroom door. "You ok in there?"

"Yeah, I just thought my new best friend had abandoned me. What took you so long?" Jim said, emerging from the bathroom wrapped in a towel.

"Man, are you kidding me? I hate shopping, especially for somebody else. And I guess I've been in the Army too long. Uniforms are simple, man. With this civilian stuff, there are way too many choices. And the sales clerk was on me like a duck on a June bug. I must have been the first customer she'd seen in a two days. 'Do you want straight cut, boot cut, or relaxed fit? Black, blue, green or brown? New look or prewashed?' Enough already. I just wanted a pair of jeans and a couple shirts."

By this time, Jim was laughing out loud. "You're a friend indeed, Washington."

"I even got you a belt, wallet, toothbrush, comb, and most importantly, DEODORANT."

Jim quickly put on his new outfit and felt like a real person once again. Jeans, oversized belt buckle, and pearl-buttoned western shirt- Jim Harrison was a regular cowboy. He and Washington drove down Clayton's main street and found the Golden Dragon, an all-you-can-eat Chinese buffet. They both made multiple trips to the buffet bar until they were satisfyingly full. Jim leaned back in his wooden chair and smiled. "Who would've thought you'd fine good Chinese food in an out-of-the-way place in New Mexico?" he mused.

"I guess maybe we were just really hungry," Washington said, grinning. "And I don't know that I ever saw anybody put food away faster than you, man."

"Just a growing boy."

The rest of the evening was spent in pleasant conversation. Both men shared thoughts freely about their families and their upbringing, and Jim realized that Washington's easy humor was therapeutic for him. This new companion was truly a God-send.

They both slept soundly and awoke refieshed. The complimentary motel breakfast was devoured with gusto, seasoned with more conversation and Washington's humor. Shortly, they made contact with Jack Harrison again. He informed Jim that he and Stuart, Jim's older brother, were just passing through Amarillo. They estimated they would arrive to pick Jim up in two hours. "You know you don't have to wait around here on my folks, Washington. I can take care of myself."

"Not a chance. I'm on you like white on rice, if you know what I mean," he said, laughing boisterously at his own joke. "I'm looking forward to meeting the elder Harrison."

The Harrisons pulled up to the Clayton Days Inn at precisely 9:00am and soon found Jim and Washington. After bear hugs from his father and brother, Jim introduced his friend. "Guys, this is my guardian angel, Sergeant Gabriel Washington, US Army."

Jack and Stuart shook hands with the broad-shouldered black soldier. "It's truly a pleasure to meet you, Sergeant!" Jack said smiling. "It's rare to find friends like you in this day and age. We owe you big time." With that, Jack handed Washington two rolled up $100 bills.

"Sir, you don't owe me anything. I have a new friend and, hey, he laughs at my jokes."

"I insist," Jack responded. "It is the least we can do, and I'm sure you can find a way to put it to good use."

"Yes, sir," Washington smiled.

The four men shared small talk for a few moments. Then, Washington commented that it was time for him to be heading back to post. The Harrisons agreed that it was time for them to head back to Georgia as well.

Jim reached out and shook Washington's hand. "Well, I'm not sure what to say. I can't thank you enough. We'd love to have you come down for a visit some time. I promise we'll take good care of you, and my mom's the best cook in Macon." Looking the black soldier straight in the eye he said, "You've got my cell number and email address. Stay in touch, man."

"Definitely; I've made an investment in you, man, and I want to hear the *whole* story someday," Washington said.

The men parted with the soldier and began to talk in earnest. Jim motioned with his hand leading his father and brother to a small park across the road where he felt more comfortable talking. They sat at a small picnic table near a set of swings and a children's slide. Other than the Harrisons, the park was devoid of people.

Jim laid out for his family his limited knowledge of what had happened. They listened intently, but found the episode hard to fathom. They had been distraught after his disappearance and had felt helpless waiting for the authorities to get the wheels of investigation moving. They had found his car parked at the gym the next morning and otherwise had no clue as to his whereabouts. The security cameras at Doc's Gym had shown Jim's arrival and exit. What they did not show was the entrance of the shapely brunette and the altercation with the ex-boyfriend. Jack and Stuart were deeply concerned as Jim related the events in the gym.

"We've got some serious players on our hands!" Stuart concluded. "If they can tap in to the security system monitoring the gym and erase data without the casual law enforcement agent catching it, they're top tier professionals."

Jim shared with them the warnings he had been given and expressed a newfound sense of urgency for security and secrecy. "I don't know who these guys are or what they want, except for me to forget about Greta and the journal."

"What journal?" Jack asked.

"Greta's aunt found an old journal in a trunk in the attic at their grandparents' home in Austria. It belonged to her great-grandfather. He was a *fallschirmjäger*, a paratrooper, in the German Army in World War II. Greta brought it back to Barcelona earlier this year after a weekend at home. She asked me to read it with her and see if it had any literary value. She was interested in possibly using it to write a book or something. We had just started wading through it a couple weeks ago. Put it in a Word document on my laptop as she translated it."

"So maybe that's what they were after when they ransacked your apartment," Stuart concluded.

"Yes, but why?" Jack wondered out loud.

"I don't know. But one thing they didn't count on was the thumb drive on my key chain that I had with me on my run. It has a copy of the whole journal on it. We had scanned the original just to make it easier to work with."

"Good. We'll want to look at that in detail later." Jack's mind was already formulating a tactical plan.

"It still seems incredible that they went to such great expense and trouble to impress a warning on you. Do you have any idea where they took you? Did you get a look at them?" Stuart asked.

"No, these guys are pros. And they put me through an interrogation technique like waterboarding on steroids. They basically were trying to intimidate me and assumed I would wave everybody off of Greta and her journal."

Jack looked straight at Jim. "We need to get you home. Let's think carefully about where we go from here. But let's not discuss this in the car or the house when we get there. I don't know how these guys found you, but we have to start thinking seriously about our security measures. We'll file a detailed report with the sheriff's department at home."

"I don't know, Dad," Stuart said. "If these thugs are as well connected as it appears, we might want to rethink who we talk to about this. I've got an idea, but let's talk about it later."

Just outside Oklahoma City, the trio pulled off I-40 and stopped at a quick mart to get gas and some snacks. Standing in the parking lot next to his dad, Stuart asked, "Don't you have an old school buddy who runs a private security firm?"

"Yeah, T.J. Davidson. He's the CEO of Tower Intelligence and Security Services. They're based out of Atlanta. But it's been awhile since we've talked."

Jim walked up after a restroom break and joined in the conversation. The three men concluded it would be prudent to seek the advice of a trusted friend who also happened to be one of the best in his business. And then, it was time to get back on the road.

Jim called his mom on Jack's phone and had a good long talk. The Harrisons had an uneventful trip home and arrived about 10 am the next morning. Jim was surprised but pleased to find his entire family assembled at the family home. The Harrisons were rallying around him, and he thought to himself that his captors had no idea whom they had picked on.

7 The Agency

The SunTrust Plaza building is the second tallest skyscraper in Atlanta. Built in 1992, the 869 foot structure boasts 60 stories and has a majestic view of the downtown area. The building was designed by architect John Portman. Its basic structure is a postmodern square tower with a magnificent, black, stair step crown. The international headquarters of Tower Intelligence and Security Agency is housed on its 18th floor. Ashley Nordstrom had just settled into her post at the Tower reception desk and was cuddling her second mug of hot coffee when her desk phone rang.

Jack Harrison didn't trust his home landline or cell phone. He was calling from a pay phone, no mean feat. He had finally located one after four stops. At the first two gas stations, he found pay phone boxes with rough holes where the devices had once been attached. It appeared they had been ripped out by the phone company years ago. On his third try at a truck stop, Jack walked up to the attendant, who was standing outside smoking his fifth cigarette of the shift. "You got a pay phone?"

The man, who couldn't have been a day under 40 and apparently didn't care if he made it to 50, squinted at Jack. "A pay phone? Sure, buddy. It's right inside past the disco balls, eight track tapes, shoulder pads, and Rubik's cubes."

"Thanks." Jack turned and headed back toward his truck. Looking over his shoulder he shot back at the attendant, "Well, when I find one, I'll be sure to call the eighties and let them know you've stolen their hair," poking fun at the attendant's ridiculous looking mullet.

"Tower Agency, Ashley speaking, how may I direct your call?"

"Jack Harrison for Mr. Davidson, please."

"Mr. Davidson is in a meeting this morning. May I take a message?"

Jack paused, "Is there a time I can call back and catch him?"

"Let me check his schedule," the secretary said. She returned to the line momentarily. "Why don't you try back at 12 noon. He'll probably check by here before he breaks for lunch."

"Great, I'll call at noon. Thanks."

At 12 o'clock sharp, Jack called back using the same phone booth, and this time his call was transferred to the office of the CEO.

"Jack, how are you?"

"I'm doing well, T.J. How about you?"

"Couldn't be better."

The two old friends chatted for a minute. Then Jack got down to business. "T.J., my family is facing some difficult decisions, and I'm calling to see if you can steer us in the right direction. Can I come by and talk to you in person?"

"Sure, but let me ask you a question. Is personal security an issue?"

"Yes, it is."

"Alright. Fine. Then let me suggest you meet me at 4:30 this afternoon at The Nautilus. It's a subway sandwich shop on the corner of Peachtree and Ellis here in downtown Atlanta. Are you familiar with that area?"

"No, but I can web search it and put it on my GPS."

"Good, see you then," Davidson closed.

"Perfect."

That afternoon Jack arrived early at the subway shop. Davidson, however, was already there seated at one of the small tables nursing a Coca-Cola on crushed ice. "Good to see ya," Jack said shaking Davidson's hand as he rose from his chair. Davidson slipped a folded piece of paper into Jack's palm and sat down. Jack opened the note and read. *Say nothing of importance. In one minute excuse yourself and proceed to the men's room. I will follow momentarily. Wait for me. Probably not necessary but just being careful.*

Jack made small talk and then said, "I'll be back in a minute, need to wash up."

Davidson followed a minute later. He and Jack were the only patrons in the small men's room. Davidson locked the door and quietly reached inside his suit pocket and pulled out a hand held electronic bug detector. Without a word he swept Jack slowly from head to toe. "You're clean," he said finally.

"Well, that's comforting," Jack smiled. "You treat all our old school buddies this way?"

"No, not all, but some. I've learned to trust few situations to chance. It's the times we find ourselves in. Anyway, it's how I make my living. Now, unless you're hungry for a sub sandwich, we'll drive over to my office and get down to business." Jack nodded, "Sure, but I could just follow you in my truck."

"No, but if you don't mind, give me your keys. One of my guys is waiting in my car. He'll take yours over to a warehouse we use and give it a thorough going over."

Jack handed him the keys. Davidson unlocked the restroom door and returned to their table in the sandwich shop. Jack followed a few seconds behind.

Both men left the shop together and walked down the street to a parking garage. They entered and climbed the stairs to the second level. Davidson pointed to a navy blue 2005 Lexus LS430 parked in a corner next to a Jeep Cherokee. "The Lexus is mine," he said.

As they approached the car, the passenger door opened and a Hispanic man in his mid-thirties stepped out. Davidson tossed the man Jack's keys. "Here. I'm taking Jack over to the office. How long will it take you?"

"Oh, driving over to the warehouse, sweeping the car, and coming back, about an hour," the man responded nonchalantly.

"Fine. We shouldn't be much longer than that. Oh yeah, sorry, Jack. This is Reynaldo. Reynaldo Cintron, one of my best operatives. Reynaldo, meet Jack Harrison. One of my buds from high school."

"A pleasure, Mr. Harrison," Reynaldo beamed. "So you knew the boss a long time ago?"

"Yes, a very long time ago. He and I shared several adventures."

Davidson injected, "Jack's driving a white Ford F-150 pick-up. It's parked at the Nautilus."

"Great. I'll take care of him."

Jack and Davidson arrived at the Sun Trust Plaza within minutes and rode the elevator up to the 18th floor. "We're in suite 1810," Davidson said as they stepped out of the elevator onto the plush carpet. Jack was impressed by the opulence of the building, but Davidson was down to earth. The lavish surroundings reflected the expectations of the firm's clients, not any narcissistic tendency on Davidson's part. He apparently hadn't allowed his success in business to go to his head. Davidson seemed genuinely interested in Jack and his wife and their children. He peppered Jack with questions about the challenges of raising a large family. Jack realized and appreciated the fact that his old friend was a good listener.

"Here we are," Davidson commented as he stepped up to a paneled, dark oak door with a bronze number 10 at the top center. He punched in an entry code on a keypad attached to the wall to the right of the door and turned the brass handle. The door opened and the men entered a bright, small office. "Hi, Ashley."

"You're back."

"Your skills of observation are certainly improving," Davidson said with a grin.

"Mr. Harrison, I presume. I'm Ashley Nordstrom. You'll have to excuse my boss's rude manner. We're all working on his people skills, but he's a hard case." She smiled, and Jack could see that the staff at Tower was comfortable enough with each other to swap tongue-in-cheek comments. "I'll be leaving in a few minutes. Do you need anything before I go, boss?"

"No, we're fine. See you in the morning, and drive careful."

"See ya tomorrow."

"Jack, make yourself at home in our conference room," Davidson instructed as he opened a door off the entry office and flipped on a light switch. "There's juice and water in this fridge," he pointed to a small refrigerator on a table to the side of the door. "And the bathroom is down this hall and first door on your left."

"Thanks."

"I'll get some pads and pens and be right back. I also have to make two brief calls."

"Great. Take your time. I'm in no hurry. I just appreciate your meeting with me." Jack surveyed the conference room as

Davidson left. The spacious room had an oblong oak table in the center surrounded by eight black executive chairs. He stepped over to examine a large oil painting which dominated the back wall of the wood paneled room. The art piece was a DeRuyters original commissioned especially for Tower. The artist had captured a stone castle turret standing sentinel on a forested hill. The turret was bathed in the vivid light of a low slung sun. Flanking woods knelt in rich, dark hues. Jack stood quietly in the room pondering the exquisite textures of the stone and foliage captured by the oil on canvas.

"Captivating isn't it?" said Davidson, who had slipped up behind Jack unnoticed.

"It really is a striking piece. I don't recognize the artist, though. Who is this DeRuyters?" Jack asked.

"He is a young college kid from New York. I saw some of his work a couple years ago when we were on an assignment for his father. I decided to ask him to produce a painting just for Tower ISA and just for this room. And I think he did a great job. When he gets to be an acclaimed artist someday, there's no telling what this'll be worth."

"Well, I know your time is valuable, T.J., so I'll cut to the chase."

Both men sat down at the table, and Jack told his story, beginning with his first distress call from Jim in Barcelona. T.J. listened carefully, taking notes on a yellow legal pad. Occasionally he asked a question for clarification.

"Well, that's quite an account." He paused reflectively and then spoke quite deliberately, "I'll help you all I can. But this may take a lot of patience and could involve some degree of danger."

"We're aware of that and are willing to accept the risk. Jim's already been through the grinder. And we're coming to believe a girl's life may be in the balance!" Jack said soberly.

"You mean Greta?"

"Yes, that's right. Jim still hasn't heard a thing from her for more than a week."

"Alright, then, let's begin. I'd first go ahead and file a report with the local authorities. If you don't, the bad guys will assume you're up to something else. Guessing they're still monitoring you, you need to put on a show, acting how they expect you to. Once you've filed a report, and the cops turn up nothing -- they may not even believe such wild tale anyway-- the abductors may accept that you finally give up. We'll attempt to propagate that idea while we work back channels to find out who and where they are and what they're really up to. Are you prepared to go into acting?"

"Sure," Jack replied, smiling for the first time since their discussion began.

"Next, I want you to call this number in the morning at 7:30 and tell 'em about your water leak under the kitchen sink."

"We don't have a leak, as far as I know," Jack said, puzzled.

"Yeah, well, you need a plumber anyway, so call 'em in the morning. We must assume that all your electronic forms of communication have been compromised. If we're careful, we can use their success, so far, against them. I'll have a team out there first thing in the morning to sweep your home, office, and the rest of your vehicles for bugs. They'll be driving a service van. In the meantime, the whole family needs to act as natural as possible knowing all the while that someone may be listening. Until we clean your whole place, if you need to have a secure conversation, go on a walk around the block or a hike in the woods. Your cell phone is ok to use since I checked it. But the rest of the family shouldn't count on theirs until we sweep 'em. When you call for the 'plumber' in the morning, use your land line. Your adversaries are definitely not amateurs. But remember, *pride goes before a fall.*"

Davidson looked at his wristwatch. "Uh oh, 6:30. I better quit talking and get you back to your truck. We're both gonna be in trouble with the family for being late for supper. I've got enough info to get the ball rolling. But I'd like to meet with you again in a couple of days and have you bring Jim with you. We'll go over everything he remembers and begin to formulate a strategy. Also, have him bring that memory stick. Obviously, somebody thinks the journal is a very interesting document. In the meantime, we'll start making inquiries into the disappearance of Greta Rose. We've got a number of operatives in Europe. Some of their contacts may have heard or seen something. The sooner we jump on this, the greater the chance of turning up something helpful."

The men continued to talk as they left the Tower office and drove back to the Nautilus. Davidson dropped Jack off and said, "Reynaldo texted me and your truck was clean. No bugs. See you in a couple days." Davidson's mood was confident and reassuring.

"OK, T.J., I appreciate what you're doing for us. We feel out of our element with all this," Jack thanked him and headed for his pickup.

8 The Plumbers

On Saturday morning, a white service van pulled into the driveway in front of the Harrison home in north Macon. Emblazoned on the sides of the van was a black adjustable wrench with a red handle underscored with the words, *Wrench and Trench, We solve your water problems!* A young black man in gray coveralls got out of the passenger door and walked up to the front door of the Harrison home with a work order in hand. He rang the doorbell and waited. Jack Harrison opened the door and greeted the "plumber." "Good morning. I appreciate you guys getting here so quickly."

"Yes, sir. We're here to solve your 'problem'," he said with a hint of a smile.

Jack ushered in the man and two companions who had now joined him from the van. "The problem sink is in here in the kitchen." He led the way through the living room into the adjoining kitchen. "This is my wife, Jean."

"Good morning," the three men said, almost in unison.

"Good morning to you. I'm sure glad you're here. A woman just can't function without a kitchen sink, you know," Jean quipped.

"Yes, ma'am, we've heard that before," the head plumber remarked.

At that moment, the taller of the plumber's two assistants yelped as if in pain as he jumped backwards. A furry blur of black and white bounced from his shoulder onto the floor and down the hall. "What in the world?" he exclaimed.

Jack, recovering from a barely restrained chuckle, said, "Sorry, that was Mohawk. He was just checking you guys out. He's our guard cat, a Maine Coon."

"That was too big for any house cat. He must weigh 20 pounds. 'Bout knocked me off my feet." The plumber stared at his feline assailant, now stopped in the hall and standing with his black tail erect and ending in a curl resembling an interrogatory punctuation.

"I'm really sorry. He doesn't mean any harm. If he wanted to hurt you, he would've," Jack continued.

"Where did he come from, anyway?" the plumber asked looking over his shoulder.

"Oh, he sleeps up on top of the bookshelf until he gets ready to exercise. You just happened to be in the right place at the wrong time," Jean commented, smiling. "He didn't scratch you did he?"

"No, just startled me," he admitted trying to regain his dignity as a trained professional security operative.

"Have to admit, he did get the 'drop' on you, man" the head plumber chortled.

The tall assistant cleared his throat as his leader changed back to a no-nonsense discourse, "Mr. Harrison, if you don't mind, we'll also do a whole house inspection while we're here just to make sure you don't have any other problems in the making. So, we'll be under the house and in each of the bathrooms. Do you have a sink or bathroom in your attached building?"

"Yeah, a toilet and sink is all. It's my office-shop," Jack replied sliding easily into his role of needy homeowner.

Actually, the shop had no bath at all, but Jack's acting lines gave the Tower operative a legitimate reason for going out to his shop should anyone be watching or listening.

One of the plumbers "fixed" the leaky kitchen sink. Meanwhile, the other two men inspected and swept the entire house and shop inside and out for electronic eavesdropping and spying devices. An hour later, the lead plumber approached Jack Harrison. "We're done, Mr. Harrison. Mr. Davidson will give you a more in-depth report, but here is basically what we've found: there's a tap on your landline phone, there's an electronic bug in your shop, and a camera with a transmitter on the power pole next to your front yard. Everything else is clean. Per Mr. Davidson's instructions, we have *not* removed the devices. In the past, we've used these kinds of bugs to our advantage in situations where we want to feed false information to the eavesdroppers. I also checked everyone's cell phones. They're all fine. Finally, we've put our own cameras in to watch your house. There's a total of five. No coverage of your bathrooms or bedrooms. We're not here to invade your privacy. Now, nobody comes or goes without our knowing. I hope that gives you some measure of reassurance."

"Sure," Jack answered. "We're glad for any help you can give us with security."

"We'll be in touch. And, by the way, the kitchen sink is working fine."

"Thanks. Anything we should or should not do?" Jack asked as the plumbers finished packing up to leave.

"No, sir. Just realize that somebody is watching who comes and goes and listening to all landline conversations and anything that goes on in your office-shop building. Our boss'll probably call you this afternoon and set up a strategy session.

I'll be giving him a written report before lunch," the lead plumber advised. "Have a good one."

"Thanks," Jack responded, grateful for the expertise of the men from Tower.

After the "plumbers" left, Jack asked Stuart to gather the rest of the family for a conference. Jean persuaded her husband to have the discussion over the hot brunch she had just finished preparing. She had cooked a large cheese, egg, and sausage casserole for her family and set it on the lazy Susan which filled the center of the circular dining table. Fresh cut grapefruit halves were at each place setting of the large oak table.

Glenn and Jim had slept in on this last lazy Saturday in June, but now they found themselves quietly slipping into their seats at the round table. Their mother's food had remarkable reviving powers for their sleepy bodies and minds.

Their sisters had been up for a while. Michelle and Annette had just come back from a four mile jog. "I'm starving. Let's eat!" Michelle said. "You guys get your beauty sleep?"

"Yeah, yeah," Glenn responded. "Looks like you girls *didn't* get yours. You're sweating like pigs," he kidded as he winked at his dad.

"Thanks, little brother," Michelle shot back. "You really know how to encourage a girl. And just for your information, girls don't sweat; they glisten. Keep it up and I'll sic Zach on you."

Zachary Black, Michelle's 28-year-old husband of one year sat reading a copy of the Macon Telegraph. A mug of hot coffee sat on the table directly in front of him and his newspaper. "Glenn, do you really wanna cross swords with her before breakfast?" he asked without lowering his newspaper.

"I guess not. Don't wanna ruin everybody's appetite."

"Nothing is ruining *my* appetite," Michelle said. "Let's do it before it gets cold."

The rest of the family took their chairs at the table. Jack bowed his lightly graying head, "Let's pray." Eight heads bowed, and Jack Harrison thanked God for the food set before them. "Lord, thank you for my family and for our friends who came to help today. We ask you to help us find Greta, soon. Lord, give her strength and comfort. In Jesus' name, Amen."

Jean smiled as she looked around the table. *All my kids.* The casserole, juice, and homemade cinnamon rolls were passed from person to person. She saw a scene of pure joy as sunshine streamed into her dining room. What she did not see was a pair of icy blue eyes watching her family through a pair of binoculars. The man was lurking in the darkened bedroom of the house one hundred yards away with its back yard butted against that of the Harrisons.

*****

The family ate while Jack talked. "I met yesterday afternoon with T.J. Davidson at Tower. He listened, took notes, and said they would get back to us. He sent the 'plumbers' this morning. They found a bug on our house phone, one in the shop, and a camera out front. I don't want you guys to be alarmed, but we all know that what we're up against is serious. Jim has shared his story with you. This afternoon we meet with the sheriff's office, and we'll probably be referred on to the GBI or the Feds. I don't know how much help they can or will be. We have to be responsible for our own safety and security. At least for a while, till we get these guys off our backs, whoever they are, we have to be proactive. I want all of you to stay in close touch with each other. I don't want any of you to be out by yourself. I want you to keep me aware of your schedule. And don't call us on the house phone. Use my cell. It's clean. And I want to cover a bit about situational awareness. An example of how not to do it is Jim." All eyes briefly glanced Jim's way as he winced. "Live and learn. He helped this brunette, which was the right thing to do in the circumstances. But things weren't what they appeared to be. He took her cup of tea, drugged tea. He wasn't on his guard."

Jack paused and took a drink of hot coffee. "Do you guys know what I mean by 'situational awareness'?"

"Sorta. I've heard the term somewhere," Annette answered for most of the siblings.

Stuart nodded and said, "Yeah, that was a big topic in some of our SERE training."

"Okay. Well, I don't want to bore you, but this is critical. T.J. gave me some material on it, and I also read some on the internet this morning. You all know the world we live in can be a nasty place. Terrorists and criminals can run their operations anywhere there are people. But their attacks don't come out of nowhere. They plan. They do surveillance. They execute. Pass the juice, please."

After two bites of casserole and a drink of juice, Jack continued. "I want you to be aware of what's going on around you at all times. Trust your gut. If something or someone seems out of place, they probably are. Look out for each other."

"But this all seems so surreal," Jean commented. "I mean, it sounds like something off of a movie or out of a novel. We just shouldn't have to worry about this kind of junk."

"Mom, you're right. We shouldn't have to" Stuart agreed. "But it is what it is… By the way, this food is great."

"Thanks. Anybody need another cinnamon roll?" Jean asked.

The Harrisons finished the meal with small talk, assuaging the pain of the imminent threat with the pleasure of food and company. Then everybody pitched in on the dishes. The mood in the room seemed bright, but the faint scent of premature darkness curled through the air.

*****

After meeting with the Bibb County Sheriff's office, Jack and Jim returned home. A detective with the Sheriff's Investigative Division had interviewed Jim for 45 minutes. He had listened attentively to Jim's story, taken notes, and then closed the interview promising to call the Harrisons the next week or sooner if anything turned up. The Criminal Investigation Unit would look into bringing in a technical consultant, who they used from time to time, to go over the security tape from Doc's Gym again.

"What do you think?" Jim asked his father as they drove home. "Did he believe me?"

"I don't know. They hear so much. At least he seemed to be paying attention. Looked like he was making some notes. But his questions were pretty routine." Jack stared out the side window of the '98 Ford Mustang as the Georgia countryside rushed by. His thoughts drifted. There was a lot for this father and husband to brood over. "My guess is that he was skeptical. It is very strange that someone would be kidnapped, probably taken out of country, and returned with no ransom demands. And *you* were less than candid when he asked you if you had a copy of the journal."

"I didn't lie," Jim protested.

"Yeah, but you led him to believe you *didn't* have a copy. You said all your electronics, your computer and all your disks and iPad, were taken. You failed to mention your thumb drive."

"Dad, I don't want anybody to know I have a copy of that journal. I don't think we can take for granted trusting the sheriff's office, or the GBI, or the FBI for that matter. I'm stretching just to trust your friend at Tower."

"Well, I don't like it. The truth's in short supply already."

The pair rode on in silence for a while. "Well, you didn't mention the bugs the Tower men found at our place."

"He wasn't interviewing me," Jack said in a low tone. "We've got to be discrete. 'Wise as serpents and harmless as doves.'" There was another pause. "What gnaws at the pit of my stomach is the question of what could be so crucial in a German soldier's war journal from seventy years ago."

9 The Discovery

Four days later, on Tuesday afternoon, Jack Harrison's cell phone rang. "Hello."

"This is Ashley with the Tower Agency. Mr. Harrison?" asked a cheerful voice on the phone.

"Yes, this is Jack."

"Can you hold for Mr. Davidson?"

"Yes, I'll hold."

In less than thirty seconds, T.J. Davidson picked up. "Jack, how's it going?"

"Doing fine, and you?"

"Excellent. Listen, I want to see you guys as soon as possible. I think we have turned up something. Can you come up this evening?"

"What've you got?"

"Probably best to go over it face to face. And be sure to bring Jim with you," T.J. Davidson said.

"Good. Mind if Stuart comes as well?"

"No, of course not. I may actually put him to work."

"Great. See you about seven?"

"Sure, I'll have some carry out Mexican waiting when you get here, and we'll do a working dinner," T.J. suggested. "Everybody ok with burritos and chalupas?"

"Absolutely. See you this evening."

Jack walked to the large kitchen where his wife was preparing the evening meal for her family. She was standing at the sink peeling potatoes, humming as she worked. Jack stealthily approached her from behind and wrapped his arms around her. "Gotcha," he grinned.

"Nah, heard you coming; you can't sneak up on me, Mr. Harrison," she bantered back. "You hungry?"

"I *am*," he answered nibbling on her right ear.

"Quit that," she responded with feigned outrage. "I've got work to do."

"Well, you'll have three fewer mouths to feed tonight, I'm afraid. T.J. just called. He wants to see us this evening and do a working supper. He thinks they've found something."

"Really?" she said turning to face Jack. "I hope so. Jim is worried sick over Greta. And I'm worried about Jim. He's been… so… I don't know-- just not himself. " She began slicing the potatoes placing them in a large pot. "We'll miss you for supper, but we'll have some leftovers waiting so your boys can eat again when you get back."

"I don't know how late we'll be. You don't have to wait up for us. But just leave the cookies on the table!"

"What's with you and my cookies? Didn't Doc Alexander tell you to cut back on the sweets at your last visit with him?" Jean lectured.

"I'm just a growing boy, my dear," he teased squeezing her again.

The Harrisons arrived at Tower an hour later and were ushered into the main conference room. T.J. was examining a Power Point slide displayed on the large screen which hung from the ceiling and covered most of the left side wall of the room. One of his operatives was seated at the oblong conference table and a technician was finishing the set up for the presentation. Several legal pads and pens were on the table.

"Hi, guys, ... right on time."

The three men returned the greeting, and hands were shaken all around.

"Call me if you need anything, I'll be right down the hall," the technician said to T.J. as he left the room.

"Gentlemen, I'd like you to meet one of my best my intelligence analysts, Jake Ewell. We affectionately call him 'The Snake'."

"Jake, The Snake?" Jack smiled. "Nice handle."

"Yeah, I guess it's because I've developed some expertise in identifying and retrieving valuable information by what you might call 'clandestine' methods," he grinned rubbing his chin.

Jake Ewell was indeed an exceptional intelligence operative. Born in Monte Vista, Colorado, he had joined the Army at age 17 after high school graduation in 1984. He began his military career in intelligence serving as a technical adviser to the Chief of Staff of US Central Command. He then served one combat tour in support of Operations Desert Shield and Desert Storm in 1990-91. Having been recognized by his superior officers as one with unusually keen cyber intelligence acumen, he received an assignment with the National Security Agency (NSA) at Ft. Meade, Maryland, in the Signals Intelligence Directorate (SID). His final duty station was a coveted position at the Pentagon as a senior advisor for cyber warfare to the Army Vice Chief of Staff. He retired from the Army in 2004 after 20 years of service and immediately filled a lucrative position with Tower ISA.

"Alright, let's get started," T.J. said as he handed each man a to-go box from the Mexican eatery down the street.

The men sat down at the conference table and began their meal in silence, except for murmurs of approval. Delicious aromas wafted from the hot, spicy food they found stuffed in their boxes, which were printed with the red and green *El Rio* logo. T.J. dimmed the room lighting just enough to enhance the viewing of the slide projected on the screen in front of them. "Gentlemen, this is a map of the northeast corner of New Mexico where Jim was dropped on the roadside. As you can see, this is a pretty desolate stretch of road. Jim, you estimated you were riding in the van (I suppose we're still operating under the assumption of a van) for two to three hours. From that estimate and an assumed speed of 70-80 miles per hour, we can zoom out and draw a circle." A purple circle materialized on the map. "This circle is set at a distance of 240 miles as the crow flies."

The screen shot advanced, and red dots highlighted two cities on the map. "Those cities are Colorado Springs, Colorado, and Albuquerque, New Mexico. If we include regional fields, we also have to consider Amarillo and Lubbock, Texas, and Santa Fe, New Mexico." Three blue dots now appeared on the screen. "And, finally, if Jim's time is off by 30-60 minutes, which is entirely possible given the circumstances, we would have to also consider Denver International." A green dot marked Denver. "Unless Jim's assessments are terribly flawed, these are the possibilities we have to analyze," T.J. concluded. "I'll let 'The Snake' present that analysis."

"Again, assuming that you're correct in your perception of a major international or regional airport and not a small rural or municipal airfield, we encompass only six likely candidates. You also guess you were on foot for another three hours. Backing up from the time you were picked up by Sgt. Washington, 0530, 5:30 am, we get a target time of 2330, that is 11:30 pm." Jake stood up, wiping a bit of salsa from the corner of his mouth, and cleared his throat. "Now, realizing time is often difficult to estimate when isolated from most reference points, we have added a reasonable margin of error, two hours, to either side and created a four hour window of investigation from 2100, 9:30 pm to 0130, 1:30 am."

Stuart spoke up for the first time, "Seems like that would be a huge number of aircraft arriving at possibly as many as six different locations during that time period. And, besides, how could you possibly prove which jet Jim was in?"

"Good questions. Let's give you the whole picture and then narrow things down." Jake continued. "Here's the stuff," he said, advancing to a slide with the six different locations under the title "**Aircraft Arrival Data**".

Confidential -- J. Harrison File

Aircraft Arrival Data

Colorado Spgs

1.	Hale Aerospace Industries	9:36pm	Gulf Stream III	Dallas
2.	Sherrouse Engineering Inc.	9:40pm	Beechjet 400	Chicago
3.	O'Connor Health Care LLC	9:51pm	Falcon 2000	Los Angeles
4.	Ball Food Services	11:33pm	Lear 35	OKC
5.	Kelly Power Holdings	11:41pm	Citation XLS	Houston

Albuquerque

1.	USAF	9:46pm	C20A	Omaha
2.	Gaetjens Publishing	9:53pm	Lear 55	Salt Lake
3.	Holland Farms Inc.	10:45pm	Westwind I	Kansas Cty
4.	Jones & Jones Pharma	11:01pm	Gulf Stream III	Chicago
5.	Balder Chemical	11:20pm	Citation Bravo	Houston
6.	Marr Telecom LLC	12:02pm	Lear 35	Dallas

Amarillo

1.	Snyder Automotive Inc.	9:32pm	Citation II	Houston
2.	Woods Entertainment LLC	9:34pm	Hawker Horizon	Las Vegas
3.	Eagle Drilling	10:12pm	Gulf Stream 150	Fargo

Lubbock

1.	Morrison Enterprises	9:30pm	Diamond 1A	Little Rock
2.	Hasty Ranches	9:50pm	Gulf Stream III	Denver

Santa Fe

1.	New Mexico State Gov't	9:43pm	Lear 60	Dallas
2.	Reliant Oil Inc.	10:09pm	Hawker 1000	Phoenix
3.	Arthur, Keith, and Hatton LLC	11:00pm	Premier 1A	San Fran

Denver

1.	Highwood Properties Inc.	9:37pm	Citation Excel	Cheyenne
2.	Intrepid Industries	9:41pm	Challenger 600	Vancouver
3.	Anderson Racing LLC	9:45pm	Falcon 2000	Mexico Cty
4.	Clemens Consulting	10:22pm	Beechjet 400	Santa Fe
5.	Gore, Castleman, and Gore	10:48pm	Premier 1A	Colo Spgs
6.	Curtis Construction Corp.	12:18am	Lear 55	Portland
7.	Bradley Investment Services	1:01am	Hawker 1000	OKC

"Okay, so you have a window with twenty-six aircraft arriving, owned by a hodge-podge of private and commercial entities. How does this help us find out who kidnapped and tortured my brother?" Stuart pushed.

"Another good question. We've inquired into each of these entities very discretely, so we don't tip our hand. So far, every single one of them looks legit. Now, that doesn't mean we're finished, but it doesn't help us either," Ewell conceded. "We could continue to probe carefully, but it could take weeks, or even months, to hit pay dirt."

Jim interjected, "We need to know something, and soon! If the same jerks have Greta…" he slammed his fist on the table. He looked 'The Snake' square in the eyes. "T. J. didn't call us up here just to look at a list of possibilities. Give us something."

"Alright, just cool your jets," Ewell continued in crisp, professional tone. "To summarize: because of Jim's alertness and good luck…"

"Providence!" Jack said.

"Okay, Providence; we have three pieces of information that his abductors don't know we have—the approximate time, location, and mode of his return. What we need is a fourth—which will allow sort of a 'quadrangulation', if you will."

"I think he just made that up," Stuart whispered to Jim. Jim ignored his brother and continued to listen with rapt attention to The Snake's exposition.

"Just hang with me for a few more minutes while I walk you through this and show you four more slides. Sometimes in this business you hang your hat on facts, data, calculations, et cetera. But, sometimes you just have to follow a hunch and hope and pray it doesn't waste your time and limited resources. I started with the assumption that the same guys who got you also got Greta. And I also know that all humans hate change. We all tend to be creatures of habit. We like our coffee a certain way, we have a routine for breakfast most days, we generally shop at the same stores, we usually drive the same way to work every day, and so forth. Now, of course there are multitudes of exceptions, but it is a rule of thumb.

I concluded that Greta was probably flown out of the Barcelona area on a corporate jet."

"That's a leap," Jack groused.

"Go on," Jim insisted.

"I looked at the major airports within modest driving time of Barcelona and came up with these three. And, just for completeness, I have included Barcelona, although I seriously doubt they would have flown out from there." A slide of northern Spain and southern France was projected. Four red dots marked Barcelona and the cities of Tarragona and Lleida in Spain and Pirigana, France.

'The Snake' advanced to a new slide. "I arbitrarily used a six hour window from 6:00 am until noon the day she disappeared, postulating that an aircraft leaving any earlier in the morning might draw attention --the last thing they would want-- and departing any later might give the authorities opportunity to stumble on to her." Ewell projected the next slide.

"This shows what we turned up."

Ewell's screen shot showed the four cities and the aircraft data in the same format as before.

Confidential -- J. Harrison File

Aircraft Departure Data

Barcelona

1.	Barcelona Institute of Arts and Sciences	6:15am	Embraer 430	Paris
2	BP Refining	6:42am	Hawker 1000	Bonn
3.	Siemens	7:03am	Global Express	Berlin
4.	Norse Industries	7:45am	Citation X	Amsterdam
5.	Michelle Parfumeries	7:58am	Lear 35	Rome
6.	Bayonne Polypropylene	8:23am	Westwind I	Toulon
7.	Logic Technologies	9:11am	Falcon 2000	Zurich
8.	Vive Teleperformance	11:33am	Gulf Stream III	Madrid

Lleida

1.	Krupp	8:17am	Diamond 1A	Paris
2.	Marconi Communications	9:20am	Hawker Horizon	Lyon

Perpignan

1.	Deutsche Bank	8:30am	Citation II	Brussels
2.	Bayer	9:00am	Lear 60	London
3.	Accenture Consulting	11:12am	Embraer Phenom	Paris

Tarragona

1.	Spanish Defense Ministry	9:30am	Lear 55	Madrid
2.	Gaucho Films	11:07am	Citation X	Casablanca

"So what does all this mean?" Stuart queried.

"We looked for a common thread. No duplications in the ownership of the aircraft. There were some common aircraft used, but I doubt that means anything," Ewell continued the briefing.

"So you struck out!" Jim fired at The Snake.

Jake Ewell rubbed his chin again and smiled. "If I'd quit there, yes. Instead, I ran a search for all subsidiaries and parent corporations for all of the entities listed."

He paused and looked from man to man seated at the table.

"And?" Jim asked.

"And I found a match. Balder Chemical is a subsidiary of Orkhon Corporation which is a holding of..... Norse Industries," The Snake concluded triumphantly.

10 The Corporation

The Snake waited for a response. Each man seemed transfixed on the screen in front of him. Ewell recognized that his audience still didn't quite grasp the significance of his discovery or appreciate his work yet.

"So what?" Jim finally asked.

"Alright, let me move further." Ewell dug in and endeavored to impress this group with the real meat of his investigative cyber trek. A new screen shot appeared with a bullet point summary.

CORPORATE NAME: **BALDER CHEMICAL**

- HEADQUARTERS: HOUSTON, TEXAS

- PRODUCT LINES:
  PRIMARY – PETROCHEMICAL (R&D)
     AGROCHEMICALS
  SECONDARY – OIL AND GAS EXPLORATION AND DEVELOPMENT
     HYDROGEN FUEL CELL DEVELOPMENT

- MISSION STATEMENT: TO DISCOVER AND DEVELOP
     CHEMICALS AND FUELS FOR THE
     BENEFIT OF MANKIND.

"Through extensive open source and *other* data resources, I have learned the following about Balder Chemical and Norse Industries." Ewell read through the bullet points on the slide. "And now to the parent company," he advanced to another shot.

CORPORATE NAME: **NORSE INDUSTRIES**

- HEADQUARTERS: ZURICH, SWITZERLAND

- REGIONAL OFFICES: AMSTERDAM, HOLLAND
  SAO PAULO, BRAZIL
  SYDNEY, AUSTRALIA
  LAGOS, NIGERIA
  HONG KONG

- PRODUCT LINES:
  PRIMARY– CHEMICALS, ELECTRONICS, AVIATION, SHIPPING
  SECONDARY– INDUSTRIAL MACHINERY, PLASTICS, RUBBER

- MISSION STATEMENT: TO USE TECHNOLOGY AND INNOVATION TO HARNESS THE POWER AND DIVERSITY OF NATURE.

"So who owns these corporations and what would they want with Greta or me?" Jim demanded.

The Snake's tone was patient. "They are publicly traded companies and are owned by stockholders. As to what they want with you or Greta, I don't know. So far I haven't been able to get any deeper into their companies, but I'm working on it. We have operatives nosing around in cities where these companies have larger operations, and I'm using every *legal* means available to get electronic data. We want to find out what they're up to without their knowing we're probing. It's a bit delicate. It may take a while."

"Like forever!" Jim speculated.

Davidson interjected, "If Jake says he will get the info, he will. Just give him some time."

"I'm not sure we have much time," Stuart inserted. "Who knows how long before we get hit again -- another kidnapping, a break-in, or worse. And only God knows what Greta is going through..."

At this point, Davidson stood, "We think we know where they may have taken Greta. There is a place in Amsterdam. We have contacts. They've seen a young woman that fits her description. There are indications that this woman is being moved and held against her will."

Now Jim jumped to his feet, "Where, tell me where!"

"In due time. We don't want to go off half-cocked. There is planning and preparation. We're dealing with a consummate adversary, and we can't afford *any* mistakes." Davidson's tone now had the air of authority. "Do I make myself clear?"

Jim slowly sat down. "Yes, sir."

"As soon as we can be ready, I will be sending one of our operatives who has extensive experience in hostage rescue to Amsterdam." Looking straight at Stuart he said, "I'd like to send you with him."

Jim jumped up again, "Wait a ..."

This time his father intervened. "Sit down. Let's hear T.J. out."

"But I don't..."

"Sit... down," with a stern tone this time Jack stood and put his hand on Jim's left shoulder.

"Two things you should consider," Davidson calmly made his case to Jim. "Stuart has had extensive combatives training. You haven't. Stuart is not emotionally attached to this girl. You are. You are not physically or mentally ready to go on a mission like this. That's just the way it is. If you want my help, you've got to trust my call on this. This is our business. "

Davidson continued. "I think we risk spooking Greta into running if we send you. She might see you before we find her. She might try to run or hide to 'protect' you from the men who took her. On the other hand, she won't know Stuart, but if he gets close to her, she might notice enough of a resemblance to possibly trust him. If she is where we think she is, she will be very suspect of any one."

"So where do you think she is?" Jim asked.

"For now, all *you* need to know is Amsterdam." Davidson sat again. He seemed relaxed and confident. "Stuart, I understand you have an impressive military record as a PJ with the Air Force- Kosovo, Iraq, Afghanistan."

"We did our job."

"Are you able to make a trip to Europe?"

Stuart answered, "Well, our school is out for summer break. I'll need to check with Leigh, though. I can get back with you tomorrow."

"I really need to know something tonight. You'll be gone for possibly three days. If our intel is spot on, you could be back in 24 hours. Can you call her now?" Davidson was firm.

"Sure. If you think it's urgent. Let me step outside for a minute."

He stepped out into the hall and called his wife at their home in Stone Mountain. In a few minutes, he returned. "She took some convincing, but now she's okay with it. Anything we can do to help."

"Good. The Snake will arrange for you to meet with Frederick Michaels, my operative who'll be your partner. Hopefully, you guys can be on a plane within the next 24 hours. I assume you have a passport."

"Yes, but I haven't used it in a few years. And if we find Greta, and she agrees to come with us back to the States, how about getting her through customs?"

"Good question. We have friends in the State Department. We've worked that out with a little help," Davidson responded.

"How about her picture for the passport?" Jack wondered.

"She had a Facebook page with a suitable picture. We used that with *minor* modifications." He pulled a new United States passport from his pocket and handed it to Jim.

Jim carefully opened the blue passport. For a moment he gazed at the picture of Greta. An awkward silence hung in the room. Finally, turning to Jack, Davidson said, "I think that does it for you guys. We *do* need to get to work on translating that journal. Maybe we can figure out what is so critically interesting to the men from Norse Industries. Jim, you didn't happen to bring your copy with you did you?"

"Yes, sir," he responded stiffly trying to mask the emotion he felt in his throat. He pulled a thumb drive from his shirt pocket and handed it to Davidson. "You can keep this one. I've made another copy. Let us know what you find."

"We will. And The Snake and his team will be discretely but persistently knocking on the door of Norse Industries."

Jack cocked his head slightly, "Is that ... legal?"

Davidson smiled, "Don't ask."

11 The District

Amsterdam sits on the Amstel River on Holland's northwest coast and is crisscrossed by multiple canals. With a population of 780,000, it is the largest city in the Netherlands and boasts one of the most robust financial hubs of Europe. Having passed through the suburbs of this opulent city, Frederick Michaels and Stuart Harrison stepped out of their taxi and paid the Amsterdam driver, giving a generous tip. "Dank je vel," the driver said, grinning at Stuart. The black and yellow cab pulled away, leaving the two men standing on the curb of the dingy, cobblestone street. Only 40 minutes previous they had landed at Schiphol International Airport, cleared customs, and quickly hired a ride to the De Wallen district. Michaels pulled a slip of paper from his pants pocket. With a small penlight, he read penciled writing- a simple street name but no number. Both men took a deep breath and started walking. "Let's get this over," Michaels instructed.

The air was heavy as the two Americans wandered down the concrete side walk in front of a set of row houses. The street was narrow, the building facades on either side, high. Small balconies with rusting wrought iron railings clung to the faces of the aging structures. Cheap playbills covered every lamppost. Red neon lights flashed from various street-level windows advertising the services within. Pedestrians, almost entirely men of different ages and ethnicity, roamed the streets and came and went from the various entrances. "I think I'm going to be sick," Stuart muttered under his breath.

"Keep moving, I haven't seen her yet," Michaels encouraged.

"She may not even be here," Stuart countered.

"We can only pray so."

Continuing down the gloomy alley with a sense of urgency but attempting to restrain their pace, the men passed windows trumpeting women from a variety of cities and countries-Singapore, Ukraine, Spain, Egypt, Russia, France, Japan, and Hong Kong. The two carefully examined each frontage space as they passed, but they felt revulsion, not enticement. Stuart was ambivalent, hoping to find Greta, but at the same time fearing she might actually be here, in this place of hellish bondage.

The two companions continued walking and scrutinizing. A pair of uniformed Amsterdam police strolled by apparently oblivious to the human torment being played out nightly behind the walls of this foul district of the 'Venice of the North'. "*How can this be legal?*" Stuart thought to himself.

Nearing the end of the alley, the searchers finally came to a front that advertised, "Germany." They nonchalantly gazed at the woman seated behind the window. "Is it?" Stuart whispered.

"Maybe," Michaels responded.

Both men studied the downcast face. "The make-up is so heavy and dark, I can't be sure from the picture," Stuart agonized. "But I might as well try; what's the worst that could happen?"

"You don't want to know…. I can go instead if you want," Michaels offered.

"No, I'll go; I look enough like my brother. She's more likely to be reassured by a somewhat familiar face. If this is her, this shouldn't take long. You got my six o'clock?"

"I'm not going anywhere!"

Carrying a small duffle bag on his right shoulder, he stepped up to the half door behind which sat a small olive skinned man with a black mustache. Pointing to the window, Stuart asked in German, "How much?"

"Seventy-five euros," he responded.

"Nein," Stuart haggled, "twenty-five," continuing in his limited memorized German.

"Fifty," the now frowning man rejoined. "Sehr gut," he added, looking back at the window.

Shaking his head and feigning disbelief, Stuart offered, "Forty!"

"Nein, fifty." The shop owner held firm.

Spinning quickly on his heels and heading toward a shop across the road, Stuart heard the man at the door yell, "Forty!"

He stopped, paused, and turned to face the sweaty little man again. Handing him forty euros, he entered the shop and followed the woman from the window who now ascended a narrow staircase. A single naked, incandescent bulb hung from the ceiling revealing patches of peeling red paint on the sullied walls. The wooden stairs creaked with each step Jim took. The door at the top of the stairs evinced deep scars in the once handsome wood. Stuart trailed close behind as the woman entered the small room at the top of the stairs. He closed the door and asked gently in English, "Greta?"

The woman looked up at him with a startled expression and her lower lip began to quiver, "Yes," she whispered. As an inkling of recognition passed across her face, she asked, "Who…."

Before she could finish her inquiry, Stuart opened his bag and tossed a bundle of clothes to her saying, "Jim Harrison is my brother. If you want to leave, get dressed now! Quickly!"

Large tears pooled in the girl's eyes, and she began to sob quietly.

"Stop it!" Stuart ordered. "Later. Now we must move rapidly before your handler gets suspicious. Do exactly as I say and stay right with me."

"But they said if I ever leave, they would kill my mother and my sister!"

"They are safe with friends. Now get ready. We're going home!"

Pausing briefly, her deliverance settling solidly in her mind, Greta stepped into the tiny adjoining bathroom with the bundle of clothes. In less than three minutes the bathroom door opened, and she returned neatly dressed in navy slacks and long sleeve tan blouse, tears dried, and wearing a look of iron determination.

"Good," Stuart said, encouraged at the transformation. He opened the door and led the way down the stairs with Greta following. She shouldered the duffle bag with her small cache of belongings stuffed within. A light 'thud' sounded as they reached the foot of the stairs as the duffle slipped off her shoulder and hit the bare wooden floor.

Stuart turned at the sound and reached to pick up the bag. He stood and began to turn when a sharp, piercing pain struck his left mid back. "Where do you think you are going with my property?" the little man snarled as he leaned on the knife he had rested against Stuart's back.

"With me," a voice answered crisply behind the pimp's head. The cold steel muzzle of the Beretta Centurion which now indented the skin of his neck impressed the man with the correctness of the answer. The pimp slowly let off of the pressure he exerted with the knife against Stuart's back.

"Yes, of course; have a good time with her," he croaked.

The swift slap across the man's left cheek knocked him off his feet. Greta stood panting looking down at the man. "Miserable wretch!"

"Roll over," Michaels barked. The man quickly obeyed now genuinely afraid that his life was worth less than forty euros to his guests. Stuart bound wrists and ankles with zip ties and a generous swath of duct tape was wrapped around his mouth leaving adequate room for air exchange via his bulbous nose.

Stuart, Greta, and Michaels quietly exited the shop locking the door behind them. Together they walked briskly down the still busy street. At the corner they hailed a cab and were soon speeding toward Schiphol. An hour later the final call for KLM flight 730 to Atlanta was made, and Greta and Stuart stood patiently at the gate waiting to board. Michaels joined them in line, returning from a nearby payphone. He had briefly advised the Amsterdam authorities that there might be a greasy little shop owner on Oudemarkt Street who needed assistance.

The flight to Hartsfield was quiet. The cabin was about half empty. Except for the time spent eating the meal KLM served, the trio slept most of the trip. The two men could not imagine the trauma their friend had suffered and felt it wise to remain silent comforters as she rested.

A hardback copy of *Bonhoeffer*, a biography by Eric Metaxas, sat open, perched on Michaels's seat tray. He was deeply engrossed but noticed Greta had roused. "Good morning," he said to her.

"Is it?" she queried. "Why didn't you kill him?"

"What?" he whispered.

"Why did you let him live?"

"Murder is ... wrong. Besides, killing him would not lessen your suffering."

"Yes, it would," Greta responded slowly and deliberately. "What do you know about abuse and exploitation, cruelty and mistreatment? You don't know what they have done to me."

In the quiet cabin of the KLM flight, Greta stared at Michaels ... and waited for a response.

Michaels looked at his book but was not reading. "Does my name have any significance to you?"

Thinking he was changing the subject, she answered, "No, but it is a *nice* name."

"My ancestors, any guesses?"

"I would hate to speculate."

"Jews, Greta, Austrian Jews."

As Greta looked at Frederick, tears began to well up in her eyes again. "I ... am ... sorry."

"Forgiveness. You must sometime come to forgiveness. Your body will heal, but if you do not forgive them, your soul never will."

Greta closed her eyes, and leaned back against her seat. Frederick Michaels did not know if she slept or simply chose to shut him out.

The KLM flight arrived in Atlanta on time and the two men closely escorted their friend off the plane. When they reached the airport reception area, the entire Harrison family was waiting for them, and there was a large bag of chocolate chip cookies.

12 The Lake

Greta stood back as Stuart and Frederick waded into the Harrison family throng. She felt overwhelmed as she witnessed the hand shaking, smiles, and bear hugs showered on the pair of men who had effected her rescue. As if a dam cracked and then burst, tears trickled down her cheeks and then poured from her eyes. Jean Harrison rushed over and wrapped her arms around the girl. Unable to gain control, Greta sobbed without restraint. She was too tired, too empty, too raw to feel embarrassment in front of her new friends and the somewhat curious crowd in the airport. Jean whispered, "It's OK. Just let it come… It's OK. We love you, and we're gonna take care of you." She held Greta's head tight against her shoulder as she stood firmly planted in the center of the Arrivals waiting area.

Jim slowly walked over, feeling an awkward mix of relief and helplessness for his friend. He encircled both his mother and Greta with his long, muscular arms and looked around at passersby with a gaze that said, "Don't even try to interfere with this."

Momentarily, Greta staunched the tears and sighed deeply. She looked up at Jean and wiped her face with her shirtsleeve. Smiling, Jean asked, "Feel better?"

"Yes. I'm very sorry."

"You have nothing to be sorry for. You are safe with us now. I'm Jim's mother, Jean. And this is most of the rest of the tribe," she said motioning, toward her husband and two daughters who were standing in a cluster next to Stuart and Frederick Michaels.

The travelers and their welcoming committee made their way to the parking garage. There, Michaels bid the Harrisons and Greta good bye, found his car, and headed for his home in the Atlanta suburb of Conyers. The girls rode in Jean's car and the guys in Stuart's Toyota 4 Runner.

*****

The Toyota and the Lexus pulled into the asphalt driveway of the Harrison home. The family unloaded and welcomed Greta to their modest home. Within the hour, Greta showered, ate a steaming bowl of Jean's potato soup, called her mother in Austria, and went to bed. She slept for over twelve hours. Jean and Jack talked things over and decided that Greta needed time away. And they knew the perfect place.

Lake Sinclair sits in rural central Georgia northeast of Macon. Uncle Keith Harrison built one of the first cabins on the manmade lake in 1953, the year he returned from serving with the American Army as a combat engineer in the Korean War. Constructed of Georgia pine logs, the cabin was simple, sturdy, and comfortable. After a day and a half at the north Macon home, Michelle and Annette drove with Greta to the family cabin on Lake Sinclair. The sisters had another three or four days before they had to return to their respective responsibilities. They hoped some time alone with Greta in the tranquility of the cabin site would be a nurturing start to her recovery.

Mosby, the Harrison's golden retriever, insisted on accompanying the women. He piled into the back of the car with Greta and found a comfortable spot on the seat with his head resting in her lap. At first put off by the boldness of the canine, Greta slowly warmed to the idea of the big dog using her as a pillow. It seemed his trust in her came as naturally as his slow, unlabored breaths.

After the three girls and the retriever left, Jack received a text on his cell phone from T.J. Davidson: *"call when you get a chance."*

"T.J., Jack. How are you?"

"Fine, how's Greta?"

"She's been through a living nightmare, but she's putting on a good front. It's gonna take a lot of love to help her heal."

"Well, I'm certain she's in just the right place for that. When she's had a few days to process everything and get back some stability, we'd like to meet with her and gently draw out any details if we can."

"I'm not sure how long before she'll be up to that," Jack said.

"Yes, well, I'm sure she wants this evil network crushed even more than we do. We'll be very sensitive in dealing with this," T.J. promised.

"I'll let you know. Right now, Michelle and Annette are taking her up to Lake Sinclair. We have an old cabin up there that belonged to one of my uncles. It's totally secluded. And we've been very discrete about this. Nobody but family knows anything about Greta being with us."

"Good. Sounds like just what the doctor ordered. Keep us posted," T.J. requested.

"Sure, and let us know if you have any breakthrough on the Norse Industries connection."

"Will do. Talk to you later."

*****

By the time the women pulled off US Highway 129 and the car rumbled down the long gravel road to Uncle Keith's cabin, it was late afternoon. An orange solar ball smoldered in the sky behind the tall pines. It cast long, soft shadows over the pine needles blanketing the ground. Annette's red Chevy Cobalt came to a stop and the three friends stepped out and stood looking at the quiet scenery. Mosby woke up, jumped out, and proceeded to make the rounds of the cabin site, sniffing and marking his territory.

Greta was the first to notice something was missing- the sounds of the city. No traffic, no sirens, no lawn mowers, no airplanes, none of the "hum" of Barcelona, Amsterdam, Atlanta or even Macon. Just the pleasant chirping of different song birds, crickets, and tree frogs emanating from the woods surrounding the rustic log cabin. Michelle inhaled deeply. "Wow, ... the smell of those pines."

Her two companions agreed. "I think you're going to love this place, Greta," Annette commented.

Annette led the trio onto the wraparound porch and up to the door. She retrieved a key from under an empty flower pot to the right of the door and tried it. With some difficulty, the stiff lock yielded and the women entered. Michelle flipped on some lights and showed Greta around. The furnishings were simple. That's how Uncle Keith had wanted it. "The more stuff you own, the more stuff owns you," he used to say.

Mosby walked in as if he owned the place and went straight to his food bowl in the kitchen. Empty. He barked once at Greta as if to alert her to his impatience with the lack of service in the establishment. "You must be hungry!" Greta cooed.

"He's always hungry," Michelle responded matter-of-factly. Annette and Michelle both laughed. And then, Greta laughed too. It seemed that this quiet cabin was just right. The women could safely set their cares aside for a few days.

13 The Cabin

The aroma of frying maple-cured bacon wafted up the stairwell and into the bedroom, beckoning Greta from her lazy slumber. The bed was a large 4 poster, and was handsomely covered by a hand-stitched quilt filled with heavy batting. A large blue star centered on a field of white with a thick red border topped the quilt. Greta sat up and looked around the room. A small oak desk and chair faced the corner to her right. A brass reading lamp was attached to the wall above the desk. On the right-hand wall, gauzy white curtains covered the window through which the sunlight painted the room in warm pastels. The door to the hallway was situated immediately opposite the foot of the bed, and a floor to ceiling built-in bookcase occupied the space between the door and the right-hand wall. The bookcase was bursting with an expansive variety of books, some with well-worn bindings, others with shiny new covers. The left-hand wall was centered by the door to a small bathroom. A restored antique four drawer chest stood in the far left corner of the bedroom. On the hardwood floor beside the bed rested a large rectangular oriental rug with gold and maroon tones. Framed photographs of American lighthouses hung on two walls of the lovingly decorated room.

Greta yawned and stretched and thought how good it felt to have a fresh new day to relish. She lifted the clean white bed sheets to her face and inhaled deeply. The scent was delightful. Swinging her feet to the floor, Greta stood and slipped on her bathrobe and patted over to the small bathroom where she washed her face and combed her hair. A smiling blond-headed, blue-eyed girl gazed at her from the mirror as she thought, *"Not much to look at this morning. Well, no guys around anyway, so it does not much matter."*

The bed was neatly made and her bathroom as clean as she had found it when she stepped into the hall and headed for the stairs. Her hand rested lightly on the polished oak banister as she bounced down the wooden stairwell in her bare feet. Greta could hear a voice humming carefree in the open kitchen. Steam hovered above a hot skillet resting on a stainless gas stovetop situated in a large island breakfast bar. Michelle, who appeared to be singing to the curling strips of bacon before her, looked up as Greta walked across the large but comfortably appointed family room and seated herself at the bar.

"Good morning, Sunshine," Michelle smiled. "How'd you sleep?"

"Wonderful. I was up kinda late checking emails. Trying to keep in touch with my mother. I am surprised you have internet here."

"It's bundled with the phone service. Just got it earlier this year."

"I also spent some time reading through more of my great-grandfather's journal. It is so fascinating."

"I'd love to read it some time. I love history."

"Me too." Greta closed her eyes and inhaled deeply. "The smells coming from this kitchen are irresistible!" She noticed a pan of homemade biscuits and a bowl of sliced fresh fruit on the counter. "I'd planned to sleep in this morning, but you certainly changed my mind with your kitchen creations. How long have you been up?"

"Oh, 'bout an hour and a half. 'Early to bed, early to rise' and all that, you know."

"No, is that one of your American colloquialisms?"

"I guess; just something my Mom used to say. She was always the first one out of bed in the morning."

Michelle deftly flipped the bacon with the spatula in her right hand while opening the refrigerator with her left and grasping a pitcher of orange juice. "Pour yourself some juice and then set the dishes if you don't mind; stay around here and I'll put you to work," she said with a brief wink.

Greta stood up and walked into the kitchen. "Who taught you to cook?"

"Oh, everybody—Mom, Dad, Annette and all my brothers. I'm the runt of the litter so everybody tried to teach me. With all that culinary counseling I learned to cook everything from quiche to barbecue ribs!"

After pouring her juice and setting three places at the island bar, Greta asked "Where's Annette, anyway?"

"Oh, she's outside on the porch reading. You can join her if you like. It *is* a beautiful day out there."

A little awkwardly Greta questioned, "Why do you do all the work?"

"I don't. I cook the breakfast, she does the dishes. At supper we trade. At lunch, it's every girl for herself."

Greta wandered out onto the large wrap around porch. Adirondack chairs were set in pairs around the exterior of the cabin. Annette sat reading her Bible with pen in hand as Greta walked up. Eyes closed and breathing slow, Mosby appeared to be asleep lying on his side at Annette's feet. "Good morning," Annette acknowledged.

"Good morning. What are you reading?" Greta queried.

"My Psalms for the day. I try to read five a day. So I go through all of them once a month."

"Oh," Greta replied. Changing the subject she said, "I love watching birds," nodding toward the heaping full feeder which hung from the ceiling of the porch by a white chain. Seeds spilled onto the floor as sparrows and cardinals darted in and out from the large brass and glass container. Occasionally a blue jay whizzed in, chasing all competitors away. "Schwein!" Greta snorted. "Why can he not share?"

"It's just the way it works some times. We keep it full so everybody eventually gets their fill."

Annette continued, "So what do you want to do today?"

"It does not matter. I am just happy to be in this quiet place. It is so peaceful and secluded. You do not know how grateful I am to be here." She stood and walked over to the rail and gazed down at the lake. "And you and your family have been so kind to me."

"Well, we're glad to have you and just glad you're safe."

Turning back, Greta locked her eyes on Annette, "We are safe here, right?"

"Yes, absolutely. I doubt anyone outside of the family knows about Uncle Keith's cabin. And we have Mosby," she said, patting Mosby's soft brown head. "And I have this." Greta's eyes widened as her new friend pulled up the front of her white blouse to reveal a holster strapped to her narrow waist above her blue jean slacks. Inside was a strange looking pistol.

"What ... is that?

"This is a Taurus 'Judge'. It's the ultimate home defense weapon for women," she said as she pulled her blouse down again.

"Do you really think you will need it?"

"No, but I'd rather have it and never use it as need it some night and be at the mercy of some thug."

"Breakfast is on," Michelle called from the porch door.

The two women went inside and sat down to a delicious breakfast prepared by their own private chef; the pistol was not mentioned again.

The women enjoyed the meal and shared stories from their childhood. It seemed a tonic to Greta to be able to relate pleasant memories from her youth with her parents and sister in Austria. But her mood turned somber as she shared about the illness and death of her father three years before.

"He had cancer of the pancreas, and it was a very aggressive tumor. He only lasted four months after they *finally* diagnosed him." Her tone had a bitter edge. "He went to many doctors, but no one found out what was wrong until it was too far advanced. It was horrible for him and us. He lost fifty pounds in the months before he died, and he was literally skin and bones."

"I'm so sorry, Greta," Michelle said placing her hand on Greta's. "I can't imagine. Please believe this, though- Annette and I love you and are here for you. And we'll be praying for you." There was an awkward silence as Greta distracted herself with her fork on her plate.

"Well, let's decide what we want to do today. Do you like hiking or would you like to take the canoe out?" Michelle asked Greta.

"It does not matter. I will enjoy whatever you choose."

"Well, you ever been canoeing?"

"No, but I would love to try. Is it hard?"

"It can be challenging. But I think you'll have a blast learning. And the lake's beautiful. How's that sound?"

"Great. Let us do it."

*****

The greenish-blue waters of Lake Sinclair provided the perfect diversion for three friends trying to escape the cares of the world. Greta paddled the bow of the red canoe with Michelle instructing on technique and offering encouragement from the stern. Annette zipped around them in her own blue kayak with grace and strength.

By the time the women coasted back into the private dock at the edge of the cabin property, the sun was just beginning to slip behind the foliage of the towering trees. They had worked up an appetite, and Annette asked, "Who's up for a spaghetti supper?"

"Count me in," Michelle responded. "I'm starving!"

"Great, that means you just volunteered to drive up to Hill's Market and get some spaghetti noodles. We also need some more milk, a dozen eggs, and a loaf of bread. Think you can remember all that, Shell?" Annette asked.

"Yeah, yeah."

"I'll get the sauce going and fix a salad while you're gone." Looking at Greta she noted, "You can stay with me or you can go with Shell to help her remember the list and find her way back."

Michelle smiled patronizingly at her older sister and then stuck her tongue out. "Thanks for the confidence," she countered.

Rallying to the aid of the younger Harrison, Greta joined in their good natured banter, "I will go with Michelle. Two heads are usually better than one."

As they pulled the canoe and the kayak up to the small metal shelter adjacent to the dock, their laughter filtered through the cove and up into the woods above. What they didn't sense at that moment was the set of blue eyes that watched them through a pair of binoculars from the dense forest. The watcher remained silent, patient, and invisible.

While Michelle and Greta freshened up inside, Annette stowed the paddles and life jackets away in the small shed and padlocked the canoe and kayak with thick chains. Finished, she slowly tramped up the path to the cabin. It had been a pleasant day, and the fatigue in her muscles from her vigorous paddling actually felt good.

As Annette entered the back door of the cabin, her sister and friend were leaving through the front door.

"See ya," Michelle called.

"Alright, but don't shop all evening. I'm really hungry."

Forty-five minutes later, Michelle and Greta returned from their grocery run. It was dark as they pulled into the gravel driveway in front of the cabin. Greta grabbed the jug of milk and Michelle carried the sack full of groceries. Hill's Market was one of those family owned stores that still had brown paper bags. Michelle led the duo through the front door and into the dark living room yelling to Annette, "We're home. You ready for these noodles?" Reaching to the right of the door, she flipped on the light. Hearing no answer from her sister, Michelle called out again and proceeded toward the kitchen where she assumed Annette would be stationed.

The two women found the kitchen empty but with the light on and a pan of meat and tomato sauce simmering on the stove. Michelle set her sack on the counter, and Greta put the gallon of milk into the refrigerator. Michelle sampled the sauce with a spoon she found resting next to the stove and then asked rhetorically, "Where is that girl?"

Looking out the kitchen window Greta replied, "There she is." Michelle followed her friend's gaze and was relieved to see her sister seated on the porch in one of the Adirondack chairs.

"Must have got bored waiting on us. I'll get her," Michelle remarked opening the door to the porch. Surprised that Annette remained immobile as she stepped outside, Michelle said, "Hey, you fall asleep?" Before she could hear a response, pain exploded in her left temple. Then everything went black.

*****

A pounding headache informed Michelle that she was conscious again. She found herself sitting on the kitchen floor between Greta and Annette. All three had their arms tied behind them. A tall figure in black trained a pistol on the trio. Michelle grudgingly noted that her attacker was not the ugly scar-faced fiend stereotypically portrayed by popular novels and movies. His features, ironically, were almost pleasant. He did not amuse himself in witty conversation with the helpless captives but was silent and maintained a flat affect.

Whispering, Michelle now questioned her sister who sat next to her with her muscles tensed and her teeth clenched. "What happened?"

"They killed Mosby!"

"No, No, NO!" Michelle shrieked. Tears welled in her eyes and trickled down her cheek as she struggled to grasp what Annette had just said.

"I was in the kitchen at the stove, when I heard Mosby start barking his head off at the edge of the woods off the end of the porch. I decided to go out to see what was bothering him. I thought maybe he had a raccoon or a possum cornered, you know. Anyway, as I started down the path toward the dock, he yelped and then stopped barking. I finally found him lying in the edge of the woods down by the shore. His neck had been slashed. He was still breathing, but barely. He was so pitiful. I just held his head and talked to him until they grabbed me from behind. I was so stupid. They should never have gotten the drop on me. I never reached my gun... But I was so devastated over Mosby... They're slime, stinking slime!"

After several minutes of silence, Annette chose to engage the guard. "So what are you going to do with us?" she boldly queried. The guard, impassive as stone, looked at her and said nothing. Pushing up with her hands and feet, Annette attempted to stand, but the man's black boot struck her hard in the left thigh knocking her sideways and slamming her head and back into the cabinet door behind her. Greta and Michelle scooted close to Annette doing their best to comfort her.

"You will remain seated until given permission to stand."

Moments later, he was joined by two subordinates who ran up from the boat dock. "The supplies are here," one reported.

"Good. Take these two upstairs. I'll take this one," the taller man ordered jerking Greta up by the arm.

"We are not going anywhere without Greta!" Annette challenged the leader.

"You will do as I say or I will shoot her in front of you." He pressed the barrel of his gun under Greta's chin. "If you obey, all will be well. Now move!" Annette paused for a moment but finally yielded, acknowledging the futility of resisting with her arms tied behind her back and now unarmed.

"You'll never get away with this," Michelle promised looking over her shoulder as she trudged toward the stairs.

The tall guard locked his gaze upon her, "Yes, that seems to be what the losers always say. Good bye."

The sisters were shoved into the first bedroom off the head of the stairs and forced onto the bed. Each had their legs trussed together and then lashed to the bedframe at the foot of the bed. Wordlessly, the two men shut the door and raced down the stairs. Hurrying outside, they opened two five gallon jugs which they had carried up from a sleek ski boat which was still tied to the private dock. They immediately began emptying the contents of the jugs around the foundation of the cabin.

Meanwhile, their leader roughly escorted Greta outside and down the path toward the dock. A fourth accomplice was seated at the controls of the ski boat which sat motionless on the smooth lake, its motor idling. "Onto the dock," the leader demanded. Greta made for the step as if complying but suddenly jerked and slipped from the man's grip, falling to her knees.

"Get up, now!"

"I will never let you take me away again. I will die first."

The man raised his gun to Greta's head. "You *will* die if you do not move now!"

"Go ahead, shoot me! You have killed me already," she spat with sarcasm.

At that same moment, a giant fire ball ignited up at the cabin as the arsonists lit off the gasoline with which they had doused the wooden porch. Grasping their empty jugs, they sprinted down the hill past their commander and into the boat.

Tension clung to the air of the humid Georgia night. The assailant hesitated momentarily as he weighed his options. The man seated at the controls of the boat yelled furiously at him in German.

A metallic click echoed in Greta's ear as her captor finally pulled back the hammer of his Ruger SP 101 double action revolver. "This is your last chance!" he growled.

Greta did not move. Bowing her head she simply closed her eyes.

The roar reverberated through the cove. The head jerked back and the body crumpled to the ground. But the body was not Greta's. It was her attacker.

"GRETA, DOWN!! GET DOWN NOW!!"

Greta dove forward and tucked her chin as shots continued to boom out from the woods.

The harsh voice screaming at her came from the forested rise behind her and to her left. Shots methodically and steadily rang out. The boat motor roared to full throttle and the craft raced away from the dock. One of the men howled as a rifle round struck him in the shoulder. He cursed at the man at the wheel, demanding to get away from the deadly sniper who continued to spit fire at them from the dark forest.

Two figures raced from the woods toward Greta. As she recognized the one in front, she screamed, "Stuart, get them out; Michelle and Annette are in the cabin. You must save them! They are upstairs!"

Stuart dropped his Remington 700 rifle on the ground, and he and Jim flew up the hill. Hunching low they broke through the flames on the back porch and wall of the cabin and crashed through the back door into the living room. The action was critical if they were to get to their sisters in time, but it also yielded a breach through which the flames stormed into the interior of the cabin. Smoke choked the entire living room and kitchen as the men charged up the staircase coughing and gasping, but determined to save their family. Miraculously, the smoke had not penetrated the bedroom yet. They raced into the bedroom, quickly closing the door behind them. The brothers released the bonds holding Michelle and Annette with rapid knife thrusts and pushed the women toward the bedroom window. Jim slid the bottom panel up and crawled out onto the first story roof.

"Out you go," Stuart encouraged as he helped Michelle and then Annette follow their brother. Smoke swirled over the roof, and the roaring flames illuminated the surrounding woods with a hellish glow while sparks leapt high into the night sky. Stuart joined his brother and sisters immediately, realizing any effort to stay and save the cabin or its contents now would be foolish in the extreme.

Jim pulled out his cell phone and tried to dial 911. "No signal. I'll run up to the top of the driveway. Maybe it'll pickup there."

Circling to the edge of the woods, the trio of Harrisons assembled down by the dock. Jim joined them in less than two minutes. "Help's on the way."

Greta sat staring at the burning cabin entranced with the fury of the destruction before her eyes. Stuart helped Greta to her feet and released her arms from behind her back.

"Are you alright?" Michelle asked, putting her arm around her friend.

"Yes. What...what happened?" Greta asked as she wiped her face with her right hand.

"I'm not quite sure I know. But we're about to find out," Michelle said looking at Stuart. Jim reached down and picked up the rifle his brother had dropped in his haste. A Mars 2x night vision scope was attached to the top rail.

"You girls ok?" Stuart asked.

"Yes, we are, but he isn't," Annette answered pointing at the shape on the ground. She knelt beside the body and placed her fingers on the left side of the neck checking for a carotid pulse. Nothing. Standing again she observed dryly, "He's gone."

Jim Harrison walked past his siblings and over to where Greta was standing. He took her by the hand and gently placed her head on his shoulder. She threw her arms around him and began to weep. "It's ok," he whispered.

"Where did you come from?" Michelle asked.

"We've been providing overwatch ever since you got here. We didn't really expect those goons would be able to track you down, but we didn't want to take any chances. With our night vision gear we tried to stay one step ahead of them. I've been watching with this enhanced thermal scope and Jim with a pair of night vision binoculars. But they did manage to sneak a guy into the woods on the opposite side of the cabin where we couldn't see him. And I'm sorry I had to dispatch this one, but it looked like he was about to shoot Greta," Stuart explained.

"He was," Greta confirmed. "You saved my life, again," Greta acknowledged.

"And you saved ours," Michelle said to her brothers. "They'd have burned us alive!"

"Why didn't you let us know you were watching? You didn't have to keep us in the dark," Annette queried.

"Well, we thought about that, but we didn't want to worry you. It was supposed to be a quiet stay for you at the cabin— no worries."

"This high tech fire power, where did it all come from?" Annette puzzled.

"One of my old buds from service has a home that's like the National Guard armory. I knew he'd let us borrow some stuff. One of my trainers pounded into my head, 'If you find yourself in a fair fight, you've done something wrong.'"

Stuart looked at his sisters, "I wouldn't put it past those guys to come back and snatch the body. We're going to wait right here."

*****

In less than fifteen minutes, three fire trucks from the Baldwin County Volunteer Fire Department arrived on the scene with sirens screaming. Two patrol cars from the Sheriff's department tore into the now congested driveway behind them. Instantly, mutual assistance calls went out and crews from four other fire departments began arriving on the scene. A pumper crew ran a large bore hose down to the lake and poured on the water. But the best efforts of all the firefighters were not enough. Uncle Keith's cabin disappeared.

The deputies took statements from Greta and the Harrisons, called their chief investigative detective, roped off an area around the body, and notified the county coroner. Fire investigators and detectives from the GBI also showed up and began their probes into the host of crimes perpetrated on this night. Leaving their cell numbers and addresses with the deputies, the Harrisons and Greta were allowed to leave and decided to head back home to Macon. It had been a long night.

14 The Bureau

The day after the horrific night at the cabin, Jack decided it was time to pay a visit to the FBI. The FBI resident agency in Macon referred the Harrisons on to the Atlanta office for further interviews. Jim and his father arrived early for their 8am appointment with the Special Agents.

The FBI field office in Atlanta is located off Interstate 85 in the north of the city. The office is home for dozens of special agents and support staff. Special Agent Braxton Roby sat behind his plain GSA issued black metal desk on the fourth floor and leaned slightly forward. He listened intently as Jim Harrison talked. In one corner of the office, Special Agent Andrew Papadakis sat in an uncomfortable GSA issued gray metal chair taking notes on a laptop.

Roby's thin, tanned face wore an easy smile, but it veiled a professional intensity born of training and experience. He was good at many things, but his forte was the interview. He was a consummate listener. When Roby interviewed saint or sinner, he used questions as a surgeon's probe. And he was interested not so much in gathering information as in exploring the gut of the patient. He noted nuances in body language and facial muscles, subtle changes in tone of voice and speech cadence, shifts in posture, and eye movements. His colleagues swore his relaxed style of interview was more effective than any polygraph test they'd administered. Roby was passionate for mining the truth, and he was loathe to quit until he hit pay dirt.

Jim was articulate and crisp in his narrative. The story of his kidnapping and return piqued the curiosity of the two FBI agents. And the kidnapping, rescue, and second kidnapping attempt on Greta Rose seemed to captivate the listeners. Roby believed in the dictum that truth is stranger than fiction. He couldn't shake the feeling that this story had the ring of truth.

"So, Jim — tell me why you think they kidnapped you and took you out of the States."

"I don't know. They just told me to forget Greta and her journal."

"And what's with this journal?"

"Not sure. It turned up in her aunt's house. They were renovating the home and found it the attic. It was lying in the bottom of an old satchel that belonged to her great grandfather. Greta's aunt thought she might be interested in it since she was into journalism."

Roby probed further. "Where does her aunt live?"

"Austria. Same town as Greta's mom and little sister-Oberndorf. Except now, an operative from Tower has quietly moved them to a safe house in Vienna."

"And what are their plans now?"

"We're working with Immigration to sponsor them to come here. Greta is living with us for now and looking for a job in Macon."

"And do you have any idea why the journal is so valuable to the men who snatched you?"

"Not a clue. Greta and I had just started wading through it in our spare time after classes. She translated it, and I entered it into her computer. I found it kind of interesting just because I enjoy history, especially military history."

"Tell me about her great grandfather."

"He was a Fallschirmjäger, that is, a German paratrooper. He apparently died in March of 1945 of wounds he received in the battle for Cologne, Germany. Greta had heard stories about him from her grandfather, but nothing really unique as far as WWII veterans."

"Except that he was on the other side."

"Yeah, right," Jim agreed.

Next, Jim related the facts that Ewell had compiled on Balder Chemical and Norse Industries. Jim sensed that Roby's easy demeanor stiffened ever so slightly at the mention of Norse Industries. "Those corporate names ring any bells with you guys?"

Papadakis looked up from his laptop and cut his dark brown eyes toward Roby. "Maybe," Roby answered carefully. "But … I really couldn't give you any details. Sorry."

Hoping to move the interview along, Jack Harrison spoke up. "So how *can* you help us?"

"Mr. Harrison, at this point I'm not sure. Of course, we don't have any jurisdiction in Europe, but we *will* get in touch with some of our colleagues at Interpol. It's fortunate that Jim and Miss Rose have both been released. We've started a file on this case, and we'll see what turns up. However, I encourage you to keep realistic expectations. With all the recent federal budget cutbacks, our resources are tight. Our current caseload has a fairly heavy backlog, and there's no hint of significant improvement in funding coming any time in the near future. If we can uncover more hard evidence of the involvement of specific individuals or organizations, we'll certainly prosecute. To be perfectly candid, because both Jim and Miss Rose have been returned, this case will not receive as high a priority as some of our other active cases. I'm sorry. For the time being, we'd advise keeping a low profile and continuing the security measures you've already implemented with the help of your friends at Tower. It sounds like they know their business."

"What about the guy that burned down our cabin and tried to kill my daughters?"

Agent Papadakis answered this time. "After you first called us last week, we contacted the GBI. They have no positive identification yet. Nothing on his person provided any clues. Nobody has tried to claim the body. No matches turned up on either U.S. or Interpol databases. It's like he just dropped out of the sky."

"Okay, what about his gun?" Jim asked.

Papadakis continued. "Yes, the gun. It's a Ruger SP 101. Tracking the serial number revealed it was manufactured in Prescott, Arizona and first sold in 2004. It was part of a cache of weapons stolen from a gun store in Huntsville, Alabama, in 2010. That case is still unsolved. So that's a dead end."

Special Agent Papadakis closed his laptop. The quiet in the small office was awkward. Jim looked down at the floor, disappointed. He had been hoping for something tangible-some new information, some help. His father broke the silence. "Well, gentlemen, thank you for your time. Please call when you find out something."

Roby answered. "We will. Thanks for taking the time to give us your information."

"No, thank you for *your* time," Jack responded. "I know you guys must be incredibly busy."

"We do have some long days," Papadakis smiled.

*****

Arriving home from Atlanta, Jim and his father discussed how they thought the interview had gone with the two agents.

"They seemed interested," Jim noted.

"Yeah, just overworked. I guess the FBI has had a full plate ever since 9/11. I'm not real surprised they can't get too excited about *former* kidnapees."

"'Kidnapees'? I'm not sure that's even a word, Dad."

"Well, if it's not, it ought to be." Both men laughed. After a few minutes of silence, Jack reached down and turned the radio on.

Jim stretched and yawned. "I'm glad you're driving. Mind if I catch a nap?"

"Be my guest."

"And if you get sleepy, let me know."

"Sure thing."

"One more thing. They *know* something about Norse Industries."

Jack agreed, "Yes, they certainly do."

15 The Journal

Blake Carter sat down at his desk in the Tower office. He flipped up the screen on his Lenovo ThinkPad and depressed the power button. He clicked his wireless internet connection and disabled it. Next, he inserted a thumb drive into his computer and brought up the file labeled "H.P. Journal". The first page of the scanned journal of Heinrich Pfeister appeared. He hit the split screen icon and brought up a blank Word document page on the right pane, leaving the printed page of neatly handwritten German on the left.

Carter was the in-house translator of German for Tower Intelligence Security Agency. Born at Tyndall AFB, Florida, where his father served with the 325th Fighter Wing as a meteorologist, he moved with his parents to Ramstein AFB, Germany, at the age of four and attended German public schools for kindergarten and the first two elementary grades. The family returned to the States when Carter was eight and moved every three to four years when his father received new stateside assignments. Carter eventually attended Hillsdale College in Michigan, majoring in history with a minor in German. After a brief stint teaching world history at a community college in Grand Rapids, he landed a job with Tower and had thoroughly enjoyed his work ever since. He had been briefed on his new project and was curious to learn what was so interesting about the forgotten journal of a German great-grandfather.

He began reading, simultaneously translating into the Word document:

The Journal of
Oberfeldwebel (Master Sergeant)
Heinrich Pfeister
1943-1945

To my children and their children
From your devoted father

These are dark days in Germany. I want you to know that I have lived and fought for you, my children, and for our people. I want you to believe that I have done my duty and have served honorably. My greatest desire is to see peace again for our land, our people, and my soul. I have seen much, heard much, felt much. If I do not survive this struggle, this journal will serve to record for you, my family, the truth, a commodity in short supply today in the third Reich.

We have been warned that it is forbidden for a soldier to keep a journal. But, many things are forbidden these days. Life is full of risks. This record of the true facts is worth the risk.

The events recorded herein are my eyewitness account of my days in the ranks of the fallschirmjäger (paratroopers) and two major operations undertaken by my unit during my service with them. The first, Operation Eiche (Oak), is known to the world. The second, Operation Ulric, has remained totally secret. When this war is over, and that must happen soon I think, we will sit down around your mother's dining table, and I will tell you these stories in person. If I must die before then, a trusted friend shall give this journal to your mother with my love.

With a desire to help save my country, I joined the Wehrmacht in December 1941 as our army suffered on the Russian front. I trained and served in the infantry until January of 1943 when I volunteered for and was accepted into the 2nd Fallschirmjäger-Division stationed in southern France. It was while we were training there that our division was ordered by General der Fallschirmtruppe Kurt Student, commander of Fliegerkorps XI, to fly to Practica di Mare airbase south of Rome. From there we were transported by truck to the German base at Frascati a few kilometers southeast of Rome.

The conditions that led to our move to Italy evolved over several months. Our Italian allies had suffered one defeat after another since 1940. The Italian Eighth army supporting our invasion of Russia was destroyed in January of 1943. All Italian forces in North Africa were defeated in May of 1943, and the Allies landed in Sicily in July of that year. Rome and Naples were bombed the same month. Mussolini, the leader of Italy for over 20 years, saw his popularity plummet. Italians were tiring of war. A conspiracy to depose Mussolini, "Il Duce", involving the military high command, the military police, the civil police, and the Italian monarch, germinated, grew, and ripened as discontent spread throughout the country.

Mussolini was summoned to see King Victor Emmanuelle III on the afternoon of July 25, 1943. Expecting to receive the King's support, Il Duce instead was advised that his services were no longer needed. He was being replaced by Maresciallo Pietro Badoglio, and his regime was dissolved. To prevent his leadership of a counter coup, Mussolini was arrested on the spot and whisked away in an ambulance.

The following day, Oberkommando der Wehrmacht-OKW (the German High Command) received orders from the Fuhrer to *find and rescue Mussolini. Simultaneously, German divisions were ordered to move into position to take control of Rome. Once freed, Mussolini was to be reinstated as leader of fascist Italy and command his forces to fight on beside the Wehrmacht.*

In order to prevent his rescue, the Italian authorities moved the former dictator six times in the next five weeks. They finally confined him in the Hotel Campo Imperatore in the isolated mountain resort area of Gran Sasso d'Italia 65 kilometers to the east of Rome.

During the two weeks following the coup that ousted Mussolini, the new Italian government of Badoglio secretly negotiated an armistice with the Allies. While Italian envoys in Portugal hammered out the details of the surrender, the government in Rome maintained the façade of continued cooperation with our forces.

At 1630 on August 8th, 1943, the armistice was officially announced by radio broadcast. General Kesselring immediately ordered German ground forces to converge on Rome and disarm the defending Italian units. The situation there became extremely chaotic as Italian units were confused as to their appropriate response. Some resisted stoutly while others surrendered without a firing a shot. The Badoglio government fled Rome, eventually setting up a pro-Allied regime in Brindisi, Italy.

Our division assisted in restoring order in the Italian capital, but I was not personally involved in that action. Instead, my company was tasked with an important mission in the second week of September. We were called to the base dining hall at Frascati on the evening of September 11, 1943. General Student entered the room from a side door and…

"Achtung," Feldwebel Eugen Abel called the company to attention.

"Be seated, gentlemen." The assemblage of Fallschirmjäger took their seats. General Student continued. "You men have been selected for a very critical mission. We believe we have found Mussolini. And you have been selected to rescue him. We will begin your briefing momentarily. But first, SS— Hauptsturmfuhrer (SS Captain) Skorzeny has asked to speak."

Skorzeny stepped in front of the men followed by his adjutant, Obersturmfuhrer (SS lieutenant) Karl Radl. General Student had a barely veiled scowl on his battle hardened face.

"Heil Hitler," Skorzeny and Radl bellowed with an enthusiastic salute.

The response from the paratroopers was a tepid, "Heil Hitler," with weakly raised hands.

Smiling broadly as if already receiving a medal in front of a fawning media, Skorzeny began, "I just wanted to take a moment to emphasize the importance of the mission you are about to carry out. Success in this endeavor will bring to your division and to each of you individually, glory and the thanks of our beloved Fuhrer and the Fatherland. To document the triumph of this mission, we will be accompanied on this raid by two of our best war correspondents." Toni Schneider and Bruno von Kayser nodded and each waved a hand from seats on the back row of the assembled group. "I have already briefed my SS detachment on their critical role in this mission. It is to provide security for Il Duce during the extraction from Gran Sasso. Gentlemen, do your duty, and remember the eyes of Germany will be upon us." Skorzeny smiled again, nodded toward General Student, and abruptly left the building with his adjutant and two sycophant war correspondents.

"Men," Student began, a trace of pain in his voice. "We are all called to do things we consider distasteful." Looking at several of his headquarters staff who had stationed themselves at the only three doors into the room, he said in a near whisper, "If any of you repeat what I am about to say, I will deny it and have you arrested for disloyalty; but then let me make myself clear. Skorzeny and his bootlickers are going on this raid against my better judgment. Their excuse for participation in this mission is to provide security for Mussolini as bodyguards. You are the real soldiers in this fight, and it will succeed or fail based on your knowledge, skill, and courage. Do not let the SS distract or intimidate you. Let them have their photographs and headlines. You get the mission done, get Mussolini out, and return safely." Motioning with his right hand toward an officer seated in the front row of chairs, Student said, "Oberleutnant Berlepsch." The lieutenant stood and spun around to face the paratroopers. General Student walked toward the exit, but stopped suddenly, a smile finally crossing his face, "And, gentlemen, one more thing- good luck!" Softly spoken "dankes" reverberated from Student's men as he left the building.

Lieutenant Berlepsch began the detailed technical briefing. "Our agents have reasonable confidence that the Italians have Mussolini sequestered in the Hotel Campo Imperatore in the mountain resort area of Gran Sasso d'Italia 90 kilometers to the east of us. The only access to the hotel is by cable car. Our mission is to rescue him before he is moved again or executed. This is an aerial photograph of the hotel." A grainy 1:20,000, black and white photographic slide was projected onto a makeshift screen set up on the wall behind the lieutenant.

"The elevation of the plateau on which it sits is approximately 2000 meters. Our intelligence personnel estimate that the Hotel itself is being guarded by approximately 100 carabinieri, Italian military police. The upper cable car station is guarded by perhaps another 50 Italians. The lower cable car station sits in the town of Assergi and is manned by an estimated 100 carabinieri. I will lead you men in an aerial assault on the hotel compound. The village and the cable car station there will be secured by a ground assault force led by Major Mors. His column will leave from here at Frascati in time to arrive simultaneously with the air assault. His force will consist of 260 troops with 20 vehicles. Two StuG-III assault guns will provide armor strength to the column."

"We have been assigned twelve DFS-230 gliders to carry the aerial assault force consisting of the entire 1 Kompanie and one platoon from the 4 Kompanie. This diagram shows the target landing area and the approaches to the hotel." Another slide depicted the hotel and the upper cable car station. The landing zone was marked in red two hundred meters to the east of the hotel.

"Surprise is key. We will also have sufficient firepower to overwhelm the Italians. There has been great variation in the willingness and capability of the Italian forces to put up resistance thus far. We must assume those guarding Mussolini are ready for a fight. We are issuing twelve of you the new FG-42-1 assault rifles. We will also be accompanied by a machine-gun section with two MG-42s, a mortar section with light mortars, and a Panzerjäger (tank-hunter) team with a 2.8 cm anti-tank gun in case we have to blow our way through the hotel entrance.

*****

Gentlemen, that is all for now. You will be packed and ready to leave for the airfield at midnight. We plan take off from Practica di Mare at 0630 hours. You will receive final details at the morning briefing. Are there any questions?"

The room was quiet. "Well, then. Get some rest. We will see you in a few hours. You are dismissed."

The lieutenant huddled with a couple of his assistants as the group of Fallschirmjäger stood. Some stretched and yawned, a few quietly left the room, and others engaged in small talk and jokes about the Italian military.

The rest of the afternoon and evening Major Mors and Lt. Berlepsch and their staff continued the final planning and preparations for the mission. Just before midnight the planners learned that the gliders would not arrive in time for an early morning assault. They approached Gen. Student who agreed to delay the assault until 1400 hours on the 12th of September. The Fallschirmjäger were advised to stand down until later in the morning.

Oberfeldwebel (Master Sergeant) Pfeister slept fitfully in the olive grove where his company was billeted. It was always this way the night before combat. A few of the newer men wore a façade of bravado, but the veterans all knew. It was a show. All the talk about glory was just that, talk. The Fallschirmjäger were not fanatics like the SS zealots. They just wanted to get the task done and get back. Most came from middle-class, hardworking German families. And most had nothing to do with National Socialism. Those who survived the war would find occupations as teachers, mechanics, craftsmen, and farmers.

Maj. Mors and his column departed Frascati at 0300 hours headed for the village of Assergi. The direct distance was only 93 kilometers. But to avoid possible interference by Italian units along the direct road, Mors chose a circuitous route which took his force first southeast and then northeast. They would eventually arrive at the outskirts of Assergi at 1300 hours. Encountering only light resistance from the carabinieri guarding the village, Mors' men attacked and captured the lower cable car station easily, suffering no casualties. Two Italians were killed and two wounded during the brief encounter with their former allies. By 1400 hours, the lower cable car station was safely in German hands.

Back at Frascati, at 0415 hours the company first sergeant roused the troops. Familiar with the vagaries of glider flight, the Fallschirmjäger consumed a light breakfast and gathered up their gear and weapons. Shortly, Berlepsch's company and the tagalong SS men were transported to the Practica di Mare airfield by truck, arriving at 0500 hours.

The Fallschirmjäger checked their equipment as they waited for the tardy gliders coming from the 12thStaffel/LuftlandeGeschwader based at Grosseto, north of Rome. Finally, at about 1100 hours, one of the Fallschirmjäger shouted, "Here they come!" Sgt. Pfeister looked up from cleaning his MP40 (Schmeisser machine pistol). He thought the green and grey gliders were a beautiful sight flying lazily in trail behind their tow planes.

The Gotha DFS-230 glider plane entered service with the Wehrmacht in October of 1939 and remained a workhorse through the balance of the war. With a wing span of 22 meters (71.5 feet) and a length of just 11.5 meters (37 feet), it was able to maintain a descent rate of just 74 meters/minute (240 feet/minute). The crew consisted of a single pilot seated directly in front of the nine Jäger who uncomfortably straddled a wooden bench which ran the length of the narrow fuselage from the cockpit to the tail. The normal tow speed was 180 km/h (100 mi/h), but the glider could reach a maximum glide speed of 290 km/h (174 mi/h).

To the chagrin of Lt. Berlepsch, only ten gliders showed up from Grosseto. His assault force of 120 had just been reduced to 100 men. There was no time to wait for the additional gliders; he would have to make do with what was available.

The ten gliders all landed safely, and, while the Hs-126 tow planes were refueled, Berlepsch gave his men the bad news of the deficiency of transport craft and then briefed them on the final details of the attack. "Unfortunately, we will have to trim 20 of you men from the assault." A chorus of groans rose from the group of paratroopers. "It's just too late to postpone the mission. Our glider assault force will be divided into four *ketten* (flights) of gliders. I will lead the first *kette* which will transport 27 members of the first platoon for the initial assault on the hotel compound. I expect our *kette* in gliders 1, 2, and 3 to land almost simultaneously.

The second *kette* in gliders 4 and 5 will insert Skorzeny and the SS contingent. I am assigning them to secure the landing zone and to guard any Italians we capture. Once we have freed Mussolini, the SS will protect him until we are able to get him off the mountain.

Kette 3 carrying 2nd platoon in gliders 7, 8 and 9 will be led by Feldwebel Abel and will take control of the upper cable car station.

Luetnant Gradler will lead *kette* 4 in gliders 6 and 10 with 3rd platoon and part of 4 Kompanie and gain control of the area surrounding the hotel. They will provide a reserve for the hotel assault group if necessary.

After the initial three gliders in *kette* 1 land, the remaining seven gliders will land at approximately one minute intervals. We should have the entire force on the ground within ten or twelve minutes."

Sgt. Pfeister was relieved to hear that he still had a spot in glider 3 with the main assault force. He looked with disgust at the cluster of arrogant SS men who had bumped several of his friends from the mission. Skorzeny's team had carelessly gorged themselves on their breakfast which had included a generous helping of rum. They would soon regret their lack of restraint.

The assault force divided into their *ketten* and were queued up to load into their gliders when an air raid siren began wailing. Pfeister ran for cover with his companions jumping into one of the sandbagged dugouts at the perimeter of the field. For several minutes they watched the western sky and waited. As it turned out, the airfield was not bombed, but the departure of the force was delayed another half hour.

Finally, at 1305 hours Lt. Berlepsch's group lifted off in glider 1 pulled by the first Hs-126 tow plane. It was followed immediately by gliders 2 and 3. The remaining seven gliders launched at two–minute intervals.

Sgt. Pfeister was third man back on the passenger bench in glider 3 and realized he had forgotten how tightly confined the interior of the glider felt. He and the eight Jäger with him were like herring stuffed in a narrow tin. Fortunately for him, none of the SS gluttons were on board. He would learn later that most of them had decorated the floors of their gliders with their rum-laden breakfasts.

Encountering headwinds approximately twenty minutes after take-off, Hauptman (Captain) Gerhard Langguth, the commander of the tug aircraft group, instructed his lead pilot to perform a slow circle maneuver to gain altitude before they passed above a high ridgeline near Tivoli. The first three tow craft executed the maneuver, but the following tug planes simply plunged straight ahead. This put Skorzeny and the SS in the lead of the assault force.

One half hour later, the first tow-glider pair containing Skorzeny and his SS men reached Gran Sasso and remained below the dense cloud cover. The winds across the mountain were gusting, which gave the glider occupants a few anxious seconds. The Campo Imperatore plateau was barren except for a single black dot which Leutnant (Lieutenant) Meyer, pilot of glider 4, assumed was the hotel. At 1403 hours, Meyer cut loose the towrope and began his descent. Seeing that the adjacent sheer cliffs invited disaster, he bypassed the intended landing zone, and chose to land higher up the plateau. Making a sharp left turn which jammed his passengers hard against the wall of the fuselage, Meyer brought glider 4 around into a near-flat trajectory. This non-powered portion of the flight ended with a screeching slide on the rocky ground stopping with an abrupt jolt just 40 meters from the hotel. The time was 1405 hours.

A less than enthusiastic passenger in Skorzeny's glider had been coerced into joining the mission on a last minute whim by the SS captain. He was one Generale di brigata Fernando Soleti. Skorzeny had calculated that a prominent Italian general might be able to help Skorzeny's men bluff their way past the guards at Gran Sasso. He had Soleti brought from Rome supposedly to provide information on the makeup of the security force guarding Mussolini. Once at Practica di Mare airfield, however, Soleti learned that he was being included in the mission. He was not given the option of declining.

Glider 4 had landed safely, but the combination of air sickness and the rough landing temporarily indisposed Skorzeny's men. They exited the glider through the one hatch on the aft port section but milled around without apparent direction for several moments. Skorzeny, on the other hand, immediately made his way through the exit hatch and rushed up the hill toward the hotel. Forgetting to carry his machine pistol or to issue any orders to his men, he instead headed toward the rear of the building, ignoring the shouts of a nearby Italian police guard. Apparently it did not occur to the sentry to fire his rifle at the German.

The Italian defenders of the Hotel at Gran Sasso were ill prepared by their commanders for the German assault. The

Italians did suspect a German rescue attempt of Mussolini might be forthcoming, but the sentries at Gran Sasso had been given no specific instructions as to how to respond to such an attack. And they had no inkling that a glider assault was in the works.

Overall command of the Italian security force had been given by Badoglio (Mussolini's replacement as prime minister) to Inspector General of Police Giuseppe Gueli. Under his direct command was a 30 member group of civilian police. They had been assigned a team of police watchdogs as well. A 43-man team of carabinieri under the command of Tenente Alberto Faiola had also been assigned to the Gueli's detail at the hotel. Finally, Gueli had requested and received reinforcements to the tune of 50 troops from various units including the PAI recently escaped from Rome after the signing of the armistice with the Allies. (The PAI, Polizia dell' Africa Italiana, was originally constituted to serve as a police force in Italian colonies in North Africa. Lately, the unit had provided security to the newly formed regime of Badoglio. Unfortunately for Badoglio, less than three weeks after its formation, his government had been forced to flee from Rome in disarray as the German army moved to seize control of the capital of their erstwhile ally.) The total security force under Gueli numbered approximately 120. Two thirds of these were responsible for the defense of the hotel; the remainder protected the upper cable car station.

Gueli had received specific orders from Badoglio to prevent Mussolini from falling into German hands. He was to see to it that the dictator was executed if necessary to prevent his rescue. But now the Badoglio government was on the run, and rumor had it that Hitler had ordered the death of any Italian officer who might harm Mussolini. Gueli's resolve was definitely shaken.

Skorzeny continued on his solo glory hunt by abruptly opening the door to what he assumed was a hotel entrance at the back of the building. Instead, he startled a lone Italian radio operator. The radio room was a dead end having no connection to the hotel proper. Sheepishly realizing his mistake, Skorzeny shut the door and proceeded on around the back of the hotel now joined by one of his SS men who had regained his wits. No sooner had he rounded a corner than he ran into two police dogs chained to posts in the hotel yard. Ironically, he noted, they were German shepherds. Taking a wide detour around the enraged, snarling animals, Skorzeny continued to look for a way into the hotel.

Meanwhile, glider 5 crash landed about 100 meters in front of the hotel seriously injuring several of the SS troops and badly shaking up the rest who were disabled for a few minutes. Glider 6 landed fairly smoothly between the hotel and the upper cable car station but narrowly missed sliding off the edge of the mountain. The Fallschirmjäger exited glider 6 without incident and moved swiftly to secure the station. They met no resistance from the guards who were stunned by the sudden appearance of a well-armed German contingent from the air.

Glider 7 came to a rough halt against an earth berm closer than all the other gliders to the east of the hotel. Two of the passengers of this glider were also injured. The remaining six Jäger under the command of Feldwebel (Sergeant) Abel deployed effectively to secure the front entrance of the hotel.

As the first four gliders of the assault force landed, the Italians reacted with surprise, confusion, and indecision. Tenente Faiola had been alerted to the arrival of the gliders by the shouts of the outside sentries. He ordered his men to barricade the main entrance to the hotel and ran upstairs to find Inspector Gueli. The inspector was taking his customary afternoon nap, and it was with some difficulty that he was awakened. Gueli slowly answered the loud knocking on the door to his room, and to his consternation, Faiola found the inspector totally disrobed and still groggy from sleep. Faiola pressed his commander, "Should I kill Mussolini or do we evacuate?" Gueli seemed unable to grasp an understanding of the situation.

As the inspector casually looked out the window of his room, he saw three more German gliders land smoothly several hundred meters in front of the hotel. One of these was glider number 3 with Feldwebel Pfeister and his squad. With his right hand, Pfeister instinctively grabbed the loop of webbing above his right shoulder as the pilot of his glider barked, "Prepare for impact!" He gripped his Schmeisser firmly with the left hand and leaned slightly forward into the back of the Jäger in front of him. His seasoned companions braced likewise. The quiet "whoosh" of the descent of the glider was abruptly shattered by the scraping of the underside skids of the craft on the grass covered ground of the designated landing area. The pilot had executed a perfect landing.

The Fallschirmjäger piled out of the glider and moved quickly toward the hotel. The guards who had remained outside the hotel offered no resistance after the first shouts directed at Skorzeny. Now they simply stood by passively as the professional soldiers of Pfeister's squad deployed in a cordon around the front of the hotel.

Back on the second floor of the hotel, Faiola grew impatient with the police inspector. He abruptly left Gueli in his room and proceeded with one of his lieutenants to Mussolini's room.

Mussolini was in high spirits as he too looked out the window of his room and saw the heavily armed German

Fallschirmjäger hurrying toward the hotel. As he continued to survey the situation with keen interest, Faiola and his subaltern burst into his room and demanded that Il Duce move away from the window. An argument ensued, and the dictator's mood collapsed. He sensed that the Tenente was about to end his life with a bullet to the head. Mussolini attempted one last ploy. He warned Faiola that if he were killed, Hitler would have the entire Italian security force executed. This threat gave Faiola pause and ultimately saved Mussolini.

The final three gliders, numbers 8, 9, and 10, landed at last and their occupants joined the rest of the Fallschirmjäger surrounding the hotel. They aided in the roundup of the Italian guards, but, curiously, the Italians demonstrated a spirit of cooperation and almost relief at being discharged from their duty.

Contrary to their orders from Faiola, many of the guards fled to their rooms and hid. Skorzeny and his lieutenant had by this time finally made their way to the front entrance. With the force of Fallschirmjäger who had reached the hotel now backing them up, the two SS men intimidated and brushed aside the few carabinieri remaining in the main lobby of the hotel. Amazingly, no shots were fired. They made their way upstairs and found Mussolini in his room, flanked by the two Italian officers. Faiola and his subordinate reluctantly yielded their weapons to the Germans. Skorzeny introduced himself to the dictator and professed, "Duce, the Fuhrer sent me to free you!"

"I knew that my friend Adolph Hitler would not have abandoned me!" Il Duce responded. The captivity of Mussolini had come to an end. Almost exactly twelve minutes had elapsed from the landing of the first glider until the release of the prisoner at Gran Sasso.

As the dictator gathered his things upstairs and prepared to leave his place of confinement, downstairs Lt. Berlepsch ordered his men to move the Fallschirmjäger and SS men who had been injured in the glider landings into the dining room of the hotel. The battalion surgeon, Dr. Brunner, patched up the injured as best he could, and his medics prepared to move them to the upper cable car station for transport down the mountain.

By this time, Maj. Mors, whose unit was still deployed around the lower cable car station, rode the cable car up to the hotel compound and conferred with Berlepsch. The discussion centered on the best means of getting Mussolini safely off the mountain before other Italian forces in the general area had time to respond to the rescue raid and attempt to retake him forcibly. The Germans were also concerned that an Allied air raid might materialize, jeopardizing the entire enterprise. Berlepsch and Mors were convinced that a cable car ride to the lower station with ground transport to a nearby airfield was the most prudent means of exfiltration for Mussolini. Skorzeny was about to trump this plan with his own self-promoting scheme.

General Student had arranged for two Fiesler Storch light observation planes to stand by for possible use in getting Mussolini out. One of these had landed near the lower cable car station, but had a severely damaged undercarriage from a rough landing. Skorzeny signaled the remaining Storch which was piloted by Student's personal pilot, Hauptmann Heinrich Gerlach. Gerlach skillfully landed on a short stretch of ground in front of the hotel throwing rocks in all directions. At this juncture, Skorzeny argued with Berlepsch and Mors pushing his own plan to take out Mussolini in the Storch. Outranked by Mors, Skorzeny nevertheless intimidated the two

Fallschirmjäger officers into yielding. (SS officers had certain leverage in their dealings with the regular army!)

Gerlach prepared his plane for take-off and recruited a mixed force of Italians and Germans to clear a path for a makeshift runway. The Italians were more than happy to assist. Gerlach was somewhat concerned, however, about having enough distance to gain sufficient airspeed in the rarified mountain air. But he was totally shocked when Skorzeny informed him that he would be escorting Il Duce on his flight out. The pilot was adamant that two was the maximum number his plane could safely carry given the circumstances. In typical SS fashion, coercion superseded reason, and Skorzeny once again had his way. Even Mussolini protested once he understood the gravity of the flight situation. To no avail. The SS captain *would* accompany Il Duce to his final destination. Skorzeny was making sure that credit would be given as he envisioned for the "glorious raid".

At 1500 hours, Skorzeny jammed in behind Mussolini in the tiny passenger compartment of the Storch. Gerlach pushed the throttle of the small engine to maximum and urged the craft forward. As the Fallschirmjäger watched...

...we were all convinced that the Storch had no chance of surviving the launch off the short plateau. It was just another example of the reckless and irresponsible decisions by those who had forced their way into positions of influence and power in the Reich. Just before the Storch lurched over the precipice at the end of the plateau, the left landing gear struck a large rock, ripping the metal strut from the fuselage. The gray aircraft disappeared below the edge of the drop off, muffling the sound of the engine. Seconds later, the Storch appeared again above the horizon, struggling to gain altitude. Hauptman Gerlach had done a masterful job

guiding the plane away from the mountain and headed westward toward the airfield at Practica di Mare.

Mussolini would eventually land at Practica di Mare and transfer to a Heinkel-111 bomber. The dictator and his SS custodian were then flown to Vienna, Austria, where Mussolini rested for two days. On September 15, he finally met Hitler at his headquarters in Rastenberg, Germany.

We Fallschirmjäger were ferried by cable car down the mountain and spent the night bivouacked in the village of Assergi. Major Mors, a wise officer, wanted to avoid a possible night engagement with any Italian forces in the area with nasty intentions. The next day our force was convoyed back to Frascati without incident.

Wretchedly, SS-Hauptsturmfuhrer (SS Captain) Skorzeny was promoted to Sturmbannfuhrer (SS Major) and propagandized as a "Nazi Commando" extraordinaire before the people of the Reich. There is nothing further from the truth. Skorzeny does not even rise to the level of the name 'soldier' much less 'hero'. Nevertheless, Himmler (head of the SS) and Goebbels (propaganda minister) both seized on Skorzeny's exaggerated and fabricated descriptions of our raid and have paraded him and his minions before our citizens. While the SS were lionized at an impressive public ceremony last October in the Berliner Sportsplast, our Fallschirmjäger received simple recognition as we stood at attention in a field outside the base at Frascati. For me, it is enough if you, my family, know the truth.

Carter pushed back in his chair and rubbed his chin with his right hand. "Amazing," he said to himself. Standing, he stepped over to the window of the small office and gazed out at the clouds rolling in from the west. "*An eyewitness account of the raid to rescue Mussolini,*" he thought. Pulling out his cell phone, he pushed 7 to speed dial his boss. "T.J., I just finished the first section of the journal. You might want to come down and see what I've got so far." He listened for a moment. "Alright, see you in a minute."

16 The Paratrooper

T.J. opened, "So what you're saying is that this journal is an account by Greta Rose's great-grandfather and that he was a German paratrooper… What did you say the German word for it was?".

"*Fallschirmjäger*, or *jäger* for short," Carter responded.

"Ok. Fallschirmjäger. And he wrote this journal in the spring of 1945 near the end of the European theater operations in World War II?"

"That's right. He relates a lot of details of his day-to-day experiences in the German Army, the Wehrmacht. But the most interesting part I've translated so far has been this eye witness account of the German rescue of Mussolini. It was about the time the Italians were getting cold feet and trying to pull out of their alliance with the Nazis. They designated it Operation Eiche. I'd never heard of it, have you?" he asked his boss.

"Yeah, I vaguely remember something about it. I mean, I enjoy history, but I really don't remember much about that incident. I guess I just always thought of Mussolini and the Italians as sort of a side show for the Axis."

Carter continued. "Well, this is a riveting account. And there's another operation he refers to in the opening of the journal—'Operation Ulric.' Ever heard of it?"

"No, can't say as I have. What was its objective?" T. J. asked, now curious.

"I don't know. So far, I haven't translated past the rescue of Il Duce, that is, Mussolini. I've used multiple search engines on the web to find Operation Ulric, but I just keep knocking against dead ends."

T.J. stood up from his black leather chair and slowly paced the maroon carpet in Carter's office. "As interesting as this journal sounds, it still doesn't explain why members of a multinational corporation would go so far as kidnapping and murder to keep it buried. I'm puzzled."

"Yeah, it's crazy. But I'll keep plugging away at translating, and maybe something will turn up."

"Good. The sooner we know what they're looking for, the better. I'm taking you off all other projects until you finish this journal. You good with that?"

"Sure, T.J. You write the checks. I'll call you as soon as I finish."

"Right. Any time, day or night."

Davidson turned and left Carters' small office. Carter sat down at his desk, took a few seconds to stretch the aching muscles in the back of his neck, and then dived again into the depths of the journal of Master Sergeant Heinrich Pfeister...

In December of last year, our fallschirmjäger unit was placed in I SS Panzer Corps reserve near Stadtkyll. We sensed something big was happening, but we were not privy to the details. Hundreds of trucks and armored vehicles rumbled down the road just beyond our bivouac perimeter each night for a week. It turned out to be the prelude to our last thrust in the west -- the Ardennes offensive was about to crash into the Allies...

17 The Scouts

Green pine needles crusted with snow stuck into the night air. The tall trees stood like silent sentries. Sgt. Shiloh Chadwell looked straight up into the night sky. The flakes fell onto his face and into his eyes. The air was clean and cold. It was quiet, eerily quiet. Lowering his head, he looked through the forest toward the two jeeps parked at the edge of the woods. *Time to get back on the trail.*

A few hours earlier, Lt. Col. Dave Cochrane, commander of the 28th Reconnaissance Troop, attached to the 2nd Infantry Division, had called Lt. John Owen to the troop command post. He described the situation to the lieutenant bluntly. "My CP phone lines have been cut, our radios are being jammed, and I've got reports of Tiger tanks punching holes in my frontline defenses. There are rumors of Nazis disguised as American MP's causing all kinds of havoc." Slamming his fist on the map covered table in front of him, he swore furiously with one long, continuous oath. "Division demands intel, they want it yesterday, and I don't intend to give them any excuses. Now Lieutenant, unless you want to spend the rest of this war on latrine clean up duty, get your scouts, get them out there now, and don't come back without some hard information. I want to know what units are hitting us, what their strength is, and what their operational objective is. Oh… and if you really want a shot at making captain, bring me back a living, breathing, and talking kraut scumbag for interrogation. Any questions?"

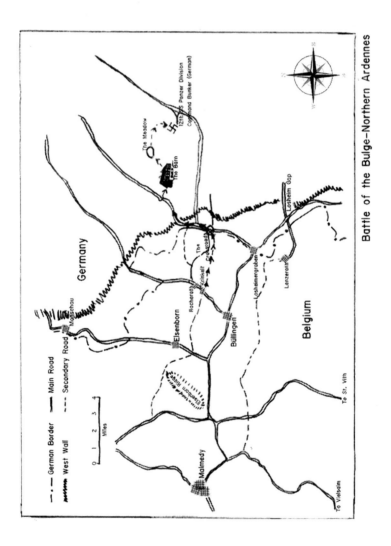

Lt. Owen rubbed his chin with his hand and looked down. "Any chance I can issue my whole squad Thompsons? I gotta feeling we may need some firepower for close in work."

"You can have 'em, but I *am not* sending you out to brawl with the whole German army. If you can avoid a firefight, do it. What I want is information, and I want it soon. Do I make myself crystal clear?"

"Yes, sir, perfectly clear."

"Anything else?"

"Yes, sir. I need the two most reliable jeeps in the troop. We want to have the speed to outrun the Krauts since we won't be able to outgun 'em."

"Alright. You can have mine and the major's here."

"Well, sir, I didn't mean to take the command staff jeeps."

"Lieutenant, shut up and take the jeeps! Just get me the information I need."

"Yes, sir."

"Good. I better see you back here in less than twenty-four hours." Major Trevor Scott stood off the colonel's left shoulder. "Major, go over what pitiful little information we do have with the lieutenant."

"Yes, sir."

"And, Lieutenant."

"Yes, sir?"

"Good luck!"

"Thank you, sir."

Major Scott leaned forward and quickly pointed out the areas where German thrusts had penetrated the 2$^{\underline{nd}}$ Division front. "We're hearing reports of German infantry here," he said, pointing to a spot on the map spread on the large table before them. "And over here there are signs of a significant Panzer force. This whole thing opened up a few hours ago with a torrent of artillery fire. We're assuming this is a local push. But fragmentary reports from other divisions north and south of us indicate bombardment along a massive portion of the front. So far, we haven't been able to confirm that. Every time we get on the radio, we get jammed by Kraut band music. We want you to get behind these thrust points and see if you can find out how serious they are, who they are, what their reserves look like. I don't know which road you should take, but assume the Krauts have control of all the routes of any size. You still have your Indian?"

"You mean Sgt. Chadwell?"

"Yeah; maybe he can work some of his magic, find a path through the woods to get behind this big Kraut drive."

"Well, he wouldn't much like hearing you call it *magic*. He calls it *Providence*."

"Okay, whatever. Just get out and get back. Here's a copy of the best tactical map we have."

Lt. Owen took the map and stuffed it into his jacket pocket.

Major Scott continued, "The colonel is desperate for info. And if things are as chaotic as it looks, you may have a time getting back through our lines. Division says the password along our front for the next 24 hours is *warthog*. In twenty-four hours, it'll change."

"Well sir, we'll do our best to be back for dinner tomorrow night. Be sure and save us a drumstick."

Lt. Owen saluted the Major who offered him a handshake instead. "Keep your head down, John."

"Yes, sir. I'll do my best."

The heavy wooden door of the village school that served as the troop command post swung open. Owen stepped out into the cold gray of the December afternoon. Shutting the door behind him, he looked at the leaden sky. "No air support today," he said to himself. The scene in the village street was just one step above chaos. Jeeps and trucks were coming and going. Diesel and gasoline fumes permeated the air. American soldiers were hurrying in all directions, each face with a determined edge. No one seemed to notice Owen. No one, that is, except a squad of GIs clustered around a table across the street from the command post. They were seated at one of the two outdoor tables of the village's only café. Owen's exit from the CP aroused the keen interest of the small group as he headed toward them, threading his way through the military traffic choking the street.

Owen's scout squad was the best in the troop. He and his seven men had been together for over a year. They had landed with the 2ⁿᵈ Division at Omaha Beach on D-Day plus 1, 7 June, 1944. The division gained a reputation for excellence as it fought the determined German defenders in the hedgerows of Normandy and then broke out of the beachhead. The men of his squad knew and trusted each other. Simply put, they were family.

A raven haired, olive skinned sergeant was seated on a small wooden box honing his combat knife. His back resting comfortably against the frontage wall of the café, his body partially obscured the hand painted sign identifying the establishment, *La Brouette (The Wheelbarrow)*. At 26, he was the "old man" of the group. Sgt. Shiloh Chadwell, a Cherokee Indian from western North Carolina, had joined the Army in 1940 as he presciently saw the American involvement in the war coming. Shiloh came from a family steeped in a heritage of military service. His father had served during WWI and his grandfather during the Spanish-American War. His great-grandfather had served as a scout with Confederate General Thomas J. (Stonewall) Jackson in his Valley Campaign during War Between the States. Among the ranks of the Reconnaissance Troop, Shiloh, a quiet and humble man, had the reputation of a fierce fighter and a dauntless scout.

Paradoxically to some in the troop, he was also a devout Christian.

"What's up, Lieutenant? You got the straight scoop?" asked Private Rocco Pitto. Pitto, from a family of steel workers in Cleveland, was a giant of a man at 6 foot 3 inches and 250 pounds, but he had the disposition of a hound dog. Friendly, out- going, and jovial, he had a joke or funny story for any occasion. How he came up with fresh comedy nobody knew. They just appreciated how he kept the mood upbeat even in the most difficult days of the war. His friends had only seen him truly angry one time.

Pitto had been the point man for the squad on patrol late one overcast afternoon in the hedgerow fighting in Normandy. Passing a small French farm, the squad was pinned down by a German machine gun nest on the second floor of the small stone home. The Americans were returning fire with their M-1 rifles and Thompson submachine guns when the front door of the farmhouse was flung open and two children ran out. A teenage girl had her little brother by the hand and came running toward the American GIs. Pitto's squad ceased firing and screamed for the children to get down. Apparently frightened beyond all reason, the pair kept running down the dirt path from their home toward the road where the American soldiers were taking cover in a parallel ditch. The children were cut down by the German machine gun just six feet before they reached the ditch.

In a solitary episode of unbridled fury, Pitto charged the farm house against the orders of Lt. Owen and the warnings of the rest of the squad. Pitto miraculously made it to the front of the farmhouse and caught a quick breath. Pulling the pin on a hand grenade, he hurled the explosive into the second story window. He followed it immediately with a second grenade and then charged inside and up the stairs. The firing of the

German machine gun had ceased after the first grenade exploded. Smoke poured out of the farmhouse window, and the rest of the squad could hear low moaning as they ran up to the building. Suddenly, the moaning ceased and the Americans saw the broken bodies of the three Germans who had been manning the machine gun, as they were hurled out of the upstairs window one by one. When the GIs searched the bodies of the German soldiers, they noticed the heads of all three were twisted at awkward angles.

Pitto insisted on digging a grave for the girl by himself while the rest of the team dug a grave for the little brother. Scarcely a word was spoken as the squad resumed and finished their patrol. The incident was never mentioned again.

As Lt. Owen stepped from the muddy street onto the patio of the café *La Brouette* the men of his squad fixed their gaze upon him. "Yeah, Pitto. The colonel's got a mission for us. Seems like nobody knows what the Krauts are up to, and he wants us to find out. Let's take it inside where we can spread this map out and put a plan together."

The group of GIs stood up. Some stretched, and all followed the lieutenant into the café. The room was deserted except for the proprietor who was seated next to a table in a far corner wrapping silverware place settings with white cloth napkins.

"Mind if we borrow a table?" Lt. Owen queried. The man in the corner just smiled and nodded. The lieutenant couldn't tell if the man understood or was just faking it. It didn't matter. The lieutenant spread out the map and the squad gathered around, eager to size up the situation. Owen laid out the purpose of the mission and reviewed the information he had with his team. "We've been issued white camouflage overcoats. I want you guys to paint the jeeps white as well- ASAP. The Krauts can't find what they can't see. We leave before dark." At this point, Owen asked for input. Every eye turned toward Chadwell who was still honing his knife. "Well?" the lieutenant verbalized what each man was thinking.

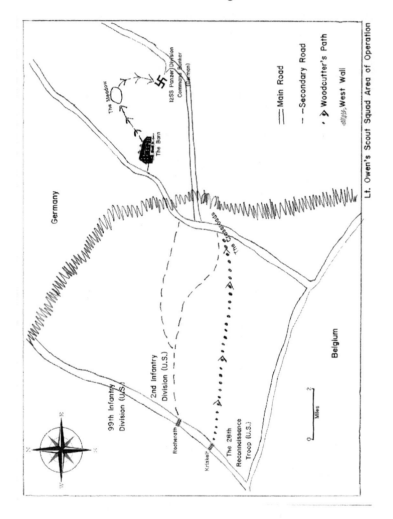

Chadwell put his knife in its scabbard and then spoke slowly and carefully but without hesitation. His mind had taken in instantly the gravity of the mission, and he evidently was already well into formulating a methodical strategy to carry it out. "The bulk of our 28th Troop is dispersed here at Krinkelt. The Germans are thrusting here at Monschau and Hofen to the north and here at the Losheim gap to the south."

"Shiloh, I hate to interrupt, but how do you know all this?" Lt. Owen asked.

Chadwell continued to study the map. Without looking up, he said matter-of-factly, "I am a scout. I know."

The Indian resumed his description of the situation. "The Germans are using infantry and armor supported by infantry. The opening artillery barrage this morning was widespread and intense but inaccurate. They either do not have enough artillery spotters or they are poorly trained. The 99th Division elements to the south of us are having a difficult fight. The 38th Cavalry Squadron is holding well at Monschau. That is all I know."

Private Walt King whistled a low whistle. "Chadwell, you never cease to amaze me. How do you do that?"

"As I said, I'm a scout. I was out all day yesterday and some of the night. I watch. I see. I hear. It's our purpose here. We're all scouts."

"Yeah, well there are scouts, and then there are scouts." King sat down in one of the random chairs against the near wall. Leaning the chair backward so it rested on the two back legs, he said, "Lieutenant, I for one am glad the Indian is on *our* side!" The rest of the team murmured in unanimous agreement.

"Continue," the lieutenant urged, a wry smile now forming on his face.

Taking a sharpened pencil from his jacket pocket, Chadwell drew a curving line on the map from Krinkelt east toward the Belgian border with Germany. "This is a very narrow woodcutter's trail. It is just wide enough for a jeep. It will get us behind the enemy. They will not know of this."

It was on this path, marked by Chadwell's thin pencil line on the lieutenant's map, that the jeeps were parked. Chadwell rejoined the team as they huddled around the lead jeep. Lt. Owen was examining his map with a small flashlight and talking to himself. His men knew this was his custom when concentrating intensely. As Chadwell walked up, Owen asked, "How far 'til we cross this road? There's bound to be Kraut traffic on it!"

"One-half mile. Mel and I will go forward and see. We'll return in 30 minutes. Lieutenant, now you rest." Corporal Mel Sweringen was from Sherman, Texas. He had been raised on a cattle ranch and was the best outdoorsman of the squad, aside from Chadwell. He had learned to hunt and fish from his father and four older brothers. Whenever Chadwell wanted company on a scouting patrol, which wasn't often, Sweringen was his pick. The squad had nicknamed the pair "the Cowboy and the Indian."

In half an hour, the squad heard the soft swish of feet treading through the ankle deep snow on the trail. Thompsons were lifted to shoulders and safeties clicked off. Momentarily "the Cowboy and the Indian" were recognized and the submachine guns facing their direction were lowered.

"Howdy, boys," Sweringen greeted his friends. "Take a nice nap?"

"Cut the small talk. What do you have?" Owen cut to the chase.

Sweringen responded, "The trail comes out at a three-way junction. One road runs north and south, a main highway. The third part of the junction is a westbound paved secondary road. We saw six troop carrier trucks and a staff car pass headed south. A company of grenadiers passed by on foot headed west. For now, it's quiet. It looks like the Krauts have posted two military police at the crossroads to give directions and check IDs."

"I think we could take out two Krauts pretty easy, huh, Lieutenant?" Private Chuck Cameron commented.

"Yeah, two dead or missing German MPs and you might as well send out a big fat invitation for the rest of the Krauts to come looking for us. Come on! Use your head," Lt. Owen snapped. "What we need is a diversion to draw the MPs away from the crossroads just long enough for us to get the jeeps across to the northbound road."

All was quiet except for the faint rustle of the snow now falling heavily upon them. Each man pondered the situation. In the pale illumination of the winter night, one might have mistaken the white-clad Americans and their frosted jeeps for specters. Breaking the silence, the lieutenant said, "Cameron, pull out that box of dynamite. You, Sweringen, and Pitto hustle over to the westbound road with some of that stuff. When you get there, find two big trees next to the road and strap three or four sticks to each tree. Take enough fuse cord to give yourself ten minutes to get back here. Set them to go off about fifteen seconds apart. The explosions and trees falling across the road might be enough to rouse the curiosity of the Krauts and pull them down the road far enough and long enough for us to scoot across the intersection behind them. Just maybe, they'll think it's a couple of random artillery rounds comin' in. You got it?"

"Got it. Want us to brush out our tracks around the trees?" Pvt. Cameron asked.

"Negative. As hard as this snow's comin' down, they'll be covered up in minutes; that's even if the Krauts decide to check out the woods. Now get going!"

The trio headed off through the woods loaded with explosives. In 30 minutes they were back, all three huffing vigorously after their exhausting trek through the rapidly deepening snow on the forest floor. "The first blow should be any minute," Cameron gasped.

"Let's go," Owen said to King, who was in the driver's seat of the lead jeep. The two white vehicles, headlights out, slowly moved down the trail toward the crossroads, following Chadwell who was leading the procession on foot. The party stopped a hundred yards from the road junction, engines quietly idling. As the lead jeep came to a halt on the snow covered trail, the sound of the first explosion ripped the still night air. The splintering crash of an ancient pine followed within seconds. Shouts from the two German MPs indicated they were walking cautiously toward the west on the road to investigate. The Americans saw the enemy flashlight beams probe the westbound road as they moved away from the junction. The second explosion completed the diversion perfectly.

Owen said, "Go!" Chadwell catapulted into the rear jeep as it led the way through the crossroads into the north bound highway, completely unnoticed by the German MPs.

18 The Bunker

The two jeeps stole north into the night and German territory with headlights still out. A mile down the road, they halted, and Lt. Owen and Chadwell traded seats. The Indian was the night eyes for the squad. Anticipating a German roadblock, the Americans looked intently for a turnoff. Giant flakes continued to fall straight down. There was no wind.

"Stop!" Chadwell ordered, and King obeyed instantly. The sergeant jumped out of the jeep and trotted back about 30 feet. Stepping to the right of the road into an opening in the trees, he disappeared from sight. In minutes, he returned and spoke to Lt. Owen. "A farmhouse. Mostly burned. Abandoned. There's a barn that's ok."

"Fine. Let's hole up there for a few hours and see what we can see comin' down this road."

The jeeps backed slowly to avoid slipping into the ditch on the roadside. Turning in at the trail to the farmhouse, the vehicles had just cleared the road when the GIs heard engine noise to the north. A line of slit headlights indicated the approach of a long convoy. The roar of engines grew as King and Cameron parked the jeeps out of sight in the old barn. The remainder of the squad deployed in the woods at the side of the road. Chadwell had just slipped back into the woods after brushing out the jeep tracks with a broom of pine branches, when the headlights of the first German truck illuminated the road in front of the scouts.

The group of eight white-clad Americans lying hidden in the darkness of the snow-covered forest floor was invisible to the passing convoy. For over an hour trucks, halftracks, and Kubelwagens jammed with troops passed by. The icy road was choked with wheeled vehicles and infantry on foot. Even the highly efficient German army could not prevent the endless starts and stops of the mass of traffic. Finally, the end of the convoy approached — a rumbling line of Panther tanks.

Moments after the last tank growled off down the road, Owen ordered, "The barn." The scouts peeled away from their line of observation and shuffled off toward the barn. The snowfall continued unabated, deepening to mid-calf. Inside the barn, Cameron lit a small candle he carried with him for just such occasions. The lieutenant threw off his white overcoat and gloves and rubbed his hands together. "Well?" he said in a questioning tone, looking at King.

Private Walter King was born in Great Falls, Montana, August 31, 1923. The family name was actually Koenig. (Walt's father had changed the name in early 1942 to dodge some of the abuse that was being heaped on Americans of German descent at that time.) The elder Koenig had immigrated with his family to the United States at the end of WWI and ended up farming wheat in the Big Sky country of central Montana. As much as anything, Walt had enlisted in the U.S. Army to prove his patriotism to his native country. He had been assigned to intelligence because of his fluency in German but had become restless with an indoor desk job. He had put in for a transfer to reconnaissance troops and, based largely on the glowing recommendation of his commander in the intelligence branch, had been granted his request. He had joined the 28th Reconnaissance Troop in England in May of 1944.

King slowly kicked off the snow clinging to his boots. "Based on the few shoulder patches and vehicle markings I could see, I'd say we just watched a regiment of the 12th SS Panzers go by. They are affectionately known as Hitlerjugen, Hitler youth. Just some youngsters out for a good time." A low guffaw of laughter bubbled through the group, huddled around the candle as if it were actually a bonfire.

"I thought Kraut frontline units didn't wear unit designations," the lieutenant noted.

"Not supposed to. But I guess these guys are puffed up about who they are," King conjectured.

A silence descended over the squad as they stood gazing at the low flicker of the solitary flame and arranged their thoughts. The fatigue of the late hour settled on them like a heavy blanket. Yawns spread from man to man like a swift contagion. "Well, we need to be sharp tomorrow. Probably not much more to see tonight. It's about 0100. I want us to be up and out at 0630. Each man take 45 minutes on guard. We each get about a five hour nap. I'll take the first watch. Sergeant, set the schedule."

"Yes, sir" Chadwell responded. "We could spread out in that hay up in the loft. Hang up a couple of our tarps from the jeeps over the rafters for a canopy to hold the heat. Use Cameron's candle, and we might all actually feel half warm sleeping. You have any more of those?" Chadwell questioned Cameron.

"Yeah, Sarge, right here." Cameron pulled out three more fat stubby candles and handed them to Chadwell like a proud student at show and tell. "Just hope none of you guys catch your pants on fire while you're sleeping." Another rumble of chuckles rolled through the group.

"I don't think you'll have to worry about your pants burning with this," Chadwell remarked as he set a large, empty clay flower pot up on the hood of one of the jeeps.

"So, Sarge, you gonna plant some flowers?" Cameron asked. The members of the squad looked from the pot to Chadwell and back again wondering not *if*, but *what*, he had up his sleeve.

"No, Private. But we might just keep your cheeks rosy with this."

Chadwell looked at Pitto. "You and Cameron go over to what's left of the farmhouse and bring me back six bricks. That's where I found this pot."

Pitto looked puzzled, "Six bricks…? Okay." He and Cameron moved off and returned quickly with the bricks.

"Alright, Chadwell. Get'em bedded down," Owen instructed.

"Yes, Sir. Pitto, get those bricks up to the loft," Chadwell instructed. He followed with the pot. The rest of the curious squad came up behind.

Working quickly, the Indian set the bricks flat on the floor of the loft in an area swept clear of hay and straw, two bricks high, with large gaps at the corners. He set three of Cameron's four candles on the floor of the loft in the center of the triangle formed by the bricks and lit them. Tossing the fourth candle to Cameron, he said, "Keep this as a spare." He then set the clay pot upside down on the triangle of bricks like a dome over the candle flames. "A candle heater," Chadwell noted.

"Well, I'll be…," Pitto expressed amazement for the rest of the scouts.

Within minutes, the clay of the pot was hot to the touch and radiated warmth to the squad, now seated and reclining around the heater. The tarps and the hay bales held much of the heat in but were open enough to allow adequate ventilation for their little den.

The night passed quickly. At 0515 Chadwell nudged the members of the squad awake with the toe of his boot. "Everybody up. Eat some breakfast. Lieutenant wants to leave in 15 minutes." The sergeant's six friends yawned and stretched and grumbled a little. Lt. Owen was poring over his map which he had spread out over the hood of one of the jeeps. While the squad sorted through their packs and traded items for their brief meal, Chadwell climbed down the ladder and stepped outside. The snow had stopped falling. The sky was still overcast but growing lighter to the east. The sun wouldn't be up for a half hour.

By the time Chadwell returned, the scouts were fully awake and assembled on the floor of the barn listening to Lt. Owen. "I want to be on this hill here by the time the sun is up." Owen pointed to a spot east of their current location just inside the German border. "Any major push through this area into Belgium has got to use this highway as one of the main arteries. If we find a good observation point here, we should have the Colonel some useful intel by tonight."

"And just how do we get from here to there?" Pvt. Pete House asked with a hint of sarcasm. "I mean the roads are bound to be crawling with Krauts this morning."

"I know a way," Chadwell said calmly. "There's another trail that goes in that direction."

"How would you know that?" Pitto asked incredulously.

"I climbed a tree on that hill behind the barn. I could see for miles."

Pitto grinned and looked at Sweringen. "The guy doesn't miss a thing."

"Nope," the Cowboy agreed.

Lt. Owen focused the attention of his squad. "Alright. Check your weapons. Collect your packs." Pausing, Owen looked at Chadwell's M1 Garand. "Why is it, Chadwell, that you and Sweringen didn't pick up Thompsons like the rest of us?"

"Lieutenant, we may need a long arm," the Indian explained tersely.

A pregnant silence hung in the barn. The squad had never seen the lieutenant and the sergeant cross swords. Ignoring Chadwell's response, Owen quickly folded his map and climbed into the jeep. "Let's get outta here."

The Americans threw their gear into the jeeps and donned their white camouflage. Chadwell threw back the two heavy wooden doors of the barn, and the jeeps crawled out following the sergeant slowly onto the trail.

The "trail" would have been more accurately dubbed a "footpath." Dense, snow-covered brush evidenced a lack of use of the path for some time. Chadwell led the duo of jeeps, picking up fallen tree branches as he went. At one turn at the top of a small hill, the sergeant called for reinforcements to push a large deadfall trunk off the path. Everyone piled out into the calf deep snow and shuffled ahead. As the squad gathered on one side of the heavy pine, Pitto spread his arms and said, "Stand back, children, and let a *man* work." The "children" obeyed, stepping back and giving the giant wide berth.

Pitto planted his feet at the smaller end of the trunk and grabbed the tree with both hands. Grunting deeply and pushing hard with his legs, he lifted the end and shoved it off the path and into the woods. Patting his gloves together, he grinned and looked around at the faces of his friends.

"Remind me not to get him riled up," Cameron said to Sweringen.

"Right," the Cowboy acknowledged as the "children" and Pitto climbed back into their jeeps. Sweringen gazed skyward for a moment. He sniffed the air, relishing the heavy pine scent. It reminded him of Christmas back home in Texas. Dad and the brothers always made a day of it, riding over to the pine grove at the Van Treese Ranch and picking the perfect tree to take home to Mom.   Sweringen hadn't felt that homesick ache for a while. "*Strange,*" he thought, how just a familiar smell could stir up the emotions like that.

The eastern sky lightened slowly that morning. The cloud cover was still thick and lowering. More snow seemed likely. Chadwell continued to lead the squad along the path with the dense forest pressing in on both sides. After topping another small hill, the path finally opened into a small meadow. "End of the trail, Lieutenant. The farmer must have used it to drive livestock up here." Chadwell spoke to Lt. Owen in the first jeep which had stopped in the middle of the clearing. The second jeep pulled up alongside.

"Alright. Scouts out. Everybody back in ten minutes. Weaver, you're with me." Owen's squad was in their element now. They were to secure a perimeter, make note of the terrain, structures, and any enemy activity, and report back. All without being spotted. "Weaver, I want you to do a radio check with the rec troop."

"Yes, sir." Corporal Weaver turned on his FM radio, performed a standard check-in with reconnaissance troop headquarters, and turned the set off, all within 60 seconds. The squad did not want to arouse the interest of any eavesdropping Germans who might try to put a fix on their location.

The ghost-like figures of the squad reassembled in the meadow next to the jeeps and gave Owen their reports. The consensus was that the best position for observing the surging forces of the Wehrmacht was the ridge at the eastern edge of the meadow. Pitto summarized, "Looks like the whole German army is on a highway a couple miles to the east. They're all headed southwest towards our lines."

"OK. Cameron and Sweringen. I want you guys to spread out on the edges of this meadow. Keep a sharp eye. I don't want any surprises! Move!" Owen turned to the rest of his men. "Let's get set up on the ridge. Must be the highest spot around here. It puzzles me why the Krauts don't have a detachment up here somewhere."

King conjectured, "I think they're in such an all fired hurry that they overlooked this spot."

"Not like the *efficient Germans* to make that kind of mistake," Owen replied.

"Pride goeth before destruction," Chadwell reminded everyone.

The lieutenant paused for just a moment, as if to digest the morsel of wisdom the Indian had tossed out. "Let's go," he ordered as he led the men to the ridge and crawled carefully to the top. The scouts cut several small branches off the young pines which clung in abundance to both sides of the ridge. Apparently, a fire had denuded the ridge several years back, leaving space for new growth forest. Each man placed a layer of the foliage on his personal ground cover on top of the snow and made himself as comfortable as possible.

Lying prone on the high ridge under the cover of the thick woods, they began their stealthy vigil. Each man had a pair of binoculars fixed on the long gray stream of men and machines that choked the highway. The German army continued to pour toward the Belgian border and the ruptured American lines.

King made detailed notes for their report to headquarters. "There's at least division strength here, if not corps," he remarked to the lieutenant.

Lt. Owen lowered his glasses. "Yeah, impressive. I'm afraid it's very serious. And what's unbelievable is that G-2 (Division level military intelligence) didn't see it coming." He scanned the immediate slope which descended from their position toward the road in the distance. The incline was covered by a fairly thick pine forest and carpeted by a foot and a half of snow. As he lifted his binoculars toward his eyes, he noticed Chadwell looking in a different direction from the rest of the squad. "See something?"

"Maybe."

"What?"

"I'm not sure. Do you see a very slight wisp of smoke over there a couple thousand yards to the southwest between here and the road?" the sergeant asked, pointing.

Owen strained to see what Chadwell was seeing. "No, I guess not. What are you thinking?"

Chadwell replied, "I'm thinking I should go investigate. Could be a headquarters of some kind."

The lieutenant rubbed his now-stubbled chin. "I suppose we're here to find out what's going on with the Krauts. You want company?"

"No. I go alone, silently," Chadwell said confidently. "And you keep this?" he said, almost as a statement rather than a question, handing Owen his M1.

"You don't want your rifle? I'm sure you're going to give me a good reason," Owen said, taking the M1 from his sergeant.

"Lieutenant, we're several miles behind enemy lines. There are eight of us and who knows how many thousands of them. If I have to start shooting, we're going to have more trouble than General Custer had. All I need is my knife and my eyes. I will be back shortly." Chadwell grasped the lieutenant's gloved hand and looked him square in the eyes. "Lieutenant, you're a good man."

Lt. Owen swallowed hard and nodded. "Return safely." The white-clad Indian slipped quickly away down the slope and disappeared into the snowy forest. *A Cherokee ghost,* he thought to himself.

At the lieutenant's order, the watchers on the ridge backed away from their perch and assembled at the jeeps. Owen looked at his watch - 1130, time for lunch. He had King and Weaver break out the K-rations and carry some to the two men on the perimeter. K-rations were intensely boring but did provide the required minimum of daily calories. Fortunately for the squad, in addition to being a radio genius, Weaver was also an expert scrounger. He had somehow squirreled away a case of assorted canned meats and fruit from undisclosed sources. These treats were judiciously distributed among the men as well. For the *piece de resistance,* Weaver had cranked up one of the jeep engines and used the exhaust manifold as a stove to heat a steaming pot of coffee for the boys. Smiles and literal pats on the back were all the reward he needed. He got them and acknowledged them with smiles and nods of his own.

Snow fell again as the squad of scouts finished their lunch, but the hot coffee continued to do wonders for the men's spirits. Jokes and stories were bantered back and forth until Lt. Owen ordered the men back to their posts. This time the sentries swapped with Pitto and House. Periodic blizzard-like bursts reduced the Americans' ability to see the road traffic, but also imposed a commensurate slowing effect on the flow of German forces.

As he peered intently through his field glasses, Owen felt a pain surge through his right calf. Turning, he looked up and saw an icy wraith silhouetted against the darkening winter clouds. The wraith was wearing combat boots and had just kicked the lieutenant. "Lieutenant, you're dead," Sgt. Shiloh Chadwell remarked.

"Thanks. You sure don't make much noise," Owen observed, sitting up and rubbing his leg.

"I'm a scout. It's … "

"What you do; I know."

Cameron and Sweringen moved next to the lieutenant anxious to hear the news from Chadwell.

"Lieutenant, there's a large wooden bunker down there at the end of a narrow road which tees in to the highway. They have three strands of barbed wire around the compound, maybe 1000 yards in circumference. There are high power radio antennas, two half-tracks, and a company of SS troopers. Two FLAK cannons. I'd say it's at least a regimental headquarters, and maybe divisional," Chadwell reported. "There's valuable material in that bunker. What I don't understand is, what's SS doing here?"

"You *sure* they're SS?" King questioned.

"Yes, no doubts."

"OK, so what," Cameron inserted. "I do believe a company of SS has us outgunned. We can't just walk down there and say, 'excuse us, we're here to look inside your bunker.'"

The Indian locked eyes with the private. "'Upon the wicked He shall rain snares, fire and brimstone, and an horrible tempest'."

A curious look spread across Cameron's face as recognition of Chadwell's plan dawned on him. "You mean we're gonna call in an artillery strike on the compound?"

"Exactly. Weaver used to be an artillery spotter. That's how he got so handy with a radio. Lieutenant, do you have a good fix on our position here?" the sergeant asked.

"Pretty good, probably within 500 yards," the lieutenant assured Chadwell.

"Sir, we're gonna have to be better than that. To take out that company of guards, we'll need a time-on-target that's within 100 yards. Can you get a fix that close?" the sergeant pressed.

"Let's take a look at that map," Lt. Owen said almost to himself as the rest of the squad on the ridge followed him back to the jeeps. The men gathered around the lieutenant and consulted with him as he checked and double checked their location. With Weaver's input, the lieutenant made calculations and scribbled notes on a small pad of paper. Owen almost stabbed the map with the pencil and then slid the point to the southeast and made an 'x' with a flourish. "That's our Kraut bunker. What do you think, Chadwell?"

There was no response to the lieutenant's question. Owen looked up and scanned the faces of his men. Snow crusted, weary eyed, but seasoned faces of veteran warriors looked back at him.

"He's ... praying, Lieutenant," replied the Cowboy, almost in a whisper.

The lieutenant turned to see the lone white figure, his sergeant and his friend, standing at the edge of the clearing.

"We got one big problem, Lieutenant. How we gonna get all those SS goons to stand out in the open for the artillery barrage?" Cameron was doubtful.

King jumped in, "If there is anything about the Germans, they're predictable. They'll have almost everybody outside, lined up in formation for the changing of the guard. And I can almost guarantee it will be right before supper, 1630."

"Well, then. The good news just keeps pouring in. Scouts, let's go to work. Weaver?" Owen was ready to get the show on the road.

"Yes, sir?"

"Think you can raise HQ and get us a T-O-T for 1630?"

"Just like dialing up my girl Kate back in Chicago," Weaver smiled.

"And how much firepower can we get?" the lieutenant queried.

"If all battalions in the division get the word, 48 tubes."

"That would do," Owen said dryly.

By now Chadwell was back with the group and the lieutenant had pulled in his sentries. All six listened as Owen and Chadwell briefed the squad and asked for questions. There were none. The scouts checked their weapons, filled their pockets with extra ammo clips and headed down the slope toward the bunker, following close behind the Indian.

The squad reached a ridge in the slope and went to ground. Chadwell crept to the left and disappeared. Crawling quickly, the rest of the scouts reached the ridge line and paused silently. The compound was as Chadwell had described. A rough cut but solid looking bunker was positioned at the front of the compound facing west. There were two doors in the rear of the bunker facing a fairly large piece of open ground. The entrance to the compound was to the left. One FLAK cannon was perched at each end of the compound. The two halftracks and two staff cars were parked at the extreme rear of the compound. A score of tents set in perfect lines were pitched to the right rear of the enclosed area.

Owen checked his watch - 1618. If the message had been forwarded to divisional artillery as requested, it was precisely 12 minutes until the T-O-T. Motionless as statues, the Americans continued to watch the activity in the bunker compound intently. The SS NCOs barked orders for their company to fall in. The German storm troopers responded. The black helmeted ranks of elite SS soldiers stood stiffly at attention behind their NCOs. Shortly, the left of the two bunker doors opened. Two SS officers stepped out into the muddy snow. As they proceeded to the front of their company, the yard was in absolute silence. Darkness descended quickly as the day of thick clouds and snow came to an end.

Owen looked at his watch again —1628. *Chadwell, come on!* he thought. He looked at the rest of the squad. Sweringen was sighting his M1 on one of the guards at the bunker doors. The rest of the men had Thompsons trained on the SS company. *Where's Chadwell?*

Suddenly a white clad figure crashed through the trees behind the squad and fell down beside the lieutenant. Chadwell was breathing heavily, "Two guards at the gate, they sleep now," he said, replacing his now bloody knife in its scabbard on his hip.

One of the SS NCOs, apparently hearing something fall in the forest on the ridge, took two steps forward and was about to speak. But it was too late. The time-on-target barrage of the 2nd Infantry Division Artillery was *exactly* on time. The squad hunkered down behind the ridgeline as the five-minute barrage of devastating shells fell continuously. Assembled in the open, the SS company never had a chance. And the two guards at the bunker doors who had fallen to ground at the onset of the torrent of explosions were both shot through by Sweringen's bullets.

19 The Prisoner

The instant the shells ceased, Owen shouted, "Go!" His men scrambled down the slope to the edge of the compound and slithered through the barbed wire. The SS troopers crumpled on the compound grounds were covered in blood and either dead or dying. None were in any shape to resist the onslaught of the American scouts. The simultaneous and unexpected arrival of rounds from four American artillery battalions had totally devastated the Germans. Thompson submachine fire barked through the clumps on the ground, finishing the job started by the 2nd Division howitzers.

Sweringen and Chadwell ran to the back wall of the bunker and vaulted to the bunker roof with the assistance of Pitto and Cameron. Rapidly pulling the pins, the two scouts on the roof each dropped two hand grenades down the pair of ventilation pipes which projected from the roof. Though several artillery rounds had struck the roof of the bunker, the solid wood had protected the interior of the structure. The ventilation pipes were riddled by shrapnel but still provided the scouts a direct channel for their grenades into the German headquarters. Instantly, muffled explosions reverberated within the bunker and smoke poured out of the pipes.

The scouts on the roof jumped down and joined the rest at the left bunker door. Pitto crashed his heavy booted foot into the door but without noticeable effect. Next he rammed his giant shoulder into the door over and over. Again, the thick wood refused to yield. Pitto stood frustrated, breathing heavily, hands on hips. "Any ideas, Lieutenant?"

Owen turned toward the open yard of the compound looking desperately for something solid to ram it with! At that moment, House, who had slipped away from the group, set a plain wooden crate on the ground, squatted beside it, and opened the lid. "Think one of these might work?" he asked, looking up at the lieutenant with a smile.

Sweringen reached down and picked up one of the four tubes resting in the crate. "A Panzerfaust," House noted. The Panzerfaust was a simple but lethal anti-tank weapon, the German equivalent of the American bazooka.

"Alright, try it!" Owen ordered.

House motioned for the rest of the scouts to step back as he lined up on the door from 40 feet away. The roar of the projectile striking the wooden door was deafening but satisfying. The wood had been reduced to a gaping, splintered hole. As the gray smoke of the explosion hung heavy in the air, Pitto charged in, and the rest of the squad followed immediately behind. Sweeping the inside of the structure with machine gun and rifle fire the scouts were determined to take no chances and probably no prisoners. Then silence. The inside of the bunker was completely black except for the slight illumination entering through the four observation slits cut into the front of the building. The winter evening was now dark but still lighter than the bowels of the bunker where all lights had been extinguished by the four grenade explosions.

Owen switched on his flashlight and moved quickly to a large table in the center of the room. He eagerly examined the maps and papers scattered there. King stepped over and whistled to himself. "Unbelievable! Situation maps, orders of battle, OKW(Oberkommando der Wehrmacht- German High Command) special directives, regimental and battalion reports. This is a gold mine!"

Across the room, Cameron remarked, "Would you look at this." He held up a black and silver medal attached to a red and black ribbon he had just ripped off a dead general officer he found hunched over a desk in the corner.

"Cameron," Chadwell scolded. "We're not here for souvenirs. Check these Germans for papers, maps, letters. And then we need to get out of here."

"But, Sarge," Cameron whined, "I ... " The blast that filled the bunker pierced Cameron from the back and exited his chest. Sweringen instantly swung his flashlight to illuminate the assailant and Weaver fired a three round burst into an SS colonel. The German fulfilled the officer's dream of dying "a glorious death for the Fuhrer." His Luger pistol dropped, clattering on the wooden floor of the bunker.

Sgt. Chadwell caught Cameron as he fell forward and gently laid him supine on the map table. "Light, give me light!" Three flashlights spotted on Cameron as Chadwell opened Cameron's jacket and pulled off his sweater, shirt, and undershirt now soaked in bright red blood. Cameron tried to speak but coughed and gasped with each breath. "Be quiet," the Cherokee spoke firmly to his friend. "You've got a sucking chest wound. We'll fix it. Just try to breathe slowly." Looking at King, "Give me a pack of cigarettes!"

"What?" King asked, incredulous.

"A pack of your cigarettes, now!" Chadwell demanded in an uncharacteristically harsh voice.

King dug deep in one of his pockets pulling out a cherished pack of Lucky Strikes. Chadwell ripped off the cellophane cover and carefully flattened it on the table beside Cameron, who continued to grow weaker as he struggled for air. Chadwell sliced off a piece of Cameron's T-shirt with his combat knife and cleaned the circumference of the dark, round wound in Cameron's right chest wall. With each labored breath, air bubbled in and out through the bloody hole in the wounded soldier's chest cavity. Carefully, Chadwell placed the cellophane over the wound and then stuffed the piece of T-shirt into the hole over it, filling the hole completely. The sucking sound ceased, and Cameron immediately began to breathe easier. The squad members, except for Sweringen, were absorbed in the drama before them as the sergeant worked to save the private's life.

Sweringen worked his way around the bunker, checking to make sure the rest of Germans strewn about were dead. He collected weapons and papers as he went and set them in a pile on a desk in the corner. Chadwell and the lieutenant continued to work on Cameron, securing a tight bandage around his chest and replacing his shirts and coats. "We've got to get out of here now!" Owen ordered.

"Lieutenant, you better come look at this," the Cowboy pressed his leader. Shining his flashlight on the swollen and bloodied face of a middle-aged German, Sweringen lifted the head for Owen to examine.

"Okay, he's bruised up, still alive, so what?" Owen turned and started to head for the door.

"Look again," Sweringen urged.

The lieutenant stopped and shined his flashlight on the German's face again. "Older German, simple uniform, couple of medals. What are you thinking?"

While Chadwell helped Cameron sit up, the rest of the scouts gathered around the lieutenant and the Cowboy. Pitto moved the rest of the men aside. "What's up?"

"I don't know, Lieutenant. But I think we have just captured a general officer or maybe a high ranking civilian."

Owen jerked the wounded German too his feet. "No time to waste. The intelligence guys can sort it out when we get back." The lieutenant looked at his sergeant. "Chadwell, can Cameron be moved?"

"Yes, but he'll need help." Chadwell was cautious.

"Let me have him," Pitto boomed.

"And I've got our prisoner," Sweringen said as he pushed the German out the door and across the compound. The prisoner had been badly cut and bruised on the face and head but was otherwise uninjured and able to walk. Being used to commanding instead of being commanded, the German protested vociferously at being shoved around. However, the Cowboy made it clear with a rifle butt to the head that he would brook no resistance.

Pitto handed his Thompson to Weaver and put Cameron on his own back. "Hang in there, Chuck." The wounded scout breathed rapidly but without coughing or wheezing. Chadwell led the squad out of the compound and up the hill. He was followed by Pitto, with Cameron on his back, Owen, with a cache of Wehrmacht papers and maps, and the rest of the scouts trailing.

Weaver and House had grabbed three *jerricans* of gasoline and doused the inside of the bunker. As the squad now struggled through the barbed wire and up the snow covered hill toward the jeeps, flames roared out of the doors and the ventilation pipes. Sgt. Shiloh Chadwell reached the low ridge overlooking the bunker compound and stood transfixed by the scene. Fiery fingers reached out of the blackened bunker, illuminating the dark winter sky. The rest of the scouts climbed up beside Chadwell, pausing to catch their breath. As the American soldiers and their Nazi prisoner watched the macabre scene, Owen spoke quietly, "Blackness, fire, death ... the evil of the place ... it's like ... "

"Hell!" Chadwell finished his thought.

Owen nodded, "Yes." The men watched the conflagration a moment longer but trudged off again with urgency knowing Cameron's critical state. The Indian carefully led the squad back up to the meadow without further incident. They avoided using their flashlights, hoping to escape notice by the German forces which were drawn to the compound by the noise and the fires now raging there. Periodically, thunderous explosions ripped the night air as rounds of high explosive shells cooked off. Whether the Germans would assume the carnage was the result of a lucky American artillery strike or conclude that commandos had staged a hit-and-run raid was anyone's guess. The scouts were not sticking around to find out.

Sweringen secured the wrists of his prisoner behind his back with a piece of rope. He did the same with his ankles. Stuffing him uncomfortably on the rear floor of the lead jeep he alerted the lieutenant, "We're ready to roll."

Pitto gently set Cameron in the front passenger seat of the second jeep and supported him as best he could with folded tarps and his own overcoat. Owen gave the order to move out. Chadwell led the way with a partially muted flashlight as the squad drove the jeeps down the trail back to the barn and finally halted side by side in front of the burned out farmhouse.

Cameron, who was slipping in and out of a blood loss stupor, had groaned with each bump on the trail. "Lieutenant, I don't think he's gonna make it if we don't get him to a hospital soon!" Sweringen warned.

"And none of us will make it if get captured by the Krauts," Owen answered. "We're going as fast as we can. There's nothing else to do for him now except pray. King, you up to pulling a bluff?"

"Sure, lieutenant, what you got in mind?" King responded.

"Swap places with me and put my helmet on. I'll drive and you be the lieutenant. We'll have to stop at the roadblock, and you'll play the part of the squad leader of a Kraut commando unit infiltrating the American lines dressed as GIs and driving two captured American jeeps. Think you can do it?"

"Lieutenant, all I can do is try. But what about Cameron? He looks awful. And our prisoner? The sentries are gonna have to be blind and stupid."

"Well, we don't have any other options. King, tell the Kraut if he makes one sound, he gets the first bullet to the head and we machine gun the sentries. Can you make him a believer?"

"I think so, lieutenant." King exited the lead jeep and traded helmets with Lieutenant Owen. He then stepped over to the second jeep and spoke brusquely to the prisoner, who said nothing.

As King attempted to instill a healthy fear in the German, Chadwell walked up and conferred briefly with Owen. He then leaned over to King, "Let's ask him the password. There's gotta be a password to get through the lines."

King phrased the question in German. "He says he doesn't know."

"He lies," Chadwell said plainly. An unpleasant rasping sound echoed in the darkness as he unsheathed his combat knife. "Ask him again."

King asked again, "Same response."

The prisoner screamed in agony. His right hand spurted blood where the Cherokee had sliced off his left index finger at the first joint. "'If thy hand offend thee, cut it off and cast it from thee.' I will fulfill this verse piece by piece until he decides to cooperate." Chadwell purposefully flung the finger out of the jeep. "Ask him again," he said with no change of intonation.

King obeyed with a grave "Alright." He questioned the German one more time. "'Winter sturm'. He says it's 'Winter Sturm'."

Sweringen wrapped a rag around the prisoner's finger stump and then took one of the tarps and covered him completely. He still lay motionless in the floor of the jeep. Sweringen and Weaver rested their boots on the German with some satisfaction.

"Alright, it's show time. Let's go, and may God go with us."

Chadwell and King loaded into the jeeps and Owen drove out onto the highway, dutifully playing his part. The second jeep stayed close behind with House at the wheel. The filthy tracks of the last convoy to pass were almost obliterated by the continuing heavy snowfall. Chadwell kept his face mostly covered with a green wrap, supposedly against the cold, suspecting the number of Indians in the employ of the Wehrmacht was probably zero.

As the jeeps boldly pulled up to the anticipated check point, the German sentries spotlighted the squad with their flashlights and shouted, "Hände hoch oder ich schieße (Hands up or I'll shoot.) !"

King, who was seated in the front passenger spot of the lead jeep, shouted back in an equally rancorous tone and perfectly pitched German. The sentries lowered their MP-40's just slightly at this unexpected response. The men in the lead jeep had obediently put their hands in the air while King and the sentries hashed things out. Climbing out of the jeep, King strode defiantly toward the first sentry and shoved a wrinkled paper in his face yelling and gesticulating all the while. The second sentry kept his gun trained on King. King seemed to grow more bold with his role, the more he yelled at the

German grenadier. Chadwell was duly impressed- *The righteous* indeed *are as bold as a lion.*

At this juncture, a Wehrmacht unteroffizier (under-officer, NCO) stepped down out of the enclosed trailer the Germans were using as a temporary guard hut. Hearing the commotion, he had come out to investigate. He seemed genuinely surprised at the sight of the Americans and pulled his pistol from its holster. Joining in the heated exchange, he snatched the paper from the grenadier. King now appeared to be giving him a dressing down as well. Owen, who had at first been genuinely anxious at their prospects of making it through the German lines, suppressed smiling at the hapless sentries. Abruptly, the unteroffizier stood to attention and saluted King. He then carefully returned the paper. The American "lieutenant" huffed indignantly back to the jeep and, in fluent English, ordered Owen to drive on. The second jeep followed closely behind.

A couple miles down the road Sweringen broke the silence, "Walt, just what did you say to those guys? And what was that paper?"

King relished the attention. "Told them we were SS commandos. They demanded the password. I gave it. We had a wounded man, he was our ticket to an Allied field hospital. I shot him myself, for the Fatherland. We would drop him off and then run wild, causing chaos in "their" rear area. This would help "our" forces break through on the Meuse River. I chewed 'em out for their obstinacy and pointed out that while my commando was putting his body on the line for the Fuhrer, they were standing in the way of the most glorious victory in the history of Germany. My ace in the hole was to show them a special order paper I found at that bunker signed by SS Oberstgrupenfuhrer (Four-star General) Josef Dietrich. Basically, it informs Sixth Panzer Army that SS commando

units uniformed as Americans will be operating at the front
and behind American lines. All German elements in his area of
operations are ordered to give full assistance and cooperation
to these commando units. They still questioned me. The
sergeant wanted to see our true identity papers. I told him he
was an idiot and would be dealing with the SS if he didn't
move out of the way and quickly. No disguised commandos in
their right mind would carry German military identity papers.
I finally gave him thirty seconds to let us pass or I would call
his regimental command post and set in motion proceedings
for his court martial and execution. He said that wouldn't be
necessary.

"Alright, let's have the helmet. I think your head's too big
for it anyway," Owen joked.

The two jeeps now sped through the snowy night with
headlights on. The scouts wanted the American sentries to see
them in plenty of time to recognize the GIs as friendly forces.
It had been a very long day and a half. It was time for hot food
and some sleep- just as soon as Cameron made it to the
hospital and the prized prisoner was delivered to Col.
Cochrane.

20 The Watcher

He held the Carl Zeiss 10 x 50 dienstglas binoculars still for a long minute. A "P" class destroyer was moored in the bay next to three trawlers and a mine sweeper. Ten or twelve British sailors were employed smartly swabbing the destroyer deck. Two patrol boats slowly worked their way in a clockwise circuit around the perimeter of the harbor. Kurt smiled. *They have no idea*. A stiff breeze was up. Short white caps coated the surface of the water. A fairly dense overcast had covered the sky with light gray clouds. Rain showers had scudded their way over the islands off and on all morning- typical for the Shetland Islands at this time of year.

Leutnant zur See (German naval lieutenant) Kurt Niemiller enjoyed his work. And he was good. He had ten years of service in the Kriegsmarine. He knew ships, he knew weather, and he knew spy craft. He had spent the last four months in surveillance of the British naval base at Scalloway on the western side of the Shetland Islands. He lived simply. His home was in a cave on the southwestern end of the island. Resupply was accomplished monthly, courtesy of the U-boat service. He moved stealthily to an observation point before sunrise each morning and watched by day. His camouflaged sniper uniform served him well, and once in position, he covered himself entirely with a waterproof ghillie suit-type blanket.   He gathered detailed information on ship dispositions and activities. Then, at 0200 every fourth night, using a highly directional radio antenna, he relayed these data in terse encoded radio messages to a surfaced U-boat.

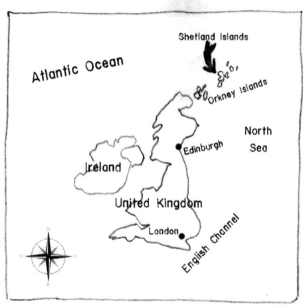

Great Britain and the Shetland Islands

Niemiller cocked his head at the faint whine of an aircraft engine. He could see nothing below the low cloud cover, but the sound was definitely of airborne origin and coming his way. Suddenly two Spitfire fighters broke through the cloud bank and began to circle slowly over the bay at about 3000 feet. Within a minute, an RNAF (Royal Naval Air Force) PBY Catalina seaplane plunged through the gray blanket of sky, followed by two more Spitfires. The seaplane leveled off and began a descent toward the relative shelter of the bay. It then landed on the slightly choppy surface and scooted toward the inner harbor. The four Spitfires circled in a vigilant rotation for another two minutes and then darted away back into the darkening cloud bank.

Niemiller watched the PBY stop and wait as the two patrol boats converged on it. The door of the seaplane opened, and a hooded figure was hustled into the lead patrol boat by four heavily armed American MPs followed by two field grade officers. *Very interesting. An important guest.* As the two patrol boats motored toward the pier, the PBY seaplane turned, revved its engines, and took off again. Within seconds the flying boat had disappeared into the dark clouds hanging over Scalloway.

That night, Leutnant Niemiller transmitted this coded message to U-122:

"PBY w/ escort. High value prisoner."

This succinct message was immediately relayed to OKM (Oberkommando der Marine- German Naval High Command) headquarters in Bremerhaven and then on to Berlin. The transmission was prefaced with an Ultra Top Secret identifier. The leutnant did not know, indeed could not have known, that the *high value prisoner* he had seen hastily unloaded from the PBY Catalina and whisked ashore to the isolated base at the village of Scalloway was none other than his Supreme Commander, Adolf Hitler.

Both the Allies and the Germans were keeping the capture of the Fuhrer strictly secret, but for entirely different reasons. The SS leadership was made aware of the Fuhrer's disappearance only after a search of the burned ruins of the bunker revealed no trace of their leader. Typical of Hitler's penchant for security, no one had been given advance notice of his surprise foray from his headquarters at the Adlerhorst in Bad Nauheim, Germany, to the forward bunker of the 12th SS Panzer Division. The dictator, a self-proclaimed military genius, had demanded to see firsthand the launch of his grand thrust toward the port of Antwerp. Only his immediate entourage and the SS escort unit had accompanied him.

Initially, the SS staff discounted the early reports coming in of Hitler's possible capture and squelched dispersal of the information. The only officials of the Nazi hierarchy immediately informed of the possible loss were Reichsfuhrer-SS Heinrich Himmler and chief of Reich Security, Reinhard Heydrich. Himmler instantly seized control of the situation and ordered a complete security blackout. With the assistance of his extensive web of SS personnel and resources, he maintained the façade of normalcy in the Reich while extreme measures were taken to establish Hitler's whereabouts. Himmler had an enormous lust for power; he also had extreme concerns over a possible coup by surviving old school Generals should any hint of Hitler's disappearance be leaked to the staff of the OKW (Oberkommando der Wehrmacht-German High Command). Radio traffic from Hitler's headquarters at the Fuhrerbunker in Berlin remained steady. Routine orders and queries flowed uninterrupted to various military commands and departments of the Reich.

Moreover, when Leutnant Niemiller's report of *a high value prisoner* reached Himmler, he had immediately set in motion Operation Ulric. His knowledge of the rescue of Mussolini the previous year led Himmler to place a direct call to General der Fallschirmtruppe Kurt Student. Although SS Hauptsturmfuhrer (Captain) Otto Skorzeny had received the press accolades for Operation Eiche, Himmler knew the real success of the operation was due to the planning and execution of the Fallschirmjäger. General Student quickly activated three squads of his paratroopers and arranged for their air transport to the North Sea port of Wilhelmshaven. A specific plan for the rescue of the Fuhrer did not exist. But contingencies for U-boat launched commando- type raids had been produced by General Student's staff at Fleigerkorps headquarters. These were now hastily adopted for use in Operation Ulric. German intelligence of the base at Scalloway was limited, and maps of the target were hopelessly out of date. Air reconnaissance was considered but rejected because of the possibility of alerting the Allies to German intentions. General Student chose to proceed with what little information he had from the coast watcher, Leutnant Niemiller. There were no other options.

On the Allied side, the German prisoner was handed over to Col. Cochrane at the Reconnaissance Troop. During the first night, he had been secretly whisked away, hooded and manacled, to SHAEF (Supreme Headquarters Allied Expeditionary Force) headquarters in Versailles, France, for further interrogation. Opinion in the hierarchy of the intelligence staff was sharply divided. Some believed this was indeed the Fuhrer, Adolph Hitler; others were highly skeptical. Tremendous swelling and inflammation disfigured the prisoner's facial features, and G-2 was well aware that the Nazis used doubles for Hitler's security. Finally, it was patently obvious that premature announcement of the *capture of Hitler* would prove to be a monumental embarrassment to the Allies should this man turn out to be nothing more than a Nazi plant. Until his identity could be verified with certainty, the Allies chose to transfer their prisoner to a remote British base for safekeeping. The fewer who knew of his existence, the better. Meanwhile, the Allied commanders in the Ardennes had their hands full. They were desperately trying to stem the massive attack launched simultaneously by three German field armies on December 16th.

21 The Raid

The U-1020 had a skeleton crew of 25, decreased from the usual contingent of 49 men. The U-boat was built by Blohm and Voss of Hamburg. The keel was laid April 30, 1943, and the submarine launched March 22, 1944. A type VIIC/ 41 U-boat, her overall length was 67 meters, and she was 6.2 meters at the beam. With a draft of only 6.74 meters, she was able to penetrate shallow coastal waters. And, with a sturdy pressure hull, she could plunge to a crush depth of 250 meters to escape British and American depth charge attacks. Her chances of survival were significantly improved over earlier model submarines. Normally carrying 14 torpedoes, she might slip away like some giant sea-snake from an Allied destroyer or corvette and strike back at her pursuer through one of four bow tubes or the single tube in her stern. Mounted on deck were an 88-mm cannon for attacking surface ships and a 20-mm FLAK gun for use against aircraft. The U-1020 had been retrofitted with a *schnorkel* which allowed her to run her diesel engines while submerged thus increasing her speed and operational range underwater.

This night she was not on the hunt for ships of the Allied navies or merchant marine. Instead, she had a special cargo. Twenty-four seasoned veterans of the 2nd Fallschirmjäger

Division were stuffed in the tight crew quarters and various compartments of the Kriegsmarine sub.

On November 22, 1944, U-1020 had sailed from the Norwegian port of Horten on her first patrol but was urgently recalled to Germany less than a month later. Forty-eight hours afterwards, on the night of December 20th, she slipped quietly into the port of Wilhelmshaven. Kriegsmarine support personnel refueled and provisioned the sub as she lay still at berth. The following evening, the U-boat slipped her moorings and secretly left the German North Sea port. Once at sea, the Fallschirmjäger commander briefed his men and the U-boat crew on their mission. They were about to launch a rescue raid to free the supreme leader of the Third Reich. The risks were extreme, but they understood their mission to be of the highest honor.

It took a total 41 hours of cruising to reach the U-boat's target, submerged by day at 7.6 knots and surfaced by night at 17.2 knots. The tiny coastal village of Scalloway, population 601, lay on the west coast of the Shetland Islands approximately 500 nautical miles from Wilhelmshaven. Scalloway was home to a Royal Navy base and the so-called Shetland Bus. (The Shetland Bus consisted of a ragtag fleet of converted Norwegian fishing boats, manned by Norwegian fishermen and supported by a small cadre of British officers and men. Their mission was to carry men and supplies to occupied Norway and evacuate endangered persons from the grasp of the Germans.) Scalloway now slept through the dark winter night, blissfully unaware of the German paratroopers who had come to rescue the village's newest guest or die in the effort.

The U-boat had rested silently on the bottom of the North Sea all day. Now the second hand of a large clock on the wall of the control room ticked rhythmically around the dial. Time for action had come. The paratroopers assembled in the sub's control room in relative darkness. Subdued red light illuminated the instrument panels and control valves covering the interior. The mood of the German Jäger (paratroopers) seemed calm, focused. But at this moment, Oberfeldwebel Heinrich Pfeister looked down at his hands. They were trembling slightly. He clenched both fists slowly. *Control.* He prayed his mind would be clear and his vision sharp. He and his comrades needed every advantage possible. Tightly clustered in the submarine's control room, the rescue team for Operation Ulric consisted of three squads of veteran Jäger. Most of these men had participated in Operation Eiche (Oak), the rescue of Mussolini in the summer of 1943. In character with the often mythical thinking of the Nazis, the squads were given the designations *Griffin, Dragon,* and *Werewolf.*

After checking the relatively calm sea with his periscope, the U-boat captain, Oberleutnant Otto Eberlein, gave the order for surfacing. Finally, just before midnight local time, the dark conning tower of the submarine broke from beneath the lightly rolling waves as the first quarter moon slipped silently below the western horizon. The night air was crisp and clear. With only starlight illuminating the wet deck of the U-boat, crewmen brought up three collapsed rubber rafts and inflated them with a high pressure air hose. The men and equipment of the Fallschirmjäger team, three squads of eight men each, were loaded into the rafts. With two sailors in each raft, they pushed away from the black metal flank of the sub. The sailors quietly paddled the three boats the quarter of a mile to the rocky beach. They would use their outboard motors during their escape from the island. U-1020 submerged and lay quietly on the flat sea bottom.

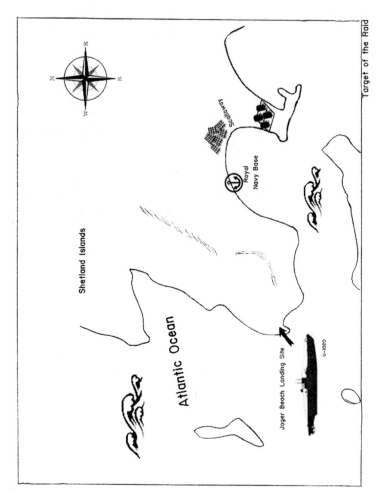

In twenty minutes, the Jäger and sailors were splashing through the low surf, pulling the rafts onto the narrow beach. The raid commander, Major Dietrich Meier, scrutinized his men and their load of submachine guns, grenades, and satchel charges. He spread out his three squads and signaled for the team to move inland. The Fallschirmjäger executed their well-practiced maneuvers with silence and meticulous timing. Meier and his squad leaders directed the team flawlessly with crisp hand signals. The time was now 0100. The six U-boat crewmen remained with the rafts and wordlessly saluted their comrades as they began to ascend a coastal hill and progress toward their target.

The Jäger moved boldly through the darkness. The gently rolling, barren ground offered no obstacle to their progress, and the softness of the turf made for a stealthy approach. The elevation rose slowly before them until they reached a flat knoll overlooking the naval base, harbor, and tiny village. The base was laid out in the shape of a 'C', opening toward the south. The harbor with its warehouses, docks, and various kinds of ship-tending tackle lay on the eastern, inner arm of the 'C'.

The first obstacle in their raid was a double run of four-strand barbed wire fence. There were no searchlights or guard towers on this remote military installation. A few muted security lights burned at various points around the base. Pairs of sentries walked leisurely back and forth along the docks and around the perimeter of the compound. Evidently an audacious commando raid was not considered a significant threat.

Team Ulric instantly went to ground just outside the fence. One of the sentry teams was moving inside the fence toward their location, apparently oblivious to the swift death which lay within a stone's throw. Their conversation was jaunty and occasionally punctuated with laughter. It was to be the last conversation they ever had. Strangely aware of his heart throbbing vigorously within his chest, Sergeant Pfeister willed himself to calmness, lying prone next to his comrades in Squad Griffin.

As the sentries passed, the beam of their single flashlight haphazardly bobbed back and forth. The camouflaged Germans remained totally motionless, barely breathing.

When the sentries had passed six to eight feet beyond the team leader, he and his sub lieutenant rose up and simultaneously squeezed off two rounds each from their silenced Luger P08 pistols. Both guards collapsed with muffled grunts. Squad Werewolf immediately cut a hole through the fence, and all three squads moved through in leap frog fashion, sprinting, pausing and covering each other. Two Jäger crept over and checked the two sentries. One picked up the still shining flashlight, stood and began to walk with the same careless stride and rhythmic motion of the flashlight.

Squad Dragon located what was presumed to be the detention area. A solid looking, single story block building sat in the center of a square yard surrounded by another set of double-stranded barbed wire. A small guard shack stood immediately adjacent to the entrance of the building. Two guards stood leaning against the door of the shack smoking and talking. Major Meier looked at his watch, *0145*, and thought, *Precisely on time, how German!*

The squads crawled to their prearranged positions and waited. Squad Dragon covered the left, Squad Werewolf the right. Squad Griffin would breach the building and rescue the captive.

A Royal Navy jeep was parked outside the detention area fence. The team leader signaled, and a Jäger of Squad Griffin tossed a rock, cracking the windshield of the jeep. One of the guards at the shack cocked his head and listened. He looked at his companion and then pulled out his pistol. He slowly walked toward the jeep and cautiously looked it over. He walked around the opposite side and noticed the chipped glass of the windshield. He leaned over to inspect it more closely. Suddenly, a Jäger who had noiselessly rolled out from under the jeep, thrust his combat knife into the man's left neck and pulled him down. The guard at the shack heard the scuffle and lifted a whistle to his mouth. It was too late; two 9-mm Parabellum bullets slammed into his chest from the leader's silenced Luger. The guard fell forward into the yard, dead.

The eight members of Squad Griffin sprinted forward, surrounded the dimly lit detention building, and waited. To the 24 German soldiers, the minutes seemed to pass more slowly than dark honey on a cold Bavarian morning. But then, a tremendous detonation sounded on the eastern side of the harbor. A series of explosions continued as U-1025, a sister U-boat to U-1020, shelled the harbor with her 88-mm deck gun from her position 3 1/2 miles to the east. She had surfaced a scant fifteen minutes earlier. The U-boat gunners had received critical targeting information by radio from coast watcher Leutnant Niemiller and were deliberately shooting at the eastern arm of the Royal Navy base.

The British naval installation came alive. Sailors and Royal marines poured out of their barracks half-dressed and sprinted toward the ships and the docks. Smoke and flames poured into the night sky as a shell hit one of the four fuel storage tanks on the eastern edge of the harbor. Sporadically, the boats and ships docked at various berths began to fire up their engines and throw off their lines. They were determined to move out of their sitting duck predicament and strike a blow at their anonymous attacker.

As pandemonium broke out as planned, the Griffin Squad leader banged on the heavy wooden door of the block detention building. He shouted, "Eh! Eh!"

One of the American MPs inside shouted back, "What's going on out there?"

The German squad leader simply repeated his exclamation, "Eh! Eh!"

Curiosity trumping caution, the MP opened the door slightly and yelled again, "What the --?"

Before he could finish his inquiry, two stun grenades were hurled through the door and the squad leader kicked the door fully open. The eight members of Squad Griffin rushed in and finished off four grenade-shocked MPs.

Two Jäger searched the guards and located a ring of keys. The rest of the squad systematically searched the interior of the building and discovered a solitary cell behind a heavy metal door. The keys were passed forward, and the team leader quickly opened the door.

A single light bulb hung from the ceiling. Seated on a simple bunk which rested against an unpainted block wall was the most feared man in the Third Reich, Fuhrer Adolph Hitler.

The man rose and Major Meier saluted him with the obligatory "Heil Hitler." The Fuhrer looked carefully at the major, a hint of a smile playing on his face.

"I knew you would come."

"Mein Fuhrer. Are you well? Are you able to travel?" the major inquired, looking at his deeply bruised and swollen face.

"Yes, I am very well," he replied in clipped German.

"Good, we must move very quickly. Your hosts will be reluctant to let you leave," he said as he gestured for Hitler to exit the room.

Any remaining formalities disregarded, Squad Griffin hustled their supreme commander out of the building and through the yard gate. Explosions rocked the harbor as 88-mm shells continued to slam into the Royal Navy base, and Squads Werewolf and Dragon detonated charges placed on adjacent buildings and vehicles. Well aimed smoke and fragmentation grenades were also hurled in tactically chosen directions. The scene of confusion and destruction on the base was well choreographed. The darkness, noise, and surprise of the raid were having their intended effect.

As the three squads withdrew with their prize, they noticed they had finally drawn some unwanted attention. An alert Royal Marine captain had been rudely awakened by the deafening chaos and knew exactly what was happening. Now he was shouting at scattered pockets of men, desperately trying to draw their awareness to the real target of the enemy. Several marines ran to the downed guards and recognized the true situation. They spotted the German Jäger running across the hill and through the outer perimeter. The marines began yelling and firing their rifles and machine guns at the rapidly retreating group. The accuracy was poor because of the thick darkness and because the Germans refused to return the fire, instead focusing on their speedy escape. The marine captain grabbed the members of a mortar team and yelled for starshell fire to illuminate the targets for his soldiers. Within a couple minutes, the team had retrieved and set up their mortar. They fired several shells illuminating the night sky and the ground beneath. But too late. The German raiders had made it across the highest hill overlooking the base and were well on their way to a rendezvous with the rafts waiting on the beach. For a measure of insurance, as their brother squads hurriedly made their way across the island and down to the rocky shore, members of Squad Werewolf placed three separate trip lines with small antipersonnel mines across the path of their retreat. Not very deadly, but enough to give pause to their pursuers.

As the last squad scrambled down the hill and onto the shore, they heard one of the trip lines go off. Within a minute however, two jeeps pulled up at the crest of the hill and the small arms fire became intense. The three rafts were quickly loaded, and the boat motors began to place precious distance between the boats and the shore. However, the water around the rafts boiled with bullet impacts, and two Jäger in the trailing raft were hit, one in the shoulder and one in the left hand. The deck gun from the U-boat now opened up and the jeeps made a short retreat down the reverse slope. The rafts roared up to the side of the U-boat and the sailors assisted the egress of their cargo of commandos and their special guest.

The deck crew now sank the empty rafts with bursts from the U-boat's antiaircraft gun. Rifle and machine gun fire continued to harass the sub from the shore, and several pings resounded as bullets bounced off the thick metal hull. Sailors and raiders were now safe in the U-boat, and Commander Eberlein slid down the ladder. Leutnant Johann Kruger, deputy commander and last man on the conning tower, came down slowly. Securing the hatch with his left hand, he supported himself on the ladder with his feet, while resting his back against the interior of the narrow conning tower. He gave a muffled "ready to dive, Kapitan" as he slipped to the bottom of the ladder and slumped to his knees. His commander looked at him with apprehension. "Kruger?"

"It is alright, Kapitan. I've done my duty."

Muffled pings continued as bullets struck the U-boat and Eberlein barked the order to dive. The captain clasped his deputy commander by the shoulders and gently lowered him to the floor of the operations deck. A fresh blood patch covered Lt. Kruger's right upper chest and shoulder. He had been hit by a chance shot from the shore. Despite the immediate attention of the sub's medical team, within three minutes Leutnant Johann Kruger of the Kriegsmarine would expire. Crew members somberly moved their deputy commander's body to the officer's ward room. The U-boat remained submerged and slipped out into the North Sea. They made the Fuhrer as comfortable as possible in the cramped quarters. He took the captain's cabin and rested for some time. After a dinner alone, he made his way through the ship personally thanking each member of the crew and the raiding party. His fabled charisma remained undimmed.

The next morning, the U-1020 surfaced and rendezvoused with a milch cow (a large supply submarine), the U-491. The Jäger were transferred to this larger sub, as fuel and food were transferred to the U-1020. As the U-491 sailed toward her home port of Bremen, the U-1020 submerged and slipped away. Official Kriegsmarine records would later report the U-1020 as *missing in action.*

Sergeant Pfeister and his team disembarked at Bremen and were met at the dock by a contingent of SS. Escorted to a secluded compound south of the city...

we were "debriefed" from our mission for three days. We were subjected to questioning and threats both individually and as a group. A certain SS colonel impressed upon us the dire consequences that would befall us and our families if we ever revealed to anyone even a whisper of Operation Ulric. I am convinced that, were it not for the intervention of the influential General Student, we would all have been secretly executed by the SS.

The authorities who know the truth have maintained the illusion of Hitler's continued presence at the head of the Reich. Doubles stand in for him now at very rare public appearances. As the Allies close in, I wonder if the fake Fuhrers have contemplated the inevitable. They most certainly will be asked to die to guard the lie. The real Adolph Hitler will live on somewhere in the New World as his Reich perishes in the Old.

22 The Translation

The NOAA weather radio on Blake Carter's desk came to life:

"**The National Weather Service in Atlanta has issued a severe thunderstorm warning for the following counties in north central Georgia: Bartow, Cherokee, Clayton, Cobb, Dekalb, Douglas, Forsyth, Fulton, Gwinnett, and Paulding. At 4:17 pm Eastern Daylight Time, National Weather Service Doppler Radar indicated a severe thunderstorm capable of producing quarter size hail and damaging winds in excess of 60 miles per hour. This storm was located one mile west of Carrollton moving northeast at 25 miles per hour. A severe thunderstorm watch remains in effect for north central Georgia until 9:30 pm Eastern Daylight Time. A flash flood warning is also in effect with heavy precipitation expected with up to 4 inches of rain through the afternoon and evening hours.**"

Carter clicked off the weather radio. He walked over to the large window that constituted the interface between his office in the Sun Trust Building and the turbulent Atlanta weather outside. He looked down at his wristwatch. 4:30. But the Georgia sky was black. Streetlights along Peachtree Street had already come on as the storm rolled in from western Georgia and engulfed the city in darkness. Carter's eyes focused on the cloud bank hanging low to the west. It was black and muscular. Periodically it slung thick cloud streamers underneath like tentacles. Carter knew from experience these formations could morph into tornado funnel clouds in a matter of seconds. Lightning ripped from cloud to ground. For several minutes he stood and marveled at the singular power of the storm. A rap on his office door startled him. "Come in," he answered.

T.J. Davidson stepped into the office. Carter remained at the window transfixed on the weather. Joining his translator at the window, Davidson said, "Bad storm coming."

"Yeah, bad."

"So how's the journal coming?"

"The translation of the journal of Heinrich Pfeister is finished." The words tumbled from his mouth with little emotion.

"You don't sound too enthused."

"I'm not. I think I've just wasted a week and a half of work."

"Why? You were pretty excited the end of last week. All that stuff about Mussolini."

"Yeah, well, I think the rest must be fiction just to make this German paratrooper look important in the eyes of his family."

Davidson turned toward Carter. "Okay, so tell me what you found."

Carter turned his back to the storm and walked over to his desk. His laptop rested on one corner of the otherwise empty desktop. He casually parked himself on the glossy wooden surface of the desk and faced Davidson. "Everybody knows Adolph Hitler committed suicide in the Fuhrerbunker under the Reich Chancellery Building in Berlin on the 30th of April 1945. Two days earlier he had married his mistress, Eva Braun. She died beside her husband – apparently suicide by cyanide poisoning."

"Short honeymoon," Davidson said with a deadpan expression.

"Yeah, very short. Two days later, the Red Army overran the last Nazi enclaves in the city. A special Soviet counterintelligence unit discovered the charred remains of the bodies of Hitler and Braun in the garden of the Reich Chancellery where they had been burned by Hitler's surviving staff."

"Sure. Those are fairly well-known facts. What's your point? Does Pfeister's journal have something to say about Hitler's final days?" Davidson's curiosity was now palpable.

"Well, not exactly. In his journal, he claims ... and I know this is ridiculous ... that the Fuhrer was somewhere near the German front lines at the onset of the Ardennes offensive in December 1944."

"Battle of the Bulge?"

"Exactly."

"Sounds plausible to me; what's so strange about that? I mean apparently the guy was an egomaniac," Davidson interrupted.

"Let me finish. He then claims that in the confusion of the first 48 hours of the German attack, Hitler was trying to observe the action first hand from the headquarters bunker of the 12th SS Panzer Division near the German-Belgian border. While he was there, supposedly an American scout unit was able to penetrate the German lines, sneak behind the command bunker, and, with the help of a time-on-target divisional artillery barrage, capture the bunker. Hitler was one of the few survivors of the American attack. He was taken prisoner and forced to accompany the GIs back through the American lines."

Davidson's mouth dropped open. "Incredible."

"There's more. Pfeister relates that Hitler was quickly and secretly moved to the British-held Shetland Islands northeast of Scotland and confined on a remote Royal Navy base for interrogation. Apparently, according to this tale, the intelligence experts in the Allied high command were concerned that this guy might have been a double, planted to create confusion. And, if they made public the 'capture of Hitler', and were then proven wrong, the embarrassment would have been extremely severe."

Davidson sat down in a chair beside Carter's desk. He turned and looked out the window. "Go on."

"The journal claims that Pfeister's paratrooper unit was activated on December 19, 1944, and flown to the port city of Wilhelmshaven. There they boarded a submarine and sailed to the Shetland Islands."

"How did they supposedly know where Hitler was being held?"

"Good question," Carter stood up again and took a stick of gum from his desk drawer. "Want a piece?"

"No, thanks."

"Pfeister mentions a coast watcher's report of a high value prisoner arriving in Scalloway in the Shetlands shortly after the alleged disappearance of Hitler. He relates that this mission, 'Operation Ulric,' was launched on a hunch that the prisoner would turn out to be the Fuhrer."

"On second thought, I will take a piece of that gum," Davidson said.

Handing his employer the foiled stick, Carter continued his narrative. "The night after they arrived off the coast adjacent to this British Navy base, the paratroopers were put ashore via motorized rafts. They proceeded to raid the small outpost, find and release Hitler, and spirit him off to the U-boat."

Davidson leaned forward and rested his chin on his palm. Slowly shaking his head, he remarked, "I just have a hard time buying it. Too many loose ends."

"Yeah, me too."

"But go ahead and finish. Is there more in the journal?"

"Yeah. Apparently, the U-boat rendezvoused with a larger supply sub, a so-called milch cow, to which the paratroopers were transferred. Hitler stayed with the original submarine, U-1020, and sailed away to parts unknown. Pfeister and company were met at the port of Bremen by the SS and threatened with death for them and their families should they ever reveal the story of 'Operation Ulric'."

"Garbage! I don't believe it."

"Right," Carter agreed. "Like I said, I just wasted a week and a half."

Davidson stood and slowly moved to the window. Carter joined him in silence. For several minutes they gazed at the storm without saying a word. The rain was pelting the window now, and rumbles of thunder reverberated through the small room.

"Undoubtedly a fictitious account. But there's one problem," Davidson mused.

"I know. You've gotta wonder ... why would anyone be willing to kidnap or kill for an old journal that turns out to be largely a piece of fiction?"

23 The Proposal

The crisp scratching of the red Montegrappa pen pierced the quiet of the chambers of Federal District Judge Vanessa Kavulla. She finished her abbreviated signature with an understated flourish and handed the single sheet of paper to Special Agent Braxton Roby. She had just executed a court order authorizing Federal Agents to tap into the computers and data of Balder Chemical Corporation, Houston, Texas.

Her no-nonsense *cut the garbage* manner had earned her the admiration of every prosecutor and the respect of most, not all, attorneys for the defense in the greater Atlanta area. Those who entered Judge Kavulla's court for the first time quickly learned she had no interest in *fairness*, and she would brook no malarkey. Her passion was *justice*, and she suffered no fools.

The judge handed Agent Roby the paper and looked him squarely in the face. "Now, go get your proof!"

Roby took the paper soberly and answered simply, "Yes, Ma'am."

The FBI agent and his partner excused themselves and left the judge's chambers. The sound of their footsteps echoed rhythmically down the marble floored corridor of the Richard

B. Russell Federal Building. Leaving the building, Roby said, "I feel like going for a Chicago dog. You in?"

Roby, who was typically stoic, felt like celebrating. He had been following elusive leads on Balder Chemical and other subsidiaries of Norse Industries sporadically for more than three years. The alleged illegal activities of these 'respectable companies' included money laundering, racketeering, insider trading, postal fraud, and a litany of other mostly white collar crimes. Most recently, the evidence provided by the Harrisons had added kidnapping and attempted murder to the list.

The two agents walked down the street and stopped at Frank's Franks sidewalk cart. "I'll take the loaded Chicago dog," Roby ordered. "And give me a large Dr. Pepper with that."

"You got it," the middle aged, slightly graying vendor replied. "How 'bout you, son?" he asked Roby's partner. The vendor worked while he talked, scooping the onions, pickle relish, peppers, and other condiments onto the steaming hot dog he had skillfully placed on the large poppy seed bun.

Agent Papadakis replied, "Ditto for me, Sir." Awed by the vendor's artistry, he asked, "You Frank?"

The vendor let out a loud chuckle. "No, son. Frank retired two years ago. He sold the best frankfurters in the city for 20 years, and now he's on easy street in Florida."

Papadakis was intrigued. "He retired on the profits from a street vendor's cart selling hot dogs?"

The vendor continued, enjoying sharing the narrative of his boss's success. "Look, his overhead was wholesale food, this frankfurter cart, and a vendor's license. No employees (except me now), no mortgage, no utilities, no advertising, essentially no insurance. He made great tasting frankfurters with lots of options and they were always hot! He treated folks like they were family. People loved it and he got tips, too. And now, he's enjoying the fruits of his labor and ingenuity."

Roby chimed in, "Well, I'll say one thing. This is about the best hot dog..er..frankfurter I ever tasted."

The two agents paid Frank's protégé, thanked him, and strolled away chomping contentedly on their fully loaded Chicago dogs.

Two days later, Agent Roby placed a call to the office of the Tower Intelligence and Security Agency. "Tower ISA, this is Ashley. How may I direct your call?"

Roby set up a meeting with T.J. Davidson the following day and met him at the Tower office in the Sun Trust Building.

"Agent Roby? I'm T.J. Davidson. Please come in."

"Thanks. I appreciate your agreeing to meet with me." Roby showed Davidson his badge, not that Davidson expressed any doubt about his identity.

"Sure. How can I help the FBI?"

"I believe we have a mutual interest in Balder Chemical Corporation, Houston, Texas."

Davidson offered Roby a seat in the conference room. "Go on."

"We've interviewed Jim Harrison and his father and understand your people have been helping them. We've been investigating Balder for some time and now have a court order for searching their computers. We're interested in having your agency work under contract to the Bureau with the authority of this court order. I'm here to see if that kind of arrangement would interest you."

Davidson *was* interested but cautious. "Why come to us? Why not just continue your investigation? What do we have that you need?"

"We understand your agency is respected for expertise in information technology; you have tenacity for seeing investigations through to the end, and a reputation for integrity. That's a good fit for our mission. And, we're currently underfunded for the volume of work we're assigned. We simply don't have the manpower to press this as aggressively as we'd like. What do you think?"

"I think you've just made my day."

Over the next hour, the men hammered out the details of the working arrangement. Roby ended the discussion with a final item. "I do have a technology specialist that will be on call with your people and periodically set up meetings with them to assess the information you ferret out."

"Fine. What's his name?"

"*Her* name is Regina Rhodes. She'll be by tomorrow to meet your people, if that's ok."

Davidson nodded. "Great. Ashley'll set up something convenient for both parties." He was sure The Snake would be fired up by the FBI proposal to let him loose in Balder's back yard.

24 The Infiltrator

The coffee came out of the Keurig coffee maker rich and very hot. The steam from the dark brown surface curled up and seemed to hang in the air. Chandra Rahman lifted the black mug and slowly savored the full aroma of the fresh brew. *Delicious. The simple pleasures.* He took his time drinking his first cup of the day as he sat and scanned this morning's edition of the Washington Post. He paused as he noticed an article on page two. Pundits speculated on the contents of the President's State of the Union address taking place tonight in the Capitol in the chamber of the U.S. House of Representatives. As usual, the Vice President, the members of the President's cabinet, save one (the "designated survivor"), the combined House of Representatives and Senate, the members of the U.S. Supreme Court and members of the Joint Chiefs of Staff were slated to assemble to hear the President's address. Tonight would be the one time that the exact location of the President could be predicted.

Another article on the facing page carried the headline, "Capitol Police on High Alert for SOTU." The article detailed the standard heightened security during the hours leading up to the President's State of the Union address when almost all members of the three branches of the Federal government were in one place at the same time. The security precautions included helicopters, dogs, and large numbers of uniformed Capitol Police. Plain clothes USCP would also be a presence over the entire Capitol complex. The already wide security cordon had been extended several hundred yards away from the Capitol Building.

Rahman was born in Rajshahi, Bangladesh, in the hot summer of 1977. Bangladesh, formerly known as East Pakistan, had broken away from West Pakistan in March of 1971. After a nine-month war and with the assistance of the Indian Army, Bangladesh gained its full independence in December 1971.

Brought into the turbulence of the young nation, Chandra had one stable influence in his life — his mother, Sagarika. His father, Abhik, was 1400 miles away attending medical school at Bangalore Medical College in Bangalore, India. Totally dedicated to succeeding in his studies, he rarely came home to visit his wife and young son. As the years passed and Chandra became aware that his family was different from that of most of his friends, he felt a smothering loneliness and longing for a father. Sagarika did her best to raise her only son, but she resented the life she was living. To make ends meet, during the day she taught elementary students at a local girls' school. At night, she poured her love into the growing Chandra. But the young Bengali boy would spend most of his waking hours at one of the Islamic madrasas in Rajshahi — it was the only thing Sagarika knew to do for childcare.

Doctor Abhik Rahman finally came home to Rajshahi in the summer of 1983. He worked day and night for two years manning a small clinic in the suburbs, still consumed with his work. He was seldom at home except to sleep. Sagarika and six year old Chandra were living with a stranger. Finally, in 1985, through family connections, Dr. Rahman secured a position as a fellow in cardiology at St. George's Hospital Medical School in London. In May, the unhappy little family immigrated to the United Kingdom hoping for a new start.

Initially, father and son seemed to be bonding. Dr. Rahman was at home more. He attended some of Chandra's school events and soccer matches. But something in Chandra's heart had been lost. He looked to his mother for approval, and increasingly, to his religious leaders at the mosque.

The Rahmans moved to the United States in 1991 settling in Falls Church, Virginia, a suburb of Washington D.C. Dr. Rahman, now an up and coming cardiologist, joined the medical staff of Georgetown University Medical Center. The quiet and affable Dr. Rahman developed a thriving practice and an intensely loyal referral network. He was always available for consults from colleagues and questions from patients. But what was good for his reputation as a physician was a disaster for his role as husband and father.

Chandra entered public school in Falls Church. He was a solid B student with few friends. His teachers appreciated his presence in class as he was always studious and never caused any disciplinary problems. Chandra seemed stable and content. But his calm face and winsome smile overlay a boiling heart of anger. Not only could he not gain his father's approval, he couldn't even gain his attention.

The teenage Rahman did gain someone's attention. Having become an ardent Muslim, faithful to the local mosque, Chandra was quiet, thoughtful, and desperately seeking the esteem of his elders. Through his years in high school, Chandra was carefully groomed into a good soldier for Allah. He regularly received praise from his mentors at the mosque for his devotion to the Koran. He was also encouraged to develop his skills and knowledge of all things mechanical. In the Islamic center across the street from the mosque, Chandra trained his body daily at the weight room in the basement. His handlers were cultivating a young man who was smart, tough, and committed through and through to the way of Islam. The heart that needed a father settled instead for a master.

Chandra graduated from high school in 1995. In defiance of his cardiologist father's desire for the young Rahman to go on to college, Chandra enlisted in the US Army the following spring. The plans of his handlers were moving along nicely. He was instructed to choose the MOS (Military Occupation Specialty)-91B, Wheeled Vehicle Mechanic. The young soldier completed basic training at Fort Jackson, South Carolina and attended 12 weeks of AIT (Advanced Individual Training) at Aberdeen Proving Grounds, Maryland.

For the next five years he served his adopted country at four different posts. His final assignment was repairing and driving Humvees for the 10th Mountain Division stationed at Ft. Drum, New York. Sergeant Chandra Rahman completed his duty with the Army in August of 2001 receiving an honorable discharge. His career was not stellar, but he had, without knowing it, achieved the desire of his Muslim handlers with whom he remained in discreet communication through contacts in mosques and Islamic Centers near his duty stations in Washington State, Germany, Colorado, and Georgia. He had served quietly and honorably in the armed forces of the United States. He had earned a record of trust, a very valuable commodity indeed.

Sergeant Rahman returned to Virginia where his mother still lived. His father had died in 2000, ironically, of a heart attack. The funeral of Dr. Rahman was attended by dozens of grateful patients and several doctors. Conspicuous by his absence, Sergeant Rahman did not bother to request bereavement leave.

The twenty-five year old veteran reestablished his strong friendship with his mentors at the northern Virginia mosque and, at their urging, was soon applying for a position with the US Capitol grounds maintenance unit. In the era of political correctness, a native Bengali, an Army veteran, honorably discharged, with work experience and desirable maintenance skills, Chandra Rahman had a job offer three days after he applied.

25 The Breach

T.J. Davidson's smart phone chirped. He quickly slid his finger over the security pattern on the screen, and the home page appeared. He had a text from The Snake.

Have some new info when u r ready

Davidson's fingers slid nimbly over the letters of his virtual keyboard and responded.

Be right over

Tapping the 'send' icon, he replaced the phone in his belt holster on his left hip. He closed his laptop computer on which he had been composing a memo to a client in St. Augustine, Florida, and slid back his black leather captain's chair. His desk top pad was a checkerboard of sticky notes from Ashley demanding attention. Some had smiley faces, some exclamation points, and some stars. But they would have to wait. The Snake had a reputation for understatement. If he had some "new info," Davidson was sure it was of great interest. He could literally feel his heart rate rising in his chest as he rose from his chair and headed for the door of his office.

The Snake's office was in a suite shared with Blake Carter on the same floor as the main Tower offices, but in the opposite corner of the building. Davidson knocked on the door and let himself in.

"What've you got?" he asked without the usual pleasantries.

"Well good morning to you too, Boss," Ewell remarked.

"Good morning," Davidson responded, only barely chastised for his abrupt entry. "Sorry for the attitude. Guess I've just been on edge about the Harrison case. I can't help but think that we're not done with the guys from Norse."

Ewell said, "You're probably right. But I've got some news for you."

"Like what?"

"Well, actually, I have two things. First off, yesterday morning, one of my techs was using a new antivirus program and stumbled on to some code that had an interesting coincidence."

"What was that?" Davidson asked.

"He found the phrase 'Operation Ulric' which Carter noted was in the paratrooper journal. Using this as a starting point, he uncovered a Trojan imbedded in his computer that sits quietly in the background and does nothing."

"A Trojan that does nothing. Really?"

"Well, *almost* nothing." Ewell was enjoying the give and take. Davidson, however, was just below a slow boil.

"Come on, Jake. Stop playing with me. Get to the point."

"Sure. Since yesterday morning, we have found this Trojan, on every single computer- desktop and laptop- in the office!"

"You're kidding." Davidson was incredulous.

"No, I'm dead serious."

"So, why is it there?"

Ewell continued. "It's curious. It's a surveillance program. It's looking for one particular phrase or set of words. Our preliminary conclusion is it's looking for the phrase 'Operation Ulric'. Once found, it sends an alert to someone, along with any available user identity or location information."

"How long's it been on our computers?"

"No idea. And it's a fluke we found it at all. It hasn't been discovered before because it does nothing, except watch. None of the antivirus/ antispyware programs clean it because no one has had any problems with it. It's just there. And it has quietly spread from computer to computer across the net. Who knows what percentage of computers have it?"

Davidson slowly paced back and forth in the Snake's eccentrically decorated office. On one wall was an original movie poster for *The Magnificent Seven* with Yul Brynner. On the facing wall was a poster for the annual Savannah Music Festival. On a corner table rested a terrarium with a scarlet kingsnake as its only tenant. Its red, black, and yellow color bands were striking. In another corner of the room rested a sophisticated metal detector. Two framed displays adorned the wall immediately behind Ewell's desk. One was a first day cancelled stamp and envelope from the Apollo 8 mission. The other was a stamp from the Free City of Danzig issued in 1939 featuring geneticist Gregor Mendel. In several piles distributed haphazardly around the floor of the office were computer tech magazines and throw away journals.

"If there's a theme to your office, I sure don't get it."

Ewell smiled, "Yeah, there's a theme. I'll explain it over coffee someday."

"Ok. Back to your computer Trojan. What about Macs?"

"Yeah, Cintron has a Mac, and he's infected too. Best I can tell, this Trojan has been around for months. And that's how the Norse/Balder guys were able to find Jim Harrison and Greta in Barcelona."

"Amazing."

"Secondly, the gal from the FBI and I breached the Balder Chemical firewall last night. At first, we worked on getting in to the Norse computers in Amsterdam. But their system is almost impregnable. We finally decided to attack Balder and see where that took us. The Balder setup is tough, but not quite as advanced. I've been downloading data all night long. Turns out they change their password daily. We had a limited window to get the stuff before we had to start over at square one again."

"OK. I appreciate you putting in an all-nighter. Especially arduous with the beautiful Ms. Rhodes. So what did you find?"

"What we've got, we gleaned from e-mail accounts, financial records, travel documents, and purchase orders. What look like corporations every savvy investor would want in his diversified portfolio are actually companies involved in some very questionable activities and alliances. They have investments in very dark places."

"Such as?" T.J. asked.

"If my first impressions are correct from the tangled connections we've unwound so far, these corporations are in bed with some people who definitely don't play nice. They've invested funds in companies, charities, and individuals with probable ties to this list of baddies..." The Snake pointed to his computer screen and Davidson began to read:

Al-Qaeda

North Korea

Iran

The Taliban

Cuba

Venezuela

Hezbollah

Hamas

Abu Sayyaf- Philippines

Al Shabaab- Somalia

Chechen Rebels

Syria

Revolutionary Armed Forces of Colombia-(FARC)

Davidson let out a low whistle. He then murmured under his breath, "What a catalog of cutthroats and murderers! How in the world are these totalitarian regimes and terrorist groups connected to a chemical corporation like Balder?"

"Good question. I get the impression, although she hasn't said so in as many words, that Miss Rhodes knows a lot about this corporation. She was pretty intense about getting into Balder's files. Hopefully we get out without leaving any traceable fingerprints so to speak. We really don't want 'em alerted to the fact that we've been playing in their sandbox."

"And what *does* Ms. Rhodes from the FBI think about the stuff you've dug up?"

"You know, that's curious. She acted as if this was no surprise. I guess they've had suspicions about these guys for a long time. She said they've found hints of ties between shadowy neo-Nazi groups in South America and all kinds of terrorist organizations. Apparently, and this was news to me, the Nazis had links to and influence with various Muslim leaders and their followers even during World War II."

Davidson pondered for a moment. "So the FBI gives some credence to rumors of neo-Nazis in Latin America?"

"Yeah. I guess some of those people are still sore about the Versailles Treaty that ended World War I and bitter over the split up of the German nation at the end of World War II. And some of them must still have some delusional thinking about resurrecting an Aryan Reich. Anyway, she rushed back over to her office for something. She's instructed me to call as soon as the downloads are complete. It's gonna take a while to comb through all the data."

Davidson scratched at a small, dark, irregular raised lesion on the right side of his head just in front of his retreating hair line. "I just hope we got enough incriminating evidence for the Feds to shut these guys down for good."

"Yeah. And, T.J."

"Yes?"

"You really need to get that skin thing checked out. It looks funny to me."

"Right, soon as I get time. It's probably just a mole," Davidson answered nonchalantly.

26 The Journey

Four months later.

Fall had come and gone from Macon, Georgia. Jim had enrolled at Mercer University and continued working on his degree in journalism. Greta found an apartment three miles down the road from the Harrison home and shared it with the kid sister of one of Michelle's old college roommates.

Greta had taken a job at the county library and was finding solace in the quiet walls of books and periodicals and reference tomes. The library was her refuge. She had much free time, and, as long as her assigned work was caught up, she was at liberty to read, think, or just sit and daydream. Very slowly, she was learning to trust people. Certainly, Jim and his family had earned her confidence. Others were always suspect. Greta kept them at arm's length, at least emotionally. Unfortunately, she was still haunted by nightmares. Often, she would wake up drenched in cold sweat, sobbing. Jim was seeing Greta daily and trying hard to encourage and console her without being pushy. Some days she seemed fine. Other days she seemed cold and distant, even bitter. He had offered a meeting with the pastor at Faith Bible Church where his family attended. Greta was polite but firm in her refusal to meet with a minister.

Over the Christmas and New Year's holidays, the Harrisons hosted Greta several times. She seemed to enjoy the time with the family. But, occasionally, in the midst of the laughter, food, board games, and family conversation, Jim would catch a glimpse of sadness in Greta's eyes. He surmised she had a toxic mix of home sickness, worry over her family, and anger over her earlier ordeal in Amsterdam. He struggled with his own sense of impotence in helping her. He often asked God for wisdom and patience.

Then, on the first Tuesday of the New Year, Greta received a certified letter from the US Customs and Immigration Service (USCIS). A meeting with officials in Washington D.C. was requested the last Wednesday of January to "address immigration issues." She shared the letter with Jim the following day and asked his advice. "Should I go? What do you think they want with me?"

Jim wore his most reassuring smile. "I'm certain they're gonna try to help you with getting the proper paperwork completed to get you and your mom and sister permanent citizenship here. This is what we've been hoping for all winter."

"I know but … "

"Look, the Tower people have been working hard on some way to get your family here from Europe. I mean, I know they're safe where they are, but you all really need to be back together, permanently. So in a few weeks we'll journey up to our nation's capital, take care of business, and see the sights."

"You'd go *with* me?" she asked haltingly. "I couldn't ask you to do that. You're so busy."

"You *didn't* ask, and I'm not so busy I couldn't take a few days to accompany a beautiful girl to the nation's capital. Have you ever been to D.C.?"

"No," she answered quietly. Greta was sitting at the dining room table in her small apartment. Jim stood with his back resting against the kitchen counter, a glass of water in his hand, watching her carefully. With her hands clasped tightly together in front of her, she stared at her fingers as if they belonged on someone else's hand. "I long to see my family, but… I'm not sure I *deserve* to be really happy again," she said in a hushed voice.

*****

Two weeks later, in a plush office 800 miles to the west, Mr. David Braun sat at a mahogany desk with his hands clasped together in front of him. His reverie was interrupted by a light tapping on his office door. "Mr. Braun?"

"Yes, Derrick. Come in."

The door opened. A middle-aged man in a black suit and crimson tie entered. "Excuse me, sir. The men are ready for the final briefing."

Braun looked up. "Good." Braun, who was wearing a white, open-collared shirt and stylish blue slacks, stood and led his executive assistant out of the office and down the hall to a large conference room. As he entered, the team of six men assembled there stood and snapped to attention. "Thank you, gentlemen. Please take your seats." The men resumed seated positions around the long conference table. All faces focused intently on Braun and waited. "I am here to encourage you as you begin the culmination of your mission. All the time, money, and work you-we-have invested for years is now riding on your shoulders. You have before you the chance of a generation. By your skill, intelligence, strength, and training you will succeed. Failure is not an option. You must triumph or perish in the effort." Each man nodded in assent.

"I won't bother to go over the details. You each know your assigned targets and timetables. You must function not as a set of individuals; instead, you must act as a single, cohesive organism. Rely on your training and your instincts. What you are about to accomplish will clear the stage for the emergence of something truly grand and good. This world is in great need of a deep cleansing breath. You, my friends, will provide mankind with a stiff draft of fresh air." Braun looked at each man. He saw determination in the young, well chiseled faces, and he felt satisfaction. "Any questions?" There were none. "Alright. Gentlemen, you are dismissed."

After a few hours of sleep, Braun's team of men rose, dressed, and breakfasted in the company dining hall. The lighting was subdued, but the mood was confident. Shortly after 1:00 am, the team loaded the last of their gear in their fleet of five vehicles. Two service vans took the lead as the convoy left the secure and strongly fenced grounds of Balder Chemical outside of Houston. Following the two vans, a large sewage pumper truck with a shiny stainless steel tank pulled out. Bringing up the rear of the caravan were another service van and a late model BMW. This column of five assorted vehicles drove into the night and eased onto Interstate 10 heading east toward Baton Rouge, Louisiana. Their pace was moderate as they maintained a speed within the posted limit. The last thing they wanted was a Texas State Trooper nosing through their meticulously prepared arsenal of killing implements.

*****

Early on Monday morning before Greta's scheduled Wednesday meeting in D.C., Jack and Jim Harrison pulled up to Greta's apartment. Jim went to the door and knocked. Jack stayed in the Lexus and kept the engine running and the heater on. In a moment, Greta hurriedly opened the door, spoke briefly to Jim, and shut the door again. Jim stood looking at the door in the dark cold of the pre-dawn January morning and shoved his gloved hands deeper into the pockets of his winter coat. Greta, embarrassed, opened the door again and panted, "Sorry, I just can't get it together. My hair dryer quit, I stubbed my toe on the chest of drawers, and I spilled a cup of coffee in the bedroom. Please don't be mad at me."

"I'm not mad. Just let me come in from the cold."

"Sure." He stepped in, and she hurried back to her bedroom. A few minutes later she returned to the den pulling a bulging piece of navy blue luggage. Jim picked up the luggage, turned, and headed for the door. He stopped short of the door and glanced at Greta's hair. Blond stalagmites protruded in random directions. *Definitely a bad hair day*, he thought, but wisely declined to verbalize. He carried the suitcase to the car and stowed it in the trunk which Jack had popped open from inside. Jim opened the rear door for Greta, and she got into the cozily warm interior. Jim sat in the front passenger seat while Jack greeted Greta, "Good morning. How are you doing?"

"Oh, I'll be so glad when we can get on the train and simply relax for a few hours. I just hate getting ready for trips. It takes me forever to pack."

Jim smiled. "I have a big sister like that. Of course, I have another sister who could travel a week on the contents of a fanny pack. Different strokes for different folks."

The three made small talk until the Lexus pulled into the Amtrak parking lot. The sky was lightening in the east, but it was still bitterly cold. Jack helped his two passengers unload their luggage. Like a troika of fire breathing dragons, the vapor of their breath trailing behind them in the frosty air, they strode toward the terminal.

*****

The operatives from Balder completed their journey, staying strictly on the interstate system via Mobile, Atlanta, and Richmond. Driving straight through, they stopped only for fuel and fast food, pulling off the interstate singly or in pairs of vehicles to prevent drawing attention to their convoy. They arrived in Arlington, Virginia, at 11:00pm on Monday and quietly pulled up to a large warehouse on North Quinn Street. A giant garage-type door rose slowly on the front of the nondescript building. One by one, the five vehicles of the convoy pulled into the dark interior. The door immediately reversed direction, closing the team within a massive crypt.

*****

Jim shook hands with his father. Greta hugged his neck. "Thank you for getting up early to bring us. Tell Mrs. Harrison 'Hi.'"

"I will. You both be careful and have fun. I'll be here to pick you up on Thursday."

Jim and Greta left Jack in the terminal and headed for their train. They quickly found their compartment in the assigned passenger car, stowed their two pieces of luggage, and settled into their seats. *The Crescent* pulled out of the Atlanta station exactly on time and proceeded northeast. Gratefully, Greta noted that the other seats in their compartment were empty. She was ready for some peace and quiet. For the next hour, Jim leafed through a couple of magazines left in the rack across from his seat. Greta read a novel she had brought with her. Drowsiness crept over Jim's mind and he rolled his seat back and closed his eyes. His early morning alarm had been an unwelcome nuisance.

Jim had just dozed off when Greta asked, "What's wrong with Glen?"

"What?"

"What's wrong with Glen?"

"Who?"

Greta now had misgivings about asking Jim anything. "Oh, never mind. I'm sorry I woke you. I just thought it would be a good time to talk."

"Sure. I'm fine. Now what's wrong with whom?"

"Your brother Glen."

Jim yawned, "Nothing. Glen's fine. Has a great job in New York. Makes good money. Got the looks. He's fine."

Greta persisted. "No. There's something there. An anger, a sadness, something."

Jim was slightly irritated. "You've been around him, what, twice? And now you've analyzed him psychologically?"

Greta looked out the window. "Okay, if you don't want to talk about it."

Jim looked at her and pondered which way to go with the conversation. "Alright. You're very perceptive, Miss Rose. It's a personal issue. But I guess if I tell you, it may help you be patient with him when he's around."

He gazed out the large compartment window. The sun peeked over the frozen horizon, silhouetting the sharp branches of leafless trees. Greta whispered, "Go on."

"It happened three years ago." He paused, still unsure whether he was treading on sacred ground.

"*What* happened?" Greta blurted.

Jim looked hard at her. "If you'll give me a chance, I'll tell you."

"Men!" Greta murmured and folded her arms across her chest.

"As I was saying, it happened three years ago. Glen married Christine when he was 20 and she was 19. She was from Virginia."

Greta unfolded her arms and leaned forward. "I didn't realize he was married."

"Yes, *was* married."

Her face drooped into a frown. "Oh, I'm so sorry, they got a divorce?"

"No. Will you please just let me tell this?"

"Okay. I'm only trying to help."

"They met at a 4-H competition in Chicago while they were both teenagers. They corresponded and visited each other off and on for three years and finally got married after Glen completed his sophomore year of college. In March of the next year during spring break, they went to Florida for a week, near Miami. She loved the sun and the beach, but she really didn't enjoy swimming."

Greta listened intently. Jim continued to stare out the window as the wakening southern countryside zoomed past. "Glen loved to swim and wanted Christine to go out into the surf with him. *She* was happy just to sunbathe and read a book. But he persisted, and finally, on their last day of vacation, he talked her into going out into the ocean. For a while everything seemed fine. They were having a great time. But, just after noon, Christine was caught in a rip tide and dragged out away from the shore. Glen swam like a man possessed trying to catch her, all the while yelling for her to swim crosswise to the current. That would have saved her. But she was either too tired or couldn't hear him or both. And he couldn't reach her in time. They found her body a little way down the beach a couple hours later. And this is probably the most heart wrenching part of all… They discovered she was eight weeks pregnant."

"Oh, no!" Reaching over to clasp his hand, Greta said softly, "I am truly sorry. Please forgive me…"

"It's okay. I haven't talked with anyone about it in a while. But, as you can imagine, Glen's never been the same. At first, tremendous guilt for talking her into going swimming. Then shock and anger at losing her. And now, horrible loneliness. Some days all of those emotions are churned up together at the same time." He looked at Greta with a hint of moisture in his dark brown eyes. "It was a gut punch and a reality check for the whole family."

Jim pulled his back pack onto his lap. "You hungry? I got some granola bars."

Now Greta's mind seemed to be in a far off place as she looked out the glass of the speeding Amtrak train. "No. But you go ahead."

"Sure." He munched and thought about his brother, his deceased sister-in-law, and a thousand other mental images that seemed to tumble out of his subliminal mind. To Jim, the barely perceptible rocking of the train was reminiscent of the front porch swing at his grandma Danley's. He remembered sitting there by himself on hot summer evenings, swinging back and forth listening, but not really listening, to the crickets and tree frogs in the woods.

"Do you believe there's a God?"

Jim roused from his daydream and looked up. Greta was still staring out the window.

"What's that?"

"Do you believe there's a God?"

He paused. *Dear Lord, give me the right answer.* Taking a deep breath, he said, "I do."

"Then why does He let absolutely horrible things happen to people like Christine and Glen… and me?"

Jim hesitated, thinking. Greta continued, opening a vent on emotions that had fermented deep within. "Is He cruel? Or is He impotent? Or both?"

"That's a little strong isn't it?"

"Just to be candid with you, I'm angry. And, if there is a God, I'm furious with Him. But I really don't think He's there anyway." Now her voice was more strident than Jim could ever remember.

He paused, allowing her words to hang in the air. "So... you're angry with a God that you're convinced is not real?"

"That's right, Mr. Harrison!"

"Okay. You've been through more pain in a few months than most people suffer in a life time. But that doesn't mean there's no God. In fact, it validates His existence. "

Greta calmed slightly as if just talking about it mollified her deep hurt. "Explain that. I don't see it at all."

"Well, I can't give you a simple answer as to why there's so much pain in the world. But I know some of it is the result of the evil choices that men make. For example, the men who abused you. And the guys who drugged me and dragged me down to who knows where, probably South America." Jim relaxed a little as he sensed a genuine longing for explanations in Greta's eyes. He now asked her a question, "Do you believe there are good and evil?"

"Of course," she shot back.

"Well, let me ask you this. How do you define evil? Is it cultural, or personal, or something else? Are there actions that are recognized by all people as reprehensible?"

She gazed at the compartment ceiling. "Like murder, rape, or torturing children?"

"Exactly. Aren't these things absolutely wrong?" His tone was patient and controlled.

Pausing, Greta looked at Jim, wavering between her desire to air her bitterness and her need to come to some kind of healing, some understanding.

"I guess so. I'm not sure I see where you're going with this."

He continued. "The very things you mentioned as evil are defined as evil because there is a God. He carefully created men and women in His image."

"I just don't believe that. We're here by chance, by accident."

"If that were true, our lives would *truly* be tragic. We would be without hope or even choice. If Naturalism were true, and that's the philosophy you're proposing, then there would be no right and wrong, no freedom of will, and men would have no more responsibility for their actions than an earthworm. They would choose and speak and act because of their environment and their inheritance and no more. We would have to look at all the heinous crimes and atrocities of all the ages and be compelled to say, 'Oh well, boys will be boys. They just can't help themselves.'"

Jim stood up and walked over to the window. He thought he detected a very slight thawing in Greta's icy demeanor. "But we all know that some things humans do are just wrong. We know it deep inside. Likewise, we recognize other acts as true and good and noble. I believe it's because there's a God who made us and cares about us and has put inside our very fiber a recognition of the value, the sacredness of life."

"I wish that were true. I wish there was some purpose, some meaning to my life! But I suppose I'm with Nietzsche. He taught that God has died."

Jim responded before she could proceed, "Yes, and he also articulated the consequences of that belief. He said that if God were dead, the horizon would be wiped away, there would be no up or down, and men would have to light a lantern in the day to see."

She seemed amazed now. "You read Nietzsche?"

"Yes, and Plato, Saint Augustine, Blake, Lewis, Chesterton and others."

"I'm surprised."

For a moment there was an uncomfortable hiatus in the conversation.

Taking the initiative, Jim addressed what he knew she was thinking, which surprised her again. "And you're thinking, 'What about natural disasters, and accidents, like Christine; if there is a God, why does he let that happen?'"

"Yes, why?"

"The short answer is—'I don't know'. I don't think anybody knows for sure. We can guess. But, when those things happen, I believe it's important that we be there for each other and give it time. Tragedies catch all of us off guard. We think we have our future all mapped out, and, boom, our plan is smashed by the hard edges and corners of life. Then we grieve." Silence punctuated the last point.

Jim kept going. "Personally, I think God knows what He's doing. I can't see all the ins and outs, the consequences of this event and that choice, but He can. I believe He is good and He is all powerful. If He chooses to let something happen to me, it's ultimately for my good."

Greta sighed and asked, "But how on earth could Christine's tragic death bring any good to anybody? Two lives snuffed out, a marriage destroyed. How can you possibly say that about this evil?"

"Well, it's true. This tragedy changed my family forever. I've seen them at their worst and, even then, seen them love each other and grow closer than ever before. And it brought redemption to my brother. Before the accident, he was generally what people would call a 'good' person. Decent, honest, a hard worker. But he was also selfish and arrogant. His priorities were messed up. He worked all the time. He chased the 'good life'. He loved things and used people, even his gorgeous wife."

Greta looked at the floor for no particular reason and swallowed hard. And she kept listening hard.

"The death of his wife and unborn baby changed all that. He saw love poured out by our family and their friends, by people from all over the world, by old people and young, by people from college, business, and the military, by neighbors and his church family. This tragedy, this 'evil' as you called it, brought Glen Harrison to Christ. Christine had known Jesus for a couple years. She was a magnificent person, articulate, funny, athletic. But even she could not break down the coldness, the egotism in Glen's heart. Yet her death and that of their child humbled Glen. The man who thought he could do everything realized he could do nothing to bring back his wife and child. He came to Christ a week later. He's been a different man ever since. Sure, he still grieves. But he has a purpose in life. He's serving others and giving. He's sober, but joyful. He looks to help other men realize the truth about life without having to suffer the terrible blow he did."

Greta leaned back in her seat and closed her eyes. The conversation was over… for now. Jim sat across from her and looked at her features. *Such a beautiful woman.* He wondered now if he'd said too much.

They ate a late lunch in the dining car in silence. They arrived at the station in Washington D. C. shortly after eight o'clock that night. It seemed to Jim it had been a very long journey.

27 The Nexus

It was 8:20 Tuesday morning, January 28. Snow fell softly on the city of Arlington, Virginia. Inside the warehouse on North Quinn Street, Eric Riddell stood and looked at his men assembled around a rough wooden table consisting of a sheet of half-inch plywood resting on a large, empty wooden spool which formerly held a coil of heavy gauge electric cable. Behind him, a marker board was fixed securely to the interior wall of the warehouse.

"I'm certain each of you understands the gravity of the mission. I know you have prepared and rehearsed this multiple times over the past six months. But I want no mistakes. This operation must go off like clockwork. So I want to walk through the timeline minute-by-minute one last time. At the end of our session, ask questions; make comments. Let's get it right." Pulling a pack of cigarettes from the shoulder pocket of his blue jump suit, he sat down and pointed to one of his men. "Zed, you may begin." Riddell lit a cigarette and sat back while Zygmunt Swift detailed his part of the mission. Swift's chief and his team always called him *Zed*.

One by one, each man in the team stood and carefully reviewed his role in the plan. They were methodical, confident, and brief. There was no embellishment and no humor. Each was a professional, and this was their business.

After thirty minutes, the last man sat down. Riddell finally smiled. "Good. I want you to remember why all this is necessary. There are only two nations on earth that stand in the way of advancement. Tonight we decapitate the one, and the other will shrivel up and die as well."

*****

10am Jim and Greta ate brunch in the Article One-American Grill at the Hyatt Regency. They had checked in the night before; Jim had surprised the clerk at the desk in the posh lobby of the hotel by asking for separate rooms. "*Two* ...rooms, Sir?"

Jim had simply replied "Yes," and smiled broadly. The clerk raised his eyebrows but said nothing more and produced the two keys for Jim. "Thanks," Jim said as he turned and escorted Greta toward the elevators.

They planned out the rest of their day over Belgian waffles, sausage, and fresh fruit from Central America. They laughed and talked. Jim was encouraged to see Greta enjoying herself. Maybe she *was* healing a little. Tomorrow they had their meeting with immigration officials. Today, Jim wanted to show Greta the monuments, the Capitol Building, the White House, and Arlington Cemetery.

Looking out a large window of the restaurant, Greta saw an airliner pass across the gray sky, apparently on final approach to Reagan National. Her countenance darkened slightly. "Have you heard anything from the FBI about their investigation?"

"Actually, last Friday I heard from Agent Roby. He told me they've obtained indictments for two men with ties to Balder Chemical. But they're waiting on three more to work their way through the grand jury process. They don't want to pull the trigger on arrests until they can bag the whole group. Apparently they consider these guys a flight risk."

"Why does this take so long?"

"Justice. It's just the way it operates. I think it's phenomenal that they've made as much progress as they have with this case so far. And I get the feeling talking to the agents that they've been onto this group for years. It's big. Our episodes were just more evidence against the whole sordid network."

" 'Our episodes'. Yeah, why us? Why did they want you and me? I still can't believe it was all tied to my great-grandfather's journal."

"I know. It's hard for me to get my brain around the claim that Hitler survived and left for somewhere... South America, I guess. But, if it were true, maybe somebody was totally committed to keeping it a secret. *Why*, I don't have a clue. I just wanna get it behind us. Get some closure." He picked at his waffle with his fork. "Let's focus today on being here, together."

*****

10:15am Riddell's men carried their bags and cases of equipment from their vehicles and set them on the concrete floor of the warehouse. Mitchell Fluke unzipped his large black bag and lifted out an oxygen diving tank and regulator, diving mask, and wet suit. He opened a separate bag and examined two white blocks- C4 plastic explosive. Opening a small metal case, he lifted out three detonators. He only needed one, but his perpetual habit was to have a backup.

Walter Dyson was a short, stocky man with arms of iron. He unloaded a bazooka- length, stainless steel tube with a crystal lens apparatus fixed at one end. Two thick cables snaked from the opposite end of the tube. Riddell walked over to where Dyson was squatting by his bag. "How much power does this laser deliver?"

Dyson looked up at his leader. "5000 milliwatts. Our field trials confirmed that's more than enough!"

"No mistakes. We must knock out that tower."

"It'll be down. Count on it."

"I am."

Zygmunt Swift unsnapped the latches of the long, plastic gun case resting on the floor in front of him. He opened the case and lifted out his weapon of choice, a DSR-1 sniper rifle. Riddell turned towards *Zed*. Folding his arms on his chest and focusing his gaze on the flat black metal of the weapon, he commanded, "Tell me about your rifle."

Zed deftly attached a silencer to the end of the barrel and responded to Riddell's order without looking up. "This is a DSR-1 sniper rifle manufactured in Germany by DSR-Precision. It's a subsonic variant and fires a .308 subsonic round. I hand load my own ammunition. No room for error. Effective range- 800 meters. Weight- 5.9 kilos, length-990 mm. I use a quick-detach Kruger 2.5 Tactical illuminated scope. And *this* is a fold-away bipod," he said as he snapped the bipod into shooting position.

"Bolt action. Is that a problem?"

"Not at all. This gun has a five-round magazine. I can empty it in 9.4 seconds-with 100-percent accuracy."

"Have you factored in the windshield?"

"Yes, sir. With a .308 round, no problem. I'll dispatch the driver first, and the passenger'll be dead before he's able to undo his seat belt. The subsonic with this silencer/suppressor attached will do the job with no one on the street hearing anything more than a light thud as the bullets penetrate the glass. If the snow continues, so much the better."

Riddell mused, *Impressive.* But he restrained his comment to, "Adequate," preferring to protect Swift from the pitfall of overconfidence.

Thomas Kopf checked and rechecked the controls on the rear of the silver tanker pumper truck parked in the warehouse. The side of the tanker now wore the red and blue logo of the American Sewage and Plumbing Company, freshly painted by team member Curtis Ballinger. One of the service vans also displayed the distinctive markings of the local company. The two other service vans sported fresh, black and blue AT&T logos. "Well done, Curt," Riddell commended his art work. Ballinger acknowledged the accolade with a nod.

"Thomas, no leaks?" Riddell queried the fourth team member.

Thomas Kopf, aware of the idiocy of the question, kept a straight face. "None. If there were, we would all be very sick by now. The birds are in good health, as well," he added, pointing to a cage containing two green parakeets which hung from the bumper of the tanker truck.

"What temperature do we need for vaporization of the gas?" the leader demanded.

Kopf felt like a professor with a surly student. He resented the leadership of Riddell who was actually five years his junior. Kopf kept his distaste for the younger man muzzled, for the time being. "158 degrees Celsius."

"What's the outside temperature now?"

"Thirty minutes ago it was minus four. And it's still snowing."

"How long will it take to get the heater up to the proper temperature?"

"Twelve minutes if the temperature remains constant. If colder, a little longer."

"Twelve minutes. A very long time indeed." Riddell stared off into the far reaches of the vast warehouse ceiling.

"If we make it past the two checkpoints guarding the Capitol complex, we should have no problem with twelve minutes. Americans have come to expect simple workmen to be sluggish," Kopf observed.

"Not *if*, but *when*, Thomas." Riddell seemed to be in his lecturing persona again. Kopf was sick of it. *His day will come, soon!*

"Here is a second heater as backup, if the first fails," Kopf said pointing to a unit attached at the right rear of the tanker.

"Good."

*****

12:30 pm Jim and Greta boarded the D.C. mass transit Metrorail at the underground station nearest their hotel. Jim had purchased two-day tickets so they could have unlimited riding to see each of the monuments and other sights. They decided to start on the east side of the National Mall and work their way west, ending their tour at Arlington National Cemetery, just across the Potomac River in Virginia.

*****

1:00 pm Zygmunt Swift loaded his rifle, silencer, clip, and scope into a large green duffle bag and then filled the rest of the bag with slacks, shirts, underwear, and socks. His final addition was a shave bag. He had just exited the tiny bathroom in the corner of the warehouse where he had shaved and trimmed his sideburns. He carefully placed the bag in the trunk of the BMW and turned to face Riddell. The chief took Swift by the shoulders. "Be in place, be on time, two shots, two kills! We need those badges."

Zed closed the trunk and opened the driver side door. "Just be there to snatch the badges. They'll be waiting on you."

*****

1:07 pm The National Mall was almost empty. The snow continued to fall and the temperature held steady in the mid-twenties. Jim and Greta started on the east end of the Mall in front of the Capitol Building. Jim noticed a buzz of activity and the significant security presence around the perimeter of the Capitol campus. Dozens of uniformed and plain clothes police and security personnel moved about the snow covered concrete and grass areas surrounding the dominating architecture of the United States Capitol. There were canine units and, less obvious, sniper teams positioned on the roofs of several surrounding buildings. Jim stopped and asked one of the Capitol police what was up.

"State of the Union Address tonight." Turning, the heavily armed policeman walked away, indicating the conversation was over.

"I didn't realize that was tonight," Jim commented to Greta. "Too bad we can't get you a tour of the Capitol. But there's still more than enough for us to see on the Mall."

"It doesn't matter. It's just beautiful here. And... sharing it with you," she said looking up at Jim's athletic profile and taking his gloved hand with hers.

Jim squeezed her hand and then continued quickly, "Let's head over to the National Gallery of Art." Jim would have preferred the Air-Space Museum but suspected the art would be a greater treat to Greta.

An hour later, Jim pulled Greta away from an exhibit of Spanish art from the 18th century and said, "I'm hungry. Lets's get something to eat."

Greta agreed, and they entered the Pavilion Café near the sculpture garden. The hostess seated them at a table adjacent to the large glass windows, and a waiter brought their menus a moment later. Jim had a specialty pizza -onion, bacon, and potato. Greta ordered the chicken noodle and vegetable soup.

By the time the meal was over, the couple was refreshed and energized, ready for the cold air out on the Mall. Foregoing the Smithsonian Institution because of time limitations, they spent the next forty minutes walking around the Washington Monument, the Vietnam Memorial, and the Lincoln Memorial. Hurrying, they boarded the Metrorail and rode over to Arlington Cemetery. They arrived before the Cemetery closed with just enough time to visit the Tomb of the Unknown Soldier. Tears trickled down Greta's cheeks as she and Jim watched the sentinel 'walking the mat' at the front of the tomb. Snow fell from the overcast sky as the Cemetery closed at 5pm. Jim and Greta were the last to leave. Their mood was somber.

Jim hailed a taxi and the pair sat in silence as they rode over to The Grenadier Restaurant.

*****

5:25pm Darkness descended on the District of Colombia. Riddell gave final instructions to Fluke, Ballinger, and Dyson. "Remember, the cyber-attack will be launched from Amsterdam at 8:25. You must be in position on time in case that attack is somehow blocked. The 911 system is the most vulnerable and will be the lowest priority target for us. The members of Congress will be seated by 8:30 and the President should be on the podium by 9:00."

Fluke spoke up, "What time do we expect the call for the plumbing contractor?"

"Our man on the inside will make his move at 7:45. The call for help will probably be placed around 7:55."

*****

6:10 pm Swift carefully pulled the blue BMW into the small parking lot of The Dragoon Motel on Blackwell Street in Arlington, Virginia. The lot was empty save for two cars. The snowfall had halted for the moment. About a half-inch of wet snow separated the soles of his black boots from the crumbling blacktop of the parking lot. He opened the trunk, threw the strap of his duffle bag over his shoulder, and closed the lid. Walking toward the entrance of the low budget motel, he glanced furtively around the area. Nothing unusual. Quiet and dark. *Just right*, he thought. The stucco exterior of The Dragoon was once cardinal red. The years had faded the color to a dark pink. The windows, shutters, gutters, and door frame were dated but clean. The establishment had the look of a building trying desperately to maintain a brave face while losing the battle against old age. In one ground floor window of the two story structure a neon sign flashed "vacancy".

Swift opened the door to the motel office and entered. A bell attached to the inside door handle jingled his arrival. Stomping the snow off his boots onto the welcome mat just inside the door, he looked up and met the eyes of a medium height, balding man in his late sixties standing behind the desk. Swift set his duffle bag on the floor in front of the check-in desk.

"Evening," Swift said. "Got any rooms left?"

"Sure do, son. Just yourself?"

"Yeah, just me." Glancing briefly over the man's shoulder, he noted a wooden board with 18 protruding hooks. Traditional ovoid plastic, gold motel key tags with keys hung

from every hook but two. Both of the missing keys were for
first floor rooms.

"Still snowing?" the clerk asked.

"No, stopped a few minutes ago. Looks like it could start
again any time."

"Where you from?" the clerk continued.

Swift considered brushing off the prying man but thought
better of it. And so, the act began. "Missouri originally. Just
back in country from Afghanistan. Just need a room for one
night. I gotta catch a flight in the morning."

"Fine. You want first or second floor?"

"Second, I guess," Swift answered casually.

"You active duty?" he pursued, looking at the green bag
sitting on the floor.

"Yes, sir. Army," Swift lied. "How'd ya know?"

"Oh, just a good judge of character. Been around the block
a few times. Where you headed?"

"Uh … Starting airborne school."

"Really? Ft. Bragg, eh?"

"Yes, sir … Ft. Bragg. So I better get to bed early. I'll just go
ahead and pay now." He pulled a roll of twenties from his shirt
pocket and asked, "How much?"

"Seventy-five, and this is your lucky day. Military gets a
10% discount. I just need to see your military I.D."

Uh oh. First mistake. "I threw my wallet in here
somewhere," he said as he bent over and made as if
rummaging through his duffle bag contents.

"Oh, what the heck. I'll just give you the discount. One
soldier to another."

"You a veteran?"

"Yeah, 'Nam. I was at Bien Hoa. Gunner on a Huey. It was
rough. Anyway, here's your key. 206. Just off the stairwell on

the left. If you need anything, just dial zero. And thanks for your service."

"You too, sir." Swift took the key, picked up his green duffle, and headed for the stairs. He raced up to the second floor and found room 206. He opened the door and let himself in. The room was small and simple but clean and well kept. He checked out the room- bedroom, bathroom, and tiny closet. Swift sat back on the bed and pulled out his smart phone. He tapped his chief's number and typed in *On site.* He hit *Send.* Then he set the alarm feature to 7:30 pm. Taking his shoes off, he lay back and closed his eyes.

While Swift settled in to his room, the Vietnam veteran at the check-in desk pulled out his cell phone and dialed 911. After two rings, the dispatcher answered. "911 operator, what is the nature of your emergency?"

The veteran calmly answered, "I've seen those ads, 'see something, say something'. Well, I saw something."

"I'm sorry, but this number is for emergencies only. The number you need to call is Homeland Security." She rattled off the number.

"Just a minute. Let me get a pen ... OK, give it to me again." She repeated the number quickly with a tone of impatience. "Thanks." Click. The operator was gone.

The veteran dialed the number he had written on the motel notepad in front of him. "I'm sorry, the number you have reached is no longer in service. Please check the number and try again." Snapping his phone shut, the veteran fumed. *They sure don't make this easy.* Pulling out the D.C. area phone book, he flipped pages until he found the number for the Department of Homeland Security.

He quickly dialed the toll free number. Two rings, three rings, four rings, five rings, and then a cheerful answer. "Homeland Security, how may I help you?"

"Finally, I got someone who wants to listen!"

28 The Assault

6:15pm The crowd of patrons at The Grenadier was large but not unruly. The Colonial themed restaurant was sumptuous. Delicious smells of simple but hardy beef and potato dishes emanated from the kitchen. Richly decorated walls displayed paintings and period weapons- faithful reproductions of muskets, swords, and knives.

After a 40 minute wait, the host led Jim and Greta to a corner booth. They were seated under the watchful eyes of Patrick Henry from his portrait on the wall behind them. The pewter dinnerware set on the maroon table cloth was elegant.

*****

6:30pm   Chandra Rahman turned off the ignition of his black Nissan Maxima. He opened the door and got out of the car. Rahman pulled his backpack out of the trunk and walked across the large employee parking lot across the street from the east lawn of the U.S. Capitol complex. He had already successfully passed through two heavily guarded Capitol Police checkpoints. Smiling as he passed each policeman and homeland security agent roving the grounds, Rahman entered the Capitol building as he had hundreds of times before. Just inside the entry used by maintenance personnel, he submitted his backpack to the security scanner. Rahman was well known to the guards manning the entry area. He had seen many of them dozens of times. They checked his photo I.D. badge. No problems.

7:09pm Rahman carried his backpack to his locker in the basement of the Capitol. *Time to retrieve my toy,* he mused. Just as he walked over to an equipment bay in the corner, a door of the room opened. A two-man Capitol security detail entered with a search dog in the lead. Rahman's pulse quickened. "What's this?"

"Routine check. Anybody else down here?"

"No, sir," Rahman replied.

The German shepherd sniffed each locker briefly as he and his handler walked back and forth past the three banks of blue metallic lockers. Stopping at one, the dog turned his head to one side and sniffed excitedly. The handler pointed to the locker directly in front of his canine partner. The security detail supervisor unlocked the locker with a master key and opened it. Inside was… nothing. The supervisor pulled a dry, paper wipe towel from a pouch on his equipment belt and wiped the inside of the locker. Dropping four drops of liquid from a bottle on the towel, he announced, "Negative."

"Alright, Jesse, keep going. Let's get it right." Jesse the dog whimpered and then continued down the line, unperturbed by the false alarm. The detail finished the locker search with no more hits.

"Later, man," the supervisor said to Rahman as they exited the room. The Bengali was left alone with his thoughts and his perspiring forehead.

7:29pm Rahman looked at his watch. *Late!* He grabbed a step ladder and bounded over to his locker. Stepping up on the ladder, he pushed back a tile from the suspended ceiling and grabbed a cloth bag resting on an adjacent tile. He jumped to the floor and removed a Smith and Wesson Bodyguard 380 .38 caliber pistol and two clips of ammunition from the bag. It had taken Rahman over nine months to smuggle the disassembled pistol parts and ammunition into the building one piece at a time. He now slipped the pistol and clips into his backpack and raced out the door and up the stairs.

He slowed to a normal pace as he opened a door and entered a first floor hallway. Two congressional aides stood conversing outside a public restroom. He passed by them unnoticed. He entered the restroom and carefully checked to make sure the stalls were empty. Quickly, he pulled a shirt out of his pack and tore off one sleeve. Next, he tied a small knot in one end of the sleeve and then poured in less than a cup of powder from his thermos. After tying a knot in the opposite end of the sleeve, he lifted the seat on one toilet, placed the sleeve in the bowl, and flushed the toilet. Closing his back pack, he left the restroom and walked briskly to the stairwell leading to the next floor. Finding the second story restroom nearest the stairs, he repeated the sleeve and powder procedure and flushed the toilet. This time he exited the restroom and moved to a restroom on the opposite end of the building on the same floor. Same procedure.

Returning to the first floor restroom, Rahman entered and found a senator cursing to himself as he watched a toilet boiling over its filthy contents onto the floor of the first stall. "What's the matter, senator?" he asked, sounding genuinely concerned. The rotund senator fired several expletives Rahman's way in describing the problem of the overflowing toilet.

Rahman looked into the stall and assured the senator he would get on it right away. At about the same moment, a call came across the radio Rahman carried on his belt. It was the shift supervisor. "Chandra, this is McDougal. Gotta toilet stopped up on second floor."

"Right, chief. Got one on first floor too."

"You're kidding."

"No, sir," he said matter-of-factly.

"Great, this is all we need with everybody who's anybody here tonight for the SOTU. Well, get on it. Get 'em cleared ASAP!"

"Right." Rahman returned to the second floor and checked the third targeted restroom. He flushed two of the toilets and achieved his desired results. The floor was soon covered in water gushing from the plugged system. "Chief, we got bigger problems. Two more toilets overflowing on second floor. I think we got a system wide obstruction."

Ignoring Capitol radio etiquette, McDougal filled the airwave with a stream of profanity. "Close those restrooms to further traffic 'til I can get the contract plumbing guys out here. I guess they're gonna have to suction the whole system again."

McDougal placed an urgent call to the Capitol switchboard. He explained the appalling situation of the public commodes to the operator in the most graphic terms he could think of. The operator agreed immediately to place the call to the plumbing contractor's 24-hour phone number.

*****

7:36pm Swift looked through the peephole of the room door and saw an empty hallway. He opened the door and looked to the left and right. Still empty. He stepped across the hall and pulled a metal pick tool from a pocket of his cargo pants. The antediluvian door lock of room 207 yielded easily to Swift's skilled hand. He turned the handle and opened the door slightly. Returning to his own room, he glanced quickly at the bed and floor. He had dropped a crumpled shirt, pair of slacks, and socks on the single chair in the room. The green duffle bag sat on the carpeted floor. The worn bedspread was pulled back and the sheets were carelessly rumpled. The place looked as if he had slept, changed clothes, and left in a hurry.

Shouldering his sniper rifle, and with his ammunition clip in his jacket pocket, he left room 206, quietly closed the door, walked across the narrow hall, and entered room 207. Swift moved through the darkness toward the single curtained window. Moving a chair over to the window, the sniper seated himself comfortably and snapped the bipod of the DSR-1 into place. He grasped the frame of the window and pulled sideways. It would not budge. He examined the frame and noticed a screw which prevented the window from sliding. Pulling his multi-tool from the pouch on his belt, he removed the screw and felt the window give under his traction. Cold air rushed in, and Swift felt exhilaration.

Downstairs in the lobby of The Dragoon, two uniformed officers of the Arlington police force spoke to the proprietor in low tones. "Why are you suspicious of this guy?" the taller of the two inquired.

"He's trying to pass himself off as Army. He's not."

"How do you know?" the officer asked with a hint of impatience, having missed his dinner because of the call from The Dragoon's owner.

"Said he was going to airborne school … at Ft. Bragg!"

"Gotcha. He didn't realize it's Ft. Benning."

"Right. How'd you know?"

"Got a brother in the 82nd at Ft. Bragg. Anything else?"

"Yeah. His duffle bag had a protrusion. There's something other than clothes in that bag. Could be … well, could be a lot of things. Anyway. Thought it best to call somebody."

"Alright, let's go see Mr., what was his name?"

"I don't know. Signed the register, but it's illegible. Gave me cash. I don't always get 'em to fill out paperwork. Just do it the old fashioned way. A handshake, you know."

The veteran led the tall officer and his partner up the stairs. They arrived quietly outside room 206. The tall officer knocked firmly on the door. No answer. He knocked again, "Police!" No answer. "You have a master key?"

"Yeah," the veteran responded. "Guess you don't have a search warrant, but I can get in the room to check the plumbing, or the air, or whatever. You can just follow me in."

Across the hall, Swift heard a sharp rap on a door. He watched the scene unfold through the peep hole of room 207. Cursing the veteran under his breath, Swift watched as the trio entered the room and closed the door. He returned to his position at the window determined to fulfill his duty, concluding it unlikely that the police would waste their time searching all the rooms of The Dragoon. He had irrevocably committed himself to fate. If the police entered his room, he would shoot it out with them. If they went on their way, so much the better. He would complete his task and be gone within the hour.

Back across the hall, the police searched but found nothing of interest. "Well, looks like he went out for the evening. No I.D. Nothing suspicious." The tall officer thanked the vet for his alertness and exited the room. He and his partner descended the stairs with the proprietor. "Guess you didn't see him leave?"

"No, but there are exits at each end of the building. He could have left by any of them."

"Well, call us if you see anything else. This guy's probably just a G.I. wannabe."

The vet watched the police leave and murmured to himself, "I don't think so."

*****

7:38pm The large door of the warehouse on North Quinn rose slowly, its decrepit rollers creaking as it moved. Inside, the engines of the two ersatz AT&T vans roared to life. They pulled out of the warehouse and into the street. It was dark, and a thin layer of snow blanketed the road. The Virginia sky was clearing now, just as the team's meteorologist back at Balder Chemical had predicted hours before. The counterfeit tanker truck and van of American Sewage and Plumbing left the building moments later. The groaning door closed behind them. And then, once again, the street was silent and cold.

*****

7:59pm The call from the switchboard was received and forwarded to the two men on call for American Plumbing and Sewage in Arlington, Virginia. Within twenty minutes Ruben Ortiz and Travis Miliosek were climbing into their pumper tanker truck. Pulling out of their truck bay, they turned onto Kinard Street and headed toward their night's work at the Capitol. They joked about the irony of the situation as they pulled up to the stop sign at the intersection of Kinard and Blackwell. At that instant, Zygmunt Swift placed the crosshairs of his Kruger scope on the dark blue jacket that covered the chest of Ortiz, the driver. He had spotted the tanker as soon as it had pulled out onto the dead end street and headed towards the intersection.

Ortiz laughed, "I always knew the Capitol was full of…"

Thunk! A .308 round slammed into Ortiz's chest just right of the sternum at the sixth intercostal space, stopping him in midsentence.

"What the…" Miliosek yelled. ***Thunk!*** The torso of the driver jerked as a second round struck one inch below the first.

Blood saturated the man's jacket as Miliosek, stunned, turned to steady his friend with his right hand. Ortiz, already dead, slumped forward against the shoulder strap of his seat belt. Miliosek never knew what happened. *Thunk!* A .308 round penetrated his chest cavity through his right axilla anterior to the right scapula. He groaned and began to cough. *Thunk!* His cough was stifled by another bullet from Swift's DSR-1 one hundred fifty yards away at the window of room 207 of The Dragoon Motel.

Less than thirty seconds later, Eric Riddell jerked open the door of the American Plumbing tanker truck, engine still idling, and snatched the Federal I.D. badges clipped to the jackets of the two dead men. He unlatched Ortiz's seat belt and let the body slump forward and off to the right toward the stick shift. He turned off the engine and activated the emergency flasher. Moving to the passenger door, he removed Miliosek's seat belt and pushed the torso to left wedging it behind the body of the driver. He quickly locked and closed both doors. One final touch: he splashed water from a large bottle in his jacket on the windshield and side windows. He anticipated a layer of ice would form rapidly, concealing the occupants of the now apparently stranded plumbing tanker truck.

*****

8:02pm It seemed the good times were just getting cranked up at The Grenadier Restaurant, but Jim and Greta were ready to leave after a delicious and filling dinner. Stepping onto the sidewalk out front, the two strolled away, Greta comfortably slipping her arm into Jim's. "You wanna walk across the bridge back to Washington and our hotel? It might take an hour or so."

"Sure," Greta smiled, as content as she had been in almost six months. "I don't guess we're in any hurry are we?" she asked looking up at the clear sky.

"No, guess not. That was a great meal, huh?"

"Yes, the best. Thank you so much for coming with me and spending your day with me. I really appreciate you," she said glancing up at Jim, squeezing his arm as they walked.

*****

8:05 pm Jack Harrison was comfortably seated in his rocker recliner in the living room of his home, reading a copy of Dickens' *A Tale of Two Cities*. Jean was in another rocker opposite her husband working on a cross stitch project for one of the grandchildren. The serenity of the scene was interrupted by a buzzing sound which indicated Jack had just received a text message on his cell phone. He picked up his phone and read:

"You are the only man who ever refused me. You must have something special. Please have someone check out the warehouse at 5009 North Quinn St., Arlington, VA. Hurry. This is very serious.

A friend from BC."

Jack handed the phone to his wife. "Strange," he remarked.

She quickly read the text. "Yeah, very strange. And BC? What do you make of it?"

"I don't have a clue. But let me Google that address." Picking up the laptop computer which rested on the coffee table, he typed in the address mentioned in the text message. Sure enough, the search yielded a photo of a large warehouse. "Well, that doesn't tell us a lot. Maybe I should try to call this person and see what's up. Might have been intended for someone else."

He dialed the number, but there was no answer. "I wonder...It sounds like an emergency." And then the reality struck Jack. "BC. Balder Chemical!"

Jean gasped, "Jack, no!"

"I've gotta call Jim. Maybe he's near there."

"No, don't get him involved. You just can't!"

"Honey, we're already involved."

"But why not call that FBI agent you met with?"

Jack reached over and took Jean's hand. "First, let's pray for wisdom."

They both bowed their heads and together poured out their hearts before God- for wisdom and courage, for safety for Jim and Greta, and for justice for Balder Chemical. Jack closed, "In Jesus' name, Amen."

Taking his cell phone back, he found Roby's private cell number in the contact list and dialed it. The phone rang once and went immediately to a voice mailbox. "Hey, this is Roby. I'm away from the phone right now. Leave me a message and I'll call you back."

"What next?" Jack thought for a moment. "The Arlington Police Department. You think they'll have an interest in an anonymous text on a guy's phone in Georgia about an address for a warehouse?"

Jean raised her eyebrows but said nothing. Jack found the APD phone number quickly by an internet search. He dialed the number and reached a cheerful operator in Arlington. She connected him with the shift supervisor. The supervisor politely took down Jack's information and promised they would have a patrol car cruise by the address when one was available. Jack thanked the officer and hung up. "I don't think he senses any urgency to this. He also said they're a bit short staffed tonight." Jack took in a deep breath. "Well, I feel I should call Jim." Jean simply nodded and bowed her head again.

*****

8:07 pm Mitchell Fluke set the parking brake of the 'AT&T' van and turned on his emergency flasher. He had parked the van in the middle of Delaware Avenue just north of Constitution Avenue. Turning to Ballinger he chuckled, "They say the best way to hide is right out in the open. Okay, let's do it."

Requiring no further prompting, Ballinger exited through the passenger door and moved to the back of the van. He opened one of the doors and grabbed four emergency road flashers. Avoiding the oncoming traffic which had slowed some in acknowledgement of the flasher of the service van, Ballinger set a virtual cordon around the van with the road flashers. He left just enough room for traffic to ease by cautiously in both directions. Simultaneously, Fluke was inside the back of the van donning his wet suit, mask, and air tank. He attached a halogen lamp to his forehead and tested it one last time.

Fluke slipped on a pair of rubber pool shoes and stepped out of the van. The irony of standing in the middle of Washington D.C. on a frigid night in January wearing a wet suit, mask, and air tank was not lost on Fluke. He smiled and stepped toward the hole in the street where Ballinger had removed the manhole cover. Carefully, and with Ballinger giving assistance, Fluke descended the ladder attached to the side of the access hole. In moments, he was up to his waist in cold water. He let go of the ladder and drifted downward. His headlamp illuminated the walls of the cavern and came to rest on a large metal box totally immersed in the water. Bundles of cables entered and left the box from both sides. He quickly removed two blocks of C-4 from a bag suspended from his tool belt. Next, Fluke attached each block to the case of the box with two sheet metal screws using a compact cordless, waterproof drill. Finally, he connected the three detonators.

As Fluke ascended the ladder, Ballinger, who was standing over the hole in the street watching his partner, noticed the flash of a distinctive blue light from a police cruiser. The police car had pulled up on the side of the van opposite where Fluke was working in the hole. The officer was bundled against the cold by a dark blue coat and black stocking cap. Walking around the rear of the van, he spied the open manhole in the middle of the street and stepped towards it. By this time, Ballinger had retreated to his seat in the van. Fluke emerged from the water, below which the central phone node for all Capitol land lines was supposedly protected. As he came up to street level, the police officer slowly advanced toward the manhole. Incredulous, the officer clicked the mike button on his shoulder radio to report the scene to his dispatcher. It was his last act. Ballinger pumped two bullets into the officer from behind and moved over to catch his slumping form. As Fluke stepped out of the hole onto the street, Ballinger pushed the body of the policeman into the hole and replaced the manhole cover.

"Okay, hustle," Fluke ordered as he handed his air tank and mask to Ballinger and flipped the safety switch on one of the detonators. In a matter of seconds, Ballinger had gathered up the four hazard flashers and slipped into the driver's seat of the van. As he pulled alongside Fluke, Fluke detonated the C-4. A low rumble emanated from the hole. No pedestrians were around to hear the subterranean thunder, and the drivers of the cars moving down the avenue seemed oblivious to the sound. The node servicing the Capitol land lines was history.

The stiff and battered body of Officer Darryl Halstead would not be found until early the next morning.

*****

8:09 pm Walter Dyson parked his AT&T van against the curb on the east end of Constitution Avenue. He was 150 yards from the cell tower providing signal for the Capitol area. He activated his emergency flasher and moved into the back of the van. He took just one minute to assemble the parts of his weapon. Lastly, he set the laser onto its custom built tripod and fired up the powering sequence. Partly opening the rear doors, he switched on the small target laser installed on the top of the steel tube. A thin red beam projected from the rear of the van into the night sky. Dyson found the main parabolic antenna of the cell tower with the targeting laser and secured the tripod adjusting screws. A digital meter confirmed the rising power level of the pulse laser as the battery power source energized the weapon. In twenty seconds, it was ready. Dyson pulled the trigger and a laser pulse crashed into the dish of the antenna, effectively frying its delicate internal circuits. Anyone in the immediate area using his cell phone realized his call had been suddenly dropped.

*****

8:10pm Jim and Greta stepped off the curb and walked across Washington Boulevard toward the entrance to the Arlington Bridge. As they passed the entrance to the bridge, Jim's cell phone rang. He stopped and answered his call. "Jim, where are you?" Jack asked.

"I'm with Greta on a leisurely walk across the Arlington Memorial Bridge over the Potomac River. Just finished dinner and we're headed towards our hotel. What's up?"

"I'm not sure. I got this strange text."

"From who?"

"I don't know. It said somebody should check out a warehouse in Arlington, Virginia. Gave the address. Said it was urgent. Apparently from somebody connected to Balder Chemical."

Jim thought as he listened. "What about just alerting the police?"

"Tried that. Got the run around. Said they're short-handed tonight. I guess D.C. area security for the President's State of the Union Address has borrowed a lot of their resources. They said they can't afford to run off on a wild goose chase."

"You really think this warning is genuine?"

"I don't know. I just sense something ominous. Would you mind taking time to just drive by and check it out?"

"I guess so. I've got good company. And it's a beautiful night for a ride. What's the address?"

"I'll text it to you. But, Jim, play it safe. If you see something suspicious, call for help! Don't try to be a hero. Stay in touch with me whatever you find."

"Will do. Love ya. You and Mom pray."

Jim tapped the *end* icon on his phone and looked at Greta. "Well, you in the mood for a detour?"

"Was that your father?"

"Yeah. He got some weird text on his phone. Somebody concerned about a warehouse here in Arlington." Jim looked up into the night sky. A few bolder stars shined past the throb of lights from the combined cities of Arlington, Washington, and Alexandria. Greta watched him as he pondered for a moment.

As the couple stood silent at the entrance to the bridge, a Blue Top cab pulled up to the curb in front of them. The driver, a man in his mid-40's, of Middle Eastern descent, rolled down his window and inquired, "You need a ride?"

Jim hesitated. Turning to Greta he said, "Shall we?"

"As long as you stay with me, anywhere you want to go."

Jim nodded to the driver, "Let's go." He read the address from his dad's text to the driver as he slid into the backseat close to Greta. He noticed the light, pleasant fragrance of her perfume and was distracted for a second. He concluded she must have 'freshened up' in the ladies room before they left The Grenadier. Inhaling deeply, Jim cherished the moment but then forced his mind to focus again on the task at hand.

Somewhat puzzled, the driver said, "North Quinn? You sure?"

"Yes. And hurry."

"Okay, but nothing there but warehouses, old buildings, empty lots. What you looking for?"

Jim answered cryptically, "Just a personal matter."

*****

8:25 pm (2:25 am) Amsterdam, Netherlands The electronic signal from the mainframe computer on the sixth floor of the Norse Industries building traversed the Atlantic Ocean in less than five seconds. The dispatchers seated at their desks in the emergency communications center in Washington D.C. noticed nothing unusual on their computer displays—for the moment. Over the next fifteen minutes, however, they would both become slightly uncomfortable with the fact that they had received no 911 calls after 8:25 pm. During the subsequent twelve minutes, they would activate a well-practiced security protocol with both software and hardware checklists and scans. It would be more than 45 minutes later, however, after multiple phone calls to contract IT specialists and department supervisory personnel that the dispatchers at the center would realize they had been the target of a sophisticated cyber-attack.

*****

8:25pm The Blue Top taxi slid to a stop on the icy road in front of the warehouse on North Quinn Street, Arlington, Virginia. A lone security light at the end of the street cast long shadows on the snow covered yard surrounding the building.

"You want I wait?" the cabbie asked as Jim and Greta exited the cab.

"No," Jim answered. "We've got the company number. We'll call when we're ready to leave."

"You ask for, me, Ansar. Okay?"

"Sure. Ansar. Thanks." The taxi pulled away from the curb and made a U-turn at the end of the street before driving off into the night.

Jim took Greta's hand and led her toward the walk-in door at the front of the warehouse. Apart from the background sounds of the city of Arlington, there was silence. The single window of the building front was dark. Unsure of the appropriate next move, Jim looked in the window but saw nothing. He returned to the door and knocked. No answer. "Suggestions?" he asked, looking into Greta's face.

"Call the police?" she wondered.

"Dad tried that. I assume they would need probable cause to go further than just looking and knocking. I'm just not sure…" He sighed and then paced the ground in front of the warehouse as he thought.

Unnoticed, Greta moved over to the door and tried the knob. It turned, and she pushed on it. The metal door gave way with a creak. "How about we just take a look around?" she asked as Jim came over to her.

Jim was incredulous. "How easy was that?"

"Very. Just can't overlook the obvious," she smiled.

He hesitated at the door. "I guess I didn't see any 'no trespassing' signs. We'll take a quick look and be on our way."

"Yes. This is exhilarating," she said.

8:28pm Careful to avoid drawing attention, Jim left the warehouse lights off and pulled out his tiny keychain flashlight. He scanned the cavernous interior of the building: a crude table, a workbench, a pegboard with a collection of mechanics' tools neatly arranged, a bathroom in one corner, a dry erase board fixed to the back wall. "Looks like … a warehouse," Jim said.

"Let's just investigate a little further," Greta urged as she pulled a tiny penlight from her purse.

*****

8:30pm The floor of the House Chamber of the U.S. Congress was filled with a hubbub of obligatory glad-handing and back-slapping as Senators and Representatives wound their way to their seats in preparation for the arrival of the President of the United States. The nine justices of the U.S. Supreme Court were also seated but with more restrained greetings than their legislative colleagues. All of the President's cabinet, save the Secretary of the Interior- the designated survivor- and the Secretary of Transportation, who was trying to survive a bout with the flu, were in attendance. The United States military was amply represented by the combined Joint Chiefs of Staff and their aides.

*****

8:31pm "Look at these," Jim said as he picked up several paint stencils.

"Who would be painting something with markings for AT&T and some plumbing company?" Greta asked almost rhetorically.

"I don't know."

Continuing their clandestine search, Greta moved to the back of the warehouse. She shined her light on the wall. "What's *this?*" She touched the surface of the marker board mounted on the wall with her gloved finger. Her diminutive light slowly swept over a diagram drawn in black on the board.

"Just a minute," Jim said as he held his flashlight in his left hand and flipped through a file folder bulging with papers with his right. "These papers…they're technical bulletins, e-mails, maps, receipts."

"Where'd you find those?"

"In an old filing cabinet," he answered without looking up.

The beam of Greta's light danced around the back corners of the warehouse and came to rest on a nondescript, gray filing cabinet.

"Probably purchased new in 1963," Jim said.

"It was open?" she asked.

"It is *now*. I just used this key," he said pointing his flashlight at a crowbar resting on the crude plywood table.

Taking a deep breath, Greta said, "You're getting into this."

"It's important. There's just something not right here. I feel it." Setting down the file folder, he joined her at the marker board and studied the detailed drawing. Illegible names labeled what appeared to be streets. But in the center, he recognized the outline of the U.S. Capitol Building.

"Quick, help me finish looking through these papers," he said as he strode over to the crude table. They divided the sheaf of papers and rifled through them furiously until Greta let out a low groan.

"What?" Jim asked as he looked at the single sheet now resting in her hand.

She read aloud, "Material Safety Data Sheet- Lethal Nerve Agent Sarin (GB)."

Material Safety Data Sheet - Lethal Nerve Agent Sarin (GB)

Section I. General Information

MANUFACTURER'S NAME: Department of the Army
MANUFACTURER'S ADDRESS:
U.S. Army Chemical and Biological Defense Agency
Edgewood Research, Development and Engineering Center
ATTN: SCBRD-ODR-S
Aberdeen Proving Ground, MD 21010-5423
CAS REGISTRY NUMBER: 107-44-8 or 50642-23-4

CHEMICAL NAME AND SYNONYMS:
Phosphonofluoridic acid,ethyl-isopropyl ester
Phosphonofluoridic acid, methyl-, 1- methylethyl ester

ALTERNATE CHEMICAL NAMES:
Isopropyl methylphosphonofluoridate
Isopropyl ester of methylphosphonofluoridic acid
Methylisoproposfluorophosphine oxide
Isopropyl Methylfluorophosphonate
O-Isopropyl Methylisopropoxfluorophosphine oxide
O-Isopropyl Methylphosphonofluoridate
Methylfluorophosphonic acid, isopropyl ester
Isoproposymethylphosphonyl flouride

TRADE NAME AND SYNONYMS: GB, Sarin , Zarin

Section II: Composition

CHEMICAL FAMILY:
Fluorinated organophosphorous compound
FORMULA:
INGREDIENTS NAME: GB
FORMULA: $C_4 H_{10} FO_2$
PERCENTAGE: 100
AIRBORNE EXPOSURE LIMIT (AEL): 0.0001 mg/m3

Section III: Physical Data

BOILING POINT DEG F (DEG C): 316 (158)

VAPOR PRESSURE (mm hg): 2.9 @ 25 DEG C

VAPOR DENSITY (AIR=1): 4.86

SOLUBILITY IN WATER: Complete

SPECIFIC GRAVITY (H20=1): 1.0887 @ 25 DEG C

FREEZING/MELTING POINT: -56 DEG C

LIQUID DENSITY (g/cc): 1.0887 @ 25 DEG C/1.102 @ 20 DEG C

PERCENTAGE VOLATILE BY VOLUME:

22,000 m/m3 @ 25 DEG C, 16,090 m/m3 @ 20 DEG C

APPEARANCE AND ODOR: Colorless liquid. Odorless in pure form.

Section IV: Fire and Explosion Data

FLASH POINT (METHOD USED): Did not flash to 280 DEG F

FLAMMABLE LIMIT: Not applicable

EXTINGUISING MEDIA: Water mist, fog, foam, CO2 - Avoid using extinguishing methods that will cause splashing or spreading of the GB

SPECIAL FIRE FIGHTING PROCEDURES:

GB will react with steam or water to produce toxic & corrosive vapors. All persons not engaged in extinguishing the fire should be evacuated. Fires involving GB should be contained to prevent contamination to uncontrolled areas. When responding to a fire alarm in buildings or areas containing agents, firefighting personnel clothing (without TAP clothing) during chemical agent firefighting and fire rescue operations.

Respiratory protection is required. Positive pressure, full facepiece, NIOSH-approved self- contained breathing apparatus (SCBA) will be worn where there is danger of oxygen deficiency and when directed by the fire chief or chemical accident/incident (CAI) operations officer. In cases where firefighters are responding to a chemical accident/incident for rescue/reconnaissance purposes vice firefighting, they will wear appropriate levels of protective clothing (see Section 8).

UNUSUAL FIRE AND EXPLOSION HAZARDS: Hydrogen may be present.

Section V: Health Hazard Data

AIRBORNE EXPOSURE LIMIT (AEL): The permissible airborne exposure concentration for GB.concentration for GB for an 6 hour workday or a 40 hour work week is an 8 hour time weight average (TWA) of 0.0001 mg/m3. This value is based on the TWA or GB which can be found in "AR 40-8, Occupational Health Guidelines for the Evaluation and Control of Occupational Exposure to Nerve Agents GA, GB, GD, and VX." To date, however, the Occupational Safety and Health Administration (OSHA) has not promulgated a permissible exposure

EFFECTS OF OVEREXPOSURE: It is a lethal anticholinergic agent. Doses which are potentially life threatening may be only slightly larger than those producing minimal effects.

[Route	Form	Effect	Type	Dosage]
ocular	vapor	miosis	ECt50	less than 2 mg-min/m3
inhalation	*vapor*	runny nose	ECt50	less than 2 mg-min/m3
inhalation		severe incapacitation	ICt50	35 mg-min/m3
inhalation	*vapor*	death	LCt50	70 mg-min/m3
percutaneous		liquid	death	LD50	1700 mg/70 kg man

Effective dosages for vapor are estimated for exposure durations of 2-10 minutes.

Symptoms of overexposure may occur within minutes or hours--depending upon dose. They include: miosis (constriction of pupils) and visual effects, headache and pressure sensation, runny nose and nasal congestion, salivation, tightness in the chest, nausea, vomiting, giddiness, anxiety, difficulty in thinking, difficulty sleeping, nightmares, muscle twitches, tremors, weakness, abdominal cramps, diarrhea, involuntary urination and defecation.

With severe exposure symptoms progress to convulsions and respiratory failure. GB is not listed by the International Agency for Research on Cancer (IARC), American Conference of Governmental Industrial Hygienists (ACGIH), Occupational Safety and Health Administration (OSHA), or National Toxicology Program (NTP) as a carcinogen.

EMERGENCY AND FIRST AID PROCEDURES:
INHALATION: Hold breath until respiratory protective mask is donned. If severe signs of agent exposure appear (chest tightens, pupil constriction, incoordination, etc.), immediately administer, in rapid succession, all three Nerve Agent Antidote Kit(s), Mark I injectors (or atropine if directed by the local physician). Injections using the Mark I kit injectors may be repeated at 5 to 20 minute intervals if signs and symptoms are progressing until three series of injections have been administered. No more injections will be given unless directed by medical personnel. In addition, a record will be maintained of all injections given. If breathing has stopped, give artificial respiration. Mouth-to-mouth resuscitation should be used when approved mask-bag or oxygen delivery systems are not available. Do not use mouth-to-mouth resuscitation when facial contamination exists. If breathing is difficult, administer oxygen. Seek medical attention *IMMEDIATELY.*
EYE CONTACT: Immediately flush eyes with water for 10-15 minutes, then don respiratory protective mask. Although miosis (pinpointing of the pupils) may be an early sign of agent exposure, an injection will not be administered when miosis is the only sign present. Instead, the individual will be taken IMMEDIATELY to the medical treatment facility for observation.
SKIN CONTACT: Don respiratory protective mask and remove contaminated clothing. Immediately wash contaminated skin with copious amounts of soap and water, 10% sodium carbonate solution, or 5% liquid household bleach. Rinse well with water to remove decontaminant. Administer an intramuscular injection with the MARK I Kit injectors only if local sweating and muscular twitching symptoms are observed. Seek medical attention *IMMEDIATELY.*
INGESTION: Do not induce vomiting. First symptoms are likely to be gastrointestinal. Immediately administer an intramuscular injection of the MARK I kit auto-injectors. Seek medical attention IMMEDIATELY.

246 † The Jäger Journal

Section VI: Reactivity Data

STABILITY: Stable when pure.

INCOMPATIBILITY: Attacks tin, magnesium, cadmium plated steel, some aluminums. Slight attack on copper, brass, lead, practically no attack on 1020 steel, Inconel & K-monel.

Hydrolyzes to form HF under acid conditions and isopropyl alcohol & polymers under basic conditions.

Section VII: Spill, Leak, and Disposal Procedures

STEPS TO BE TAKEN IN CASE MATERIAL IS RELEASED OR SPILLED: If leak or spills occur, only personnel in full protective clothing (see section 8) will remain in area. In case of personnel contamination see section V "Emergency and First Aid Instructions."

RECOMMENDED FIELD PROCEDURES:

Spills must be contained by covering with vermiculite, diatomaceous earth clay, fine sand, sponges, and paper or cloth towels. Decontaminate with copious amounts of aqueous Sodium Hydroxide solution (a minimum 10 wt percent). Scoop up all material and place in a fully removable head drum with a high density polyethylene liner. Cover the contents of the drum with decontaminating solution as above before affixing the drum head.

After sealing the head, the exterior of the drum shall be decontaminated and then labeled IAW EPA and DOT regulations. All leaking containers shall be over-packed with vermiculite placed between the interior and exterior containers. Decontaminate and label IAW EPA and DOT regulations. Dispose of the material IAW waste disposal methods provided below. Dispose of material used to decontaminate exterior of drum IAW Federal, state and local regulations. Conduct general area monitoring with an approved monitor (see Section 8) to confirm that the atmospheric concentrations do not exceed the airborne exposure limit (see Sections 2 and 8).

If 10 wt. percent aqueous Sodium Hydroxide solution is not available then the following decontaminants may be used instead and are listed in the order of preference: Decontamination Solution No. 2 (DS2), Sodium Carbonate, and Supertropical Bleach Slurry (STB).

RECOMMENDED LABORATORY PROCEDURES:

A minimum of 56 grams of decon solution is required for each gram of GB. Decontaminant/agent solution is allowed to agitate for a minimum of one hour. Agitation is not necessary following the first hour. At the end of the one hour, the resulting solution should be adjusted to a pH greater than 11.5. If the pH is below 11.5, NaOH should be added until a pH above 11.5 can be maintained for 60 minutes.

An alternate solution for the decontamination of GB is 10 wt percent Sodium Carbonate in place of the 10 percent Sodium Hydroxide solution above. Continue with 56 grams of decon to 1 gram of agent. Agitate for one hour but allow three (3) hours for the reaction. The final pH should be adjusted to above 10. It is also permitted to substitute 5.25% Sodium Hypochlorite or 25 wt percent Monoethylamine (MEA) for the 10% Sodium Hydroxide solution above. MEA must be completely dissolved in water prior to addition of the agent. Continue with 56 grams of decon for each gram of GB and provide agitation for one hour. Continue with same ratios and time stipulations.

Scoop up all material and place in a fully removable head drum with a high density polyethylene liner. Cover the contents of the drum with decontaminating solution as above before affixing the drum head. After sealing the head, the exterior of the drum shall be decontaminated and then labeled IAW EPA and DOT regulations. All leaking containers shall be over-packed with vermiculite placed between the interior and exterior containers. Decontaminate and label IAW EPA and DOT regulations. Dispose of the material IAW waste disposal methods provided below. Dispose of material used to decontaminate exterior of drum IAW Federal, state and local regulations. Conduct general area monitoring with an approved monitor (see Section 8) to confirm that the atmospheric concentrations do not exceed the airborne exposure limit (see Sections 2 and 8).

WASTE DISPOSAL METHOD: Open pit burning or burying of GB or items containing or contaminated with GB in any quantity is prohibited. The detoxified GB using procedures above can be thermally destroyed by incineration in an EPA approved incinerator in accordance with appropriate provisions of Federal, state and local RCRA regulations

Section VIII: Special Protection Information
RESPIRATORY PROTECTION:

[*Concentration   Respiratory Protective Equipment*]

- less than0.0001 mg/m3   A full face piece, chemical canister, air purifying protective mask will be on hand for escape.(The M9-, or M40-series masks are acceptable for this purpose).
- 0.0001 to 0.2 mg/m3   A NIOSH/MSHA approved pressure demand full face piece SCBA or supplied air respirator with escape air cylinder may be used. Alternatively, a full face-piece, chemical canister air purifying protective mask is acceptable for this purpose (for example, M9-, M17-, or M40-series mask or other mask certified as equivalent) is acceptable. (See DA PAM 385-61 for determination of appropriate level)
- greater than 0.2 mg/m3 or unknown   NIOSH/MSHA approved pressure demand full face-piece SCBA suitable for use in high agent concentrations with protective ensemble (see DA PAM 385-61 for examples).

VENTILATION: Local exhaust: Mandatory must be filtered or scrubbed to limit exit concentration to less than 0.0001 mg/m3 averaged over 8 hr/day indefinitely. Air emissions shall meet local, state and federal regulations.
SPECIAL: Chemical laboratory hoods shall have an average inward face velocity of 100 linear feet per minute (1fpm) plus or minus 10% with the velocity at any point not deviating from the average face velocity by more than 20%. Existing laboratory

hoods shall have an inward face velocity of 150 1fpm plus or minus 20 percent. Laboratory hoods shall be located such that cross drafts do not exceed 20 percent of the inward face velocity. A visual performance test utilizing smoke producing devices shall be performed in the assessment of the hood's ability to contain agent GB. Emergency backup power necessary. Hoods should be tested semi-annually or after modification or maintenance operations. Operations should be performed 20 cm inside hood face.

OTHER: Recirculation of exhaust air from agent areas is prohibited. No connection is allowed between agent areas and other areas through ventilation system.

PROTECTIVE GLOVES: Butyl Glove M3 and M4, Norton, Chemical Protective Glove Set

EYE PROTECTION: Chemical goggles. For splash hazards use goggles and face-shield.

OTHER PROTECTIVE EQUIPMENT: For general lab work, gloves and lab coat shall be worn with M9, M17 or M40 mask readily available.

MONITORING:

Available monitoring equipment for agent GB is the M8/M9 Detector paper, detector ticket, blue band tube, M256/M256A1 kits, bubbler, Depot Area Air Monitoring System (DAAMS), Automatic Continuous Air Monitoring System (ACAMS), real time monitoring (RTM), Demilitarization Chemical Agent Concentrator (DCAC), M8/M43, M8A1/M43A2, Hydrogen Flame Photometric Emission Detector (HYPED), CAM-M1, Miniature Chemical Agent Monitor (MINICAM) and the Real Time Analytical Platform (RTAP).

Real-time, low-level monitors (with alarm) are required for GB operations. In their absence, an IDLH atmosphere must be presumed. Laboratory operations conducted in appropriately maintained and alarmed engineering controls require only periodic low-level monitoring.

Section IX: Special Precautions

PRECAUTIONS TO BE TAKEN IN HANDLING AND STORING: In handling, the buddy system will be incorporated. No smoking, eating and drinking in areas containing agent is permitted. Containers should be periodically inspected for leaks (either visually or by a detector kit). Stringent control over all personnel practices must be exercised. Decontamination equip shall be conveniently located. Exits must be designed to permit rapid evacuation. Chemical showers, eye-wash stations, and personal cleanliness facilities must be provided. Wash hands before meals and each worker will shower thoroughly with special attention given to hair, face, neck, and hands, using plenty of soap before leaving at the end of the work day.

OTHER PRECAUTIONS: Agents must be double contained in liquid and vapor tight containers when in storage or when outside of ventilation hood.

For additional information see "AR 385-61, The Army Toxic Chemical Agent Safety Program'" "DA PAM 385-61, Toxic Chemical Agent Safety Standards," and "AR 40-8, Occupational Health Guidelines for the Evaluation and Control of Occupational Exposure to Nerve Agents GA, GB, GD, and VX."

Section X: Transportation Data

PROPER SHIPPING NAME: Poisonous liquids, n.o.s.

DOT HAZARD CLASSIFICATION: 6.1 Packing Group I Hazard Zone A

DOT LABEL: Poison

DOT MARKING: Poisonous liquid, n.o.s. (Isopropyl methylphosphonofluoridate) UN2810

DOT PLACARD: Poison

PRECAUTIONS TO BE TAKEN IN TRANSPORTATION: Motor vehicles will be placarded regardless of quantity. Driver shall be given full and complete information regarding shipment and conditions in case of emergency.

AR 50-6 deals specifically with the shipment of chemical agents. Shipments of agent will be escorted in accordance with AR 740-32. EMERGENCY ACCIDENT PRECAUTIONS AND PROCEDURES: See sections IV, VII, and VIII.

"Dear Lord…" he prayed aloud as he simultaneously pulled out his cell phone and said to Greta, "You know what this means?"

At that instant, the large door at the front of the building rose with its rollers groaning, and the overhead lights switched on automatically.

"Side door!" Jim ordered as he pushed Greta toward the exit. An AT&T service van pulled onto the warehouse floor. Greta flung open the side door of the warehouse and ran straight into the black muzzle of an MP5K submachine gun.

"Put your hands where I can see them," the sharp voice of Curtis Ballinger commanded. Jim and Greta both raised their hands and slowly backed away from the MP5. Mitchell Fluke turned off the van's engine and exited the driver's seat as the warehouse front door descended once more.

"Give me that!" Ballinger said, taking the cell phone from Jim's left hand. "I told you those were fresh prints in the snow," Ballinger said to Fluke.

"Tie them up," Fluke instructed.

"Why not just kill them?"

"Just do as you're told. We'll keep them 'til Riddell gets back. Who knows, we may need a hostage or some entertainment," he said, eyeing Greta.

"Right," Ballinger answered with a smile as he set his weapon on the table. He jerked two short lengths of rope from a bin next to the workbench. Fluke kept his own MP5 pointed at Jim.

"Reading other people's mail are we?" Ballinger remarked as he noticed the loose papers on the table.

"What are you planning to do, gas the Capitol?" Jim asked.

"Shut him up!" Fluke shouted.

Ballinger finished tying Jim's hands behind his back and pushed him to the floor. Grabbing an oily rag from a pile against one wall, he gagged Jim. Just then, Jim's cell phone rang. "Don't answer that," Fluke said.

"You think I'm stupid?" Ballinger responded.

"Don't answer that," Greta chimed in, with a bravado she didn't really feel.

Spinning around, Ballinger slammed his fist into Greta's mouth, instantly drawing a stream blood. Jim grimaced and grunted, unable to defend her.

*****

8:35pm Eric Riddell sat behind the wheel of the American Plumbing and Sewage tanker truck as it rolled across the Potomac River. He crossed on the Theodore Roosevelt Memorial Bridge leaving Arlington, Virginia headed for Washington D.C. Close behind, Thomas Kopf followed in the fake American Plumbing service van.

*****

8:49pm A convoy of five black sedans departed the White House and proceeded down Pennsylvania Avenue. In the clearing night sky, two Blackhawk helicopters carried Secret Service snipers providing overwatch for the short trip to the Capitol Building.

*****

9:03pm The lights in the warehouse on North Quinn suddenly went out. Ballinger and Fluke both stood from their folding metal chairs. "Power outage?" Ballinger asked.

"No. Street lights still on." He scanned the inside of the building. "Either of you move, and you're dead," he said to his prisoners.

"That's not very nice," a new voice said.

"Who's there?" Ballinger queried.

As the attention of the two captors was diverted, Jim scooted around in the dark placing his hands next to Greta's. She had been tied and gagged in the same fashion as Jim and seated on the concrete floor beside him. Unable to see, Jim feverishly pulled at the knot which secured her hands behind her back.

"Put down the guns, boys. Cops are on the way," the stranger continued.

A muzzle flashed twice as shots exploded from Ballinger's gun and pierced the warehouse front door. "Stop it," Fluke ordered.

Fluke then spoke to the intruder he couldn't see. "Just come over here with your hands up, friend, and we won't hurt you." Whispering in German to Ballinger, he said, "Slide around the left side and get behind him. I'll cover you from here."

Ballinger moved to the left and advanced in the darkness toward the front of the building. A soft thud sounded as the newcomer tossed a bolt onto the warehouse floor. Ballinger fired blindly in the general direction of the sound. The three-round burst struck the far wall of the building. But a single pistol shot to his abdomen felled Ballinger. Fluke ducked behind the plywood table and immediately fired his MP5 at the muzzle flash from the stranger's gun. No response. He sprayed the far end of the warehouse, emptying the machine gun clip. The loud staccato of the fire was deafening to those who remained alive in the building.

Placing a fresh clip in his gun, Fluke stood. "Well now. Are you ready to be more sensible?" he asked, expecting no response. "You've got a pistol, and I've got a machine gun."

"AHHH!" a women's voice yelled as Fluke's skull crumbled under a sharp blow from behind. "And I've got a crow bar!"

Fluke never knew what or who hit him. Greta let the bar fall from her hand. A hollow clanging echoed through the building as the tool bounced on the concrete.

"Who's there?... Please help us," she said as Jim, still tied and gagged, grunted. He had succeeded in loosening her hands just enough to effect her release. She had stood silently, removed the gag from her mouth, slipped over to the table, found the crowbar, and connected the heavy metal with Fluke's cranium.

Shuffling in the still darkened warehouse, she found Jim still seated on the floor. They both concluded their rescuer had been riddled by Flukes bullets. Greta quickly released Jim's gag and set to work untying his hands. She gasped as a strong hand gripped her shoulder. "Nice job, little lady."

29 The Address

9:00pm As the President stepped to the podium, applause thundered throughout the chamber. The Speaker of the House and the Vice President stood behind him, smiling as they clapped. Raising his hands, the President motioned for the applause to cease and the crowd to be seated.

Kirk Halstead, chief of the President's Secret Service detail, stood just off the platform against the wall of the chamber. He slowly scanned the audience. A dozen of his men were strategically positioned around the House chamber, each in radio contact with Halstead. They were as unobtrusive as agents in suits and ties with ear buds and wires could be. Each had a personal side arm, loaded, with a round in the chamber.

Five minutes into the President's speech, after three applause interruptions, Halstead had a throbbing headache. He was satisfied that everything was going as well as could be expected. But he knew his pain would not ease until this annual Presidential foray into a sea of faces, bodies, and cameras was over. He would be able to breathe normally again only after the President had left the chamber and retreated to the safety of his bullet-proof, bomb-proof limousine, affectionately referred to by the Secret Service as "The Beast."

What Halstead didn't know was the grave threat moving inexorably nearer to the Capitol building.

*****

9:07pm The American Plumbing and Sewage tanker pulled up to the first roadblock at the perimeter of the Capitol security cordon. Officer Mike Wert motioned for the driver to roll down the window. "State your business," he said to Riddell.

"You guys called us! I was just getting into the Celtics/Knicks game and you dragged me away. We're here to clear the sewerage lines for all your VIPs." Riddell played the role of the inconvenienced blue collar worker with finesse.

"Let's see your I.D.," Wert requested. "You know the drill." Riddell handed the officer the stolen Federal I.D. badge. The photo was small and resembled a bad driver's license picture. At that moment Wert's radio crackled. The Capitol maintenance supervisor's systolic blood pressure was in the stratosphere and he wanted some relief. "Wert, the President is already into his speech, and in about thirty minutes, more than 600 prima donnas are gonna pour out of that chamber looking for a bathroom. Do you get my drift?"

"Yeah, I get your drift. The tanker is here, and we're checking him out," Wert answered. "Just a few minutes and they'll be on it."

McDougal lapsed into profane diction in an effort to move the process along. "We called these plumbing guys ourselves, Wert. Listen, if this thing's still messed up when the speech is over, you're out there on the limb by yourself. *Now expedite!*"

Though the temperature had fallen to 18 degrees Fahrenheit and snow was falling again, Wert felt beads of sweat on his forehead. He called over a canine team to give the tanker and the service van a once over. Although he was a *by the book* kind of guy, he was in a genuine bind for time. He had no illusions that McDougal was bluffing about pointing the finger of blame in his direction should the Capitol toilet system remain out of service.

Wert and two colleagues searched the vehicles inside and out and found nothing. "Open the top of the tank," Wert ordered. Riddell grimaced slightly.

"You sure?" he asked. "You ain't gonna like it. There's some of the 'product' in the bottom of the tank. Didn't have time to dump it."

"Open it!"

Riddell obeyed, removing the circular cap on the forward most part of the tank. The Balder technicians had done a masterful job creating a false front compartment for just this eventuality. And a generous portion of the foul 'product' had been pumped into the compartment. Wert shined his flashlight down the hole into the compartment. The stench convinced him that the tanker was genuine. "Shut it!"

"Alright. Drive on." Wert depressed the large black button on a console just inside his guard hut. The large steel teeth of the roadblock slowly lowered and disappeared in depressions in the pavement. Wert motioned the two vehicles forward but sent two of his team with them to observe the work of the "plumbers."

*****

9:08pm "Washington! Thank God for you," Jim said. "What in the world are you doing here?"

Washington turned on a pocket flashlight, illuminating Jim, then Greta, and, finally, his own smiling face. He explained his arrival as he spelled Greta at her effort at untying Jim's hands. "I tried to call your cell phone just to chat, you know, catch up. Didn't get an answer. So, I called your home. Your dad told me about that strange text he got. He was pretty worried about you. Said he wished he hadn't got you involved. When I told him I was in the D.C. area on Army business, he asked if I could possibly check on you. Told 'im I'd be glad to. Drove here to the warehouse address and started nosing around. I peeked in through the window, and what do I see but my old buddy Jim Harrison trussed up like a pig ready for the barbeque pit... There you go," he said as he released Jim's hands from behind his back.

"What about the cops? Are they really on the way?" Jim asked as he stood.

"No, just a bluff. I called 911, but that system's down for some reason. Tried the regular operator and got a busy signal. I don't know what's goin' on with the phones."

"Okay, whatever. But you've got wheels?" Jim's tone was desperate. "We've got to get to the Capitol, now!" Jim said.

"No problem. Got a new ride a few months ago. Just follow me," he said as he led the way to the side door.

"I'll fill you in as we go." Outside the darkened building, Jim breathed a whisper of thanks as they rushed toward the rugged outline of Washington's vehicle — a white 2008 Hummer H2. Washington had the 6.2-liter V8 engine roaring before Jim and Greta could get their seat belts fastened. He backed the Hummer deftly into a driveway across the street and immediately turned the massive SUV in the direction of U.S. 50, which would take them across the Potomac into downtown D.C.

*****

9:13 pm The tanker from American Plumbing backed up to the maintenance service entrance of the Capitol building. Kopf parked the service van close by. Maintenance specialist

Chandra Rahman met the trucks at the door to assist with the task at hand.

*****

9:15 pm Agent Halstead studied the audience in the gallery of the House chamber. They were again on their feet clapping and cheering the President. The President continued, "With the dawning of my administration, the era of dependency is over. The era of responsibility has begun. This country has magnificent days ahead. Each of us will contribute to prosperity and greatness by giving our best. Healthy competition will be encouraged. Ingenuity and creativity will be rewarded. We will inspire our children and grandchildren to dream again!"

*****

9:16pm Riddell spoke with Rahman about the occluded Capitol sewage system. One of the two Capitol policemen stood by, impassively watching the scene unfold. Although Riddell and Rahman had never met, they had communicated by phone and rehearsed the interaction now taking place. Kopf, outside in the now heavily falling snow, busied himself with the controls of the tanker. The second policeman watched, pretending to comprehend the maze of pipes and valves of the tanker. Rahman and Riddell walked over to the rear of the tanker and unwound the coil of large bore hose normally used to suction sewage. Tonight, however, the hose would channel Sarin gas into the ventilation system. It would take less than 45 seconds to fill the House chamber with enough of the colorless, odorless, tasteless gas to kill every man and woman present. In a moment, the chamber would reverberate with a cacophony of retching, gasping, and choking. And then …there would be silence.

Contingencies for the safety and security of the President had been meticulously prepared and practiced by the Secret Service and ancillary personnel countless times. Atropine autojectors were ready for emergency use by the President's aides should a nerve gas agent such as Sarin ever be used in an attack. But the plans envisioned by the President's guardians were for a response to a chemical strike by bomb or shell, not a silent attack through the ventilation system of a U.S. government building.

*****

9:20pm "Just show me the access point to the sewer system. We'll take it from there," Riddell instructed Rahman.

"Sure," the Bengali answered.

Riddell, dragging the end of the hose by a sturdy handle, followed Rahman down a short corridor. The curious policeman trailed the pair. Rahman opened a large door and let Riddell enter the room. "Hey, can you look at his?" he asked the policeman.

"Okay," he answered.

Riddell leaned over a floor panel and said, "What do you make of this?"

The officer leaned forward slightly. Rahman approached from behind and fired a single silenced round into the base of the man's head. With a feeble groan he slumped to the floor, and Riddell slid his body against the wall. Rahman and Riddell stepped out into the corridor and Rahman shut the door. The men moved quickly down the hallway to another door. This door, emblazoned with a large *Authorized Personnel Only* sign, led to the heart of the ventilation system. Rahman had secretly scored a circle in the sheet metal of the panel the day before. He now punched out a hole that was almost a perfect fit for the rigid end of the hose. He secured the hose to the panel with two large, self-tapping screws and sealed the circle with duct tape. Nodding to Riddell he said, "Okay."

9:21pm Outside, Kopf watched the numbers rise on the tanker's digital thermometer. He estimated the temperature would be adequate for vaporization of the Sarin gas in six minutes.

*****

9:22pm The Hummer flew across the bridge spanning the Potomac River. Washington had received only two speeding tickets in his life, but he was in emergency mode now and didn't really care. He would lead a whole cadre of squad cars to the Capitol grounds if necessary. Jim's narrative of their findings in the warehouse had convinced him that someone was committed to using Sarin gas to kill the President and the entire leadership of the Federal government during the State of the Union address. The shootout with Fluke and Ballinger had simply underscored the determination of the conspirators.

Jim and Greta both tried to reach someone in authority with their cell phones. It was useless. Cell coverage was fading in and out the closer they got to the Capitol, and the 911 system was still unresponsive. "What are we gonna do when we get there, Washington?"

"I don't know. Just pray for direction." And Jim did.

9:24pm The Hummer skidded to a halt at the first security barricade at the perimeter of the Capitol cordon. Sergeant Gabriel Washington rolled down his window and shouted, "The President, they're gonna kill the President! The tanker truck!" Washington pointed at the American Plumbing tanker sitting at the service entrance of the Capitol.

Wert barked, "Slow down. What are you saying? We called those guys. They're here at our invitation."

"They're gonna gas the House chamber. Kill everybody in there!"

Wert was skeptical. He slid his hand to his holster and gripped his pistol. "Let's see some I.D., Mister." Wert spoke into his radio mike and asked for backup. "I've got a possible threat here," he said.

"There's no time. You gotta stop 'em now!" Washington was out of patience.

Wert wasn't sure he had heard Washington clearly over the noise of the idling Hummer engine, but he wasn't taking any chances. "I'm going to have to ask you to get out of the car. Keep your hands where I can see them."

Washington's instincts took over. His career, his freedom, and his life were on the line. But, as a decorated combat veteran of two tours in Iraq and one in Afghanistan, his experience and God-given boldness forced him to act. With his most servile tone, he responded, "Yes." But with a lightning snap of his left hand, he pulled on the driver door latch and kicked the door open with a massive burst from his sturdy left leg. The door caught Wert and knocked him backward through the open door of the hut. Striking the back wall of the enclosure, he was momentarily stunned and slid to the floor. Washington took one step into the hut, slammed his fist on the black control button, and jumped back into his Hummer. With a firm grip on the wheel, Washington yelled at Jim and Greta, "Get down!" The vehicle roared ahead and banged over the still lowering steel teeth of the roadblock.

*****

9:24pm Riddell joined Kopf at the side of the tanker. He spoke to the Capitol policeman shadowing Kopf, "The other officer asked to see you inside."

"Okay, sure. Back in a minute." The officer stepped through the door into the Capitol building looking for his partner. He failed to notice the figure hugging the wall to his left. A soft report from Rahman's pistol preceded the pain in the officer's left flank just before he lost consciousness from massive blood loss from a shattered spleen. Rahman pulled the man's body a few feet to a side room and shut the door. Jerking a rag from his pocket, he made a hasty attempt to erase the blood trail. He hoped there would be no further interruptions to the night's work. It was time to join his colleagues outside at the tanker.

*****

9:25pm Washington pushed the accelerator to the floor. The Hummer lurched forward, smashing the wooden bar of the temporary checkpoint barrier into splinters. Wert, now back in commission, jerked his SIG Sauer from its holster, simultaneously yelling into his shoulder mike, "Yankee black! Yankee black! Checkpoint Bravo, east entrance."

Wert's ear piece came alive. The strained voice of the Capitol police captain responded, "Confirm, Yankee black?"

Wert yelled back, "Roger, confirmed, a white Humvee just crashed through our checkpoint, two, maybe three tangos on board."

"Roger," the captain acknowledged. "All rovers, close now!" he ordered the roving patrols distributed over the Capitol grounds to converge on the threat point at the east side of the Capitol building. "All checkpoints hold position. Be alert for follow-on threats."

*****

9:25pm Inside the House chamber, Kirk Halstead heard the radio chatter and ordered his men in the chamber to move to seal all entrances. "Nobody in or out until I say so." He was imagining the scene outside and weighing his response options. The chief concern was the President's safety, but he dreaded the thought of interrupting the President's televised address in front of a worldwide audience of millions, especially if it were just some drunk who had accidentally crashed a police barricade.

*****

9:25pm Rahman, Riddell, and Kopf all looked up at the same time. The white Humvee caromed off a concrete barrier as it crashed beyond the barricade and kept going like a fullback churning through a line of defenders. In disbelief, the trio of assassins watched the Hummer break through a second checkpoint and careen toward them. The SUV then accelerated, the growling of its engine amplified by the frigid night air.

"Shoot him!" Riddell ordered Rahman. The Bengali fired his pistol three times. The first bullet missed. But the two subsequent shots pierced the windshield of the Hummer. One of these rounds smashed into Washington's left shoulder and exited his body, lodging in the seat back. He slumped to the right, grasping his bloody left shoulder with his right hand. Simultaneously, he slammed on the brakes slewing the Hummer toward the tanker.

Kopf and Riddell stood beside the tanker momentarily transfixed by the Hummer's black brush guard which seemed to grow larger by the second. Realizing the Hummer was not going to stop, Kopf jumped to the side, pushing his boss directly into the path of the SUV. Riddell screamed as the brush guard smashed his body into the metal of the tanker's side, crushing his pelvis.

Through the confusion, Wert heard the report on his radio, "Shots fired!" Capitol police, Homeland security agents, and Secret Service personnel converged on the Humvee from all directions.

As Rahman reloaded his pistol, Kopf, ignoring the cries of his leader, pulled on the lever of the tanker's pump valve. But the lever, which would have released the Sarin gas into the hose, would not budge. The brush guard of the SUV had not only pinned Riddell, but had also wedged against the control mechanism of the tanker's pump. The lever was jammed in the *off* position. Kopf shouted to Rahman, "Move it now," as he pointed at the white SUV. Shots now popped the body of the Humvee from multiple directions as Capitol police and Federal agents sought to neutralize the perceived threat of the vehicle.

Inside the Hummer, Jim took the Glock 9-mm Washington handed him and rolled out of the passenger door onto the icy pavement. At the same instant, Rahman jerked open the driver door, pulled Washington out, and jumped in. He wrenched the transmission into reverse and mashed down the accelerator. The Hummer lurched away from the tanker, freeing the valve lever.

Kopf smiled as he grabbed the round knob at the end of the lever. But before he could activate the valve, he felt an excruciating pain at the back of his neck. Then, he collapsed into unconsciousness. Jim had delivered a covert knockout blow with the butt of Washington's Glock.

Jim took a breath and moved to assist Washington who lay on the cold ground in a heap. Rahman, still at the wheel of the Hummer, spun the SUV in a circle, unsure of his next move. He decided to take two more infidels out of the world before he went on to paradise. Rolling down the window, he pointed his pistol at Jim who knelt beside his friend. Rahman pulled the trigger, but the shot went high and wide. His aim had been ruined by the jerk of the tightening band now encircling his neck. Greta, still in the back seat, tightened the shoulder strap of her purse around Rahman's throat. He pawed futilely at the garrote until his mind faded into oblivion. The SUV came to a halt, but the engine continued to idle. Greta crouched in the backseat and wept as the friendly fire continued.

Convinced the shots would soon kill them all, Jim dropped the Glock, stood, raised his hands high in the air, and shouted, "It's over, it's over." Walking towards the contracting ring of agents, Jim kept his hands high and said, "Please, help my friend."

One of the agents nearest Jim shouted, "Get on the ground. Do it now!"

Jim obediently placed his right knee on the ground. Seeing Jim's response, Officer Wert shouted into his radio mike, "Cease fire, cease fire!"

But a single agent, a sniper, perched high on the Rayburn House Office Building, did not hear the order and did not correctly interpret Jim's posture. He would later testify he saw a gun in Jim's hand and interpreted his move as a shift into a crouched firing stance. His .223-caliber bullet hit Jim high on the left chest just below his collar bone, rupturing his left subclavian artery and vein. Falling to the wet ground, Jim said again, "It's over."

Officer Wert screamed a *cease all fire* order into the mike and this time received a response from the sniper, "Copy that."

The Capitol security men rushed in toward Jim and the motionless Humvee and pulled the weeping Greta from the back seat. Forcing her to spread eagle against the side of the vehicle, a female agent searched her for weapons. A dozen others secured the area around the tanker and the service truck and searched the dead and injured scattered on the ground.

Washington, still holding his bleeding shoulder, grunted, "Friendlies, we're friendlies. The tanker is filled with Sarin. We had to keep 'em from killin' the President."

*****

9:32pm "Talk to me! What's the situation out there, Wert?" Halstead whispered hard into his mike. He had just shed five years of longevity waiting to hear a report from Capitol grounds security.

"All clear, all clear. Three tangos and two friendlies down. Perimeter secure."

The President began his closing remarks, blessedly ignorant of the drama unfolding around him. "I would like to close with a tribute to the many men and women who have given their lives that others might live... in freedom. Those incomparable individuals who wear the uniforms of our country. Our soldiers, sailors, airmen, marines, and coastguardsmen. Our police and fire fighters. These are the citizens of this great land who deserve your applause and gratitude." The chamber erupted one last time with a standing ovation. Halstead even found himself clapping. Ironically, just after sunrise, he would receive a call telling him his little brother, Officer Darryl Halstead, had died in the line of duty on the streets of the capital the night before.

9:34pm Federal agents and Capitol police worked feverishly to restore order and ensure a secure perimeter around the Capitol grounds. Wert escorted Greta to Jim's side. Four ambulances had arrived at Wert's request with lights but no sirens and paramedics were triaging and treating the injured. Greta sat down on the pavement, wet with snow and blood, and cradled Jim's head in her lap. One of the paramedics held pressure on Jim's chest while his younger partner pulled over a gurney and an emergency field bag. Jim's breathing was rapid and shallow. He coughed every few breaths spitting up bright red blood. The first paramedic, a middle-age Asian man shouted, "Gotta move! No radial pulse!"

As the partners quickly but gingerly slipped Jim onto the stretcher and secured the safety straps across his body, Jim mouthed words that had no sound. Greta leaned over him placing her ear against his mouth. "I love you," he whispered.

She squeezed his hand. It felt as cold as the icy ground. "I love you too, Jim Harrison! Please don't leave me. You can't leave me. I need you!" Tears ran down her face as Greta begged the older paramedic, "Please let me ride with you!"

"No way, lady. No room." Before Greta could compose a further appeal, the stretcher was lifted into the back of the ambulance, and the younger paramedic thrust a large bore IV needle into Jim's arm. The older paramedic shut the back doors of the ambulance, raced around the side, and took his seat behind the wheel. Greta touched the window of the back door, sobbing. As the ambulance turned toward the street, the driver side window rolled down and the driver said, "I'm sorry. We'll do our best."

Swirling snow swallowed up Greta's heaving body as she watched the only man she truly trusted carried away in a flurry of red and white lights. The weight of her grief crushed her chest and squeezed her throat. Her sense of abandonment was total.

30 The Vigil

But Greta was *not* alone.   A strong hand gripped her shoulder. It was as if a life guard reached down to her through a black ocean and was pulling her through the suffocating grief to the surface. "He'll be okay. Don't you worry." It was the voice of Sergeant Gabriel Washington. The paramedics had bound his left arm and shoulder with a sling and swath arrangement stanching the bleeding. The .38 caliber slug had torn away a large chunk of deltoid muscle and skin.

"Come on Sergeant," one of the paramedics urged him. "You need that shoulder cleaned up pretty quick."

"Be right with ya." Washington looked Greta in the face. "I don't know which hospital they're taking me to. But I'll find Jim, and when they release me, I'll find you. Once the cops are done with you, catch a taxi to your hotel. And stay put till you hear from me. What's your cell number?" Greta took Washington's cell phone from his good hand and entered her number into the contact list. "Hopefully cell service will be back up soon."

"Please call me as soon as you know anything about Jim. I think I'll be alright." Washington climbed into the back of an ambulance and waved at Greta. She returned the wave, turned, and walked toward a knot of agents standing nearby. "Am I free to leave now?" she asked one.

"Not just yet." The lead agent had Greta follow him to a conference room inside the Capitol building where he and a female agent questioned her for about an hour. They wanted to know everything about the warehouse in Arlington and the operatives. They also reached Agent Roby in Georgia who corroborated Greta's background story. Finally, the female agent took down her phone number and the name of the hotel where she was staying. She advised Greta that someone from the FBI would be in contact with her in the morning. She was also instructed to remain in the D.C. area until further notice.

"Am I being charged with something?" she asked.

"No. But we've got a long way to go on this investigation. You probably have some information that could be useful. We'll be in touch."

Greta was escorted outside and a young agent hailed a taxi for her. He opened the door for Greta and said, "Good night."

Greta said quietly, "Thank you."

"Where to, lady?" the taxi driver asked.

"The Hyatt Regency."

*****

The President had finished his State of the Union Address on time and with a very positive reception by those in the chamber and by Americans watching on television and by live streaming via the internet. The President returned safely to the White House. Agent Kirk Halstead, head of the President's Secret Service detail, received an immediate briefing on the attack. The FBI agent in charge, Agent John Wu, had accurately pieced together the evening's events in very short order. He laid out the scenario and the timeline for Halstead who would later brief the President:

The sewerage system of the Capitol Building had apparently been sabotaged. A call had gone out to the plumbing firm that held the Capitol contract. The contract company had responded immediately, sending a tanker pumper truck. The driver and assistant had been shot and killed by a sniper who remained at large. The telephone land lines and the cell tower servicing the Capitol had been taken down almost simultaneously by conventional explosives and some kind of electromagnetic pulse, respectively. At about the same time, the local 911 system was the target of a cyber-attack. The fake tanker had passed the security barriers around the Capitol after a supposedly thorough but flawed search and moved to the service entrance on the east side of the building. The tanker had been shadowed by two Capitol policemen. They had both been dispatched by gunshot, apparently silenced pistol rounds. The details of their demise were still unclear. The execution of the plot had been interrupted by the timely arrival of an Army sergeant and two friends who crashed through the security barriers and smashed into the tanker, jamming the pump controls. One of the two plumbing operatives had died of internal bleeding resulting from the crush injury between the sergeant's Humvee and the tanker. The other operative had been rendered unconscious by a blow to the head. A confederate from inside the Capitol had been incapacitated by the soldier's female friend who had choked him with the strap of her purse. Both of the surviving operatives were in FBI custody at Medstar Washington Hospital.

"That's a summation of what we know at this time," Wu concluded. "We have a team going over the warehouse in Arlington, Virginia, right now. Two more bad guys-one dead, one with a critical head injury, in surgery as we speak."

"Incredible. The degree of coordination is beyond belief!"

"Agreed," Wu said.

"What about the tanker? Have you confirmed what's in it?" Halstead asked.

"Working on it. We're handling it as if it really does contain Sarin gas. It's a miracle it didn't leak out already. Two bullets from our people struck the tank, but at glancing angles, so they failed to penetrate."

"Is this story still under wraps?" Halstead asked with apprehension.

"Incredibly, yes. All the major news outlets were *inside* the chamber. A few miscellaneous reporters were milling around outside the building, but on the *west* side. We're playing the bedlam on the *east* side as a DUI/MVA."

*****

The assassination plot and near miss decapitation of the United States Federal government were skillfully kept hidden from the media and the public. Rumors of the attempt circulated through D.C. for days. But anyone who showed hints of taking the rumors seriously was written off as a conspiracy fanatic.

*****

11:15pm Greta took the elevator up to her room in the Hyatt Regency. She threw her purse on the bed, kicked off her shoes, and walked into the bathroom. Looking in the mirror, she saw miserable hair and a puffy face. The eyes were red from crying. She undressed and stepped into the shower. The hot water washed over her body but could not comfort her soul. Greta tried desperately to cling to Washington's hope for Jim. But fear gnawed at the edges of her mind.

Stepping out of the shower, Greta dried off and ran a comb through her hair a couple times. Stepping into the bedroom, she took a bottled water from the small room refrigerator and took a long drink. Pulling back the covers, she fell into the bed. Her brain seemed to roll, pitch, and yaw inside her skull. And then, mercifully, she slipped into sleep.

*****

Wednesday morning, January 29, 6:30am Greta was dreaming. In her dream, she was standing at the edge of a giant rock quarry. A rock crusher was across the quarry from her. It was pounding a large boulder over and over. She tried to run away from the quarry and its noise, but her feet were frozen in place. She couldn't move. The unbearable pounding persisted. And then, she came to consciousness and realized there was a tapping on the hotel room door. The room was dark except for a soft green glow from the clock radio on the night stand.

Greta sat up and looked at the clock. She felt her heart pumping in her chest. "Just a minute," she said. Getting out of the bed, she flipped on the light, and slipped a sweat suit out of her suitcase, which sat on the floor. Quickly, Greta pulled on the blue sweat shirt and pants and stepped over to the door. Looking through the peephole, she saw the tall figure of Sergeant Gabriel Washington. A sling enveloped his arm. This was, in turn, snugly bound to his torso with a wide cloth swath. He had been stabilized in the emergency room of George Washington University Medical Center and taken immediately to surgery. The team of general and orthopedic surgeons had carefully cleaned his wound and confirmed what x-rays had suggested- the humerus was intact. A large chunk of the deltoid muscle was gone, but that defect would be more cosmetic than functional. The wound was closed and dressed. The patient was transferred to the recovery room just over 90 minutes after entering the operative suite. He had been given IV antibiotics intraoperatively to prevent infection. Being active duty Army, his tetanus immunization status was up-to-date. IV narcotic analgesics were ordered postop for pain control.

"Washington," she said through the door.

"Sorry to wake ya up."

Greta let Washington in and closed the door behind him. "Where's Jim? How is he?"

Washington, who had been facing the far wall, now turned and faced Greta. She looked at his strong face and was stunned. The tough, seasoned combat veteran could not speak. His lower lip quivered slightly. Tears welled up in the big man's eyes. His chest began to heave, and a primal sob burst from deep within. Greta buried the man's head on her shoulder and asked, "What?"

"He's gone. I'm sorry... He's gone. ," he choked out into her shoulder. "They couldn't save him."

As Washington vented his grief, Greta's mind seemed to hover above the scene, seeing herself and the soldier, but shrouded in numbness. For a long time, the two stood in the room and let the tears flow. And then, Washington wiped his face with the sleeve of his good right arm and sat down in the chair next to the room's desk. The fire fight in the warehouse, the drive to the Capitol, the crash into the tanker, the wound to the shoulder, the hour in the emergency room, the hour and a half in surgery, a night without sleep, and, now, the loss of his friend had taken their toll on the man.

For these two humans who came from two different worlds, time stopped. The middle-aged, black, American soldier and the young, Austrian woman sat in silence. Eventually, the silence was broken by a soft humming. Washington had dipped into the storehouse of music deep in his heart and pulled out a hymn. The humming grew in strength; and then, Washington sang in a mellow baritone voice: "*When peace like a river attendeth my way, when sorrows like sea billows roll, whatever my lot, Thou hast taught me to say, 'It is well, it is well with my soul'.*" It was not the first time the songs of his childhood had applied balm to his soul. It wouldn't be the last.

Greta looked again at Washington's shoulder. "Shouldn't you still be recovering in the hospital?"

"Yeah, probably. When I told the nurse that I was leavin' this morning, she acted like she had a bee in 'er bonnet. She said, 'You can't leave. The doctor hasn't released you yet!' I said, 'You just watch me.' I tried to explain that I had to find my friend. She finally quit fussin' and called the doctor. He musta told the nurse I was crazy, but when he found out I was leavin' one way or the other, he conceded and prescribed some antibiotics and somethin' for pain. I went downstairs to the information desk and had 'em start huntin' for Jim. He wasn't registered as a current patient on any of the floors. I thought maybe they'd taken him to another hospital. They finally found somebody in the emergency room who would talk to me. She told me Jim had passed away last night, but she couldn't give me any details. It was still under investigation and she could only talk further with immediate family."

Greta gasped, "His family. Do they know?"

"I don't know. I didn't call 'em. I think somebody's gotta tell 'em... in person..." Washington's voice trailed off.

*****

January 29, 6:32am Jack and Jean Harrison sat at the small kitchen table nursing cups of coffee. They had tried every possible avenue to get information on Jim and Greta. The disabling of the cell tower and the synchronized cyber-attack from a European source had played havoc with communications in the D.C. area. The Harrisons had slept fitfully and were up early trying the phones again. "I'm sorry. Your call cannot be completed as dialed. Please check the number and try again," the automated recording intoned.

As Jack tried texting Jim for the umpteenth time, the darkness of the Harrison front yard was pierced by a pair of headlights. The car pulled up the driveway and stopped. Two figures emerged and walked slowly but deliberately toward the front door of the house. The doorbell rang. Jack flipped on the porch light and opened the door. The two men were wearing Bibb County sheriff's deputy uniforms.

"Good morning," Jack said, feeling a rush of adrenaline through his chest. "You guys are out early. What can I do for you fellas?"

Both deputies knew Jack Harrison by reputation, but neither had met him personally. Their duty this morning was one that they approached with dread as they spoke with the respected building contractor, husband, father, and grandfather. "Mr. Harrison?" the senior deputy asked.

"Yes, I'm Jack, and this is my wife Jean," Jack answered as his wife joined him at the door.

"Invite them in," Jean admonished

"Of course. You men come in. Cup of coffee?" he offered.

"No sir." Both deputies entered, removing their hats and standing awkwardly in the living room.

"Well, at least sit down," Jean insisted.

"Yes, ma'am," Deputy Jason Robitalle answered, and both deputies took seats on the couch. The tension in the room was thick as the Harrisons anticipated the worst, and Deputy Robitalle struggled with the words that would break the news and the hearts of the Harrisons.

"I'm afraid I have very bad news. Your son Jim was shot and killed in Washington D.C. last evening a little before 10 pm Eastern."

Jack looked squarely at the deputy without flinching. Jean grabbed his left arm and said, "No, there must be some mistake! We talked to him last night. He was fine."

Jack put his arm around Jean's shoulders and said with a strange calm, "Let's hear him out." His gazed still fixed on Robitalle, he said, "Go on."

Robitalle continued. "Your son apparently helped stop a terrorist plot to kill government officials in the Capitol. We don't have any details at this time. I'm giving you all we have. Agents from the FBI will be here to talk to you later in the morning."

Jean began to cry softly as Jack cradled her with both of his big arms. "How did he die?" Jack asked.

"Apparently a gunshot wound. He lived long enough to reach one of the hospitals there. But they told us he had lost too much blood. He slipped into a coma and died shortly after admission to the emergency room." The deputy took in a breath as he fought to maintain a professional demeanor. "I am, we are," Robitalle said, glancing at his partner, "so very sorry."

"Did he suffer?" Jean asked.

"I was told that he didn't struggle but just drifted off like he was going to sleep."

The living room was silent save for the ticking of a grandfather clock in one corner and Jean's crying. "His friends, Greta Rose and Gabriel Washington, are they okay?" Jack asked.

"As far as I know, Mr. Harrison. We were only given the information I've shared. Wish I could tell you more."

"We understand."

The two deputies stood stiffly. Both of them shook Jack's hand. "Let me say again how sorry we are," Robitalle said.

"Thank you. I know this must be difficult for you," Jack said as he let the men out.

The two deputies got back in their cruiser, and Robitalle started the engine. "Difficult for us? The guy's a rock."

"Yeah. That whole scene back there was some kind of unreal," the second deputy commented as they drove back to the Sheriff's office. "It was ... "

"A peace," Robitalle finished his sentence for him.

"Yeah. A peace."

*****

The body of Jim Harrison was returned to Georgia on January 31st aboard Delta flight DL1239. Sergeant Gabriel Washington and Miss Greta Rose were on the same flight. Washington had been granted emergency leave by his battalion commander at Ft. Lee, Virginia.

The flight arrived in Atlanta at 14 minutes before one in the afternoon. The entire Harrison family met the plane at the airport and accompanied the casket to the funeral home in Macon. Arrangements were made for visitation of extended family and friends the following evening. Sgt. Washington kept vigil with the body of his friend through the night and the next day. He refused to leave until the very last couple had paid their respects.

Epilogue

Chandra Rahman and Thomas Kopf recovered from their injuries. They were held without bond in Federal custody on a host of charges including murder and attempted murder.

Curtis Ballinger was pronounced dead at the scene from a bullet wound to the abdomen which pierced his colon and lacerated his liver.

Mitchell Fluke remained in Federal custody with a life threatening cerebral contusion/laceration and comminuted skull fracture. He would remain in physical, speech, and occupational therapy for months and would have residual disabilities for the rest of his life. That life would be spent in the Supermax Federal Penitentiary at Florence, Colorado.

Eric Riddell succumbed during surgery at Medstar Washington Hospital Center from massive internal organ damage and multiple pelvic fractures.

Walter Dyson and Zygmunt Swift disappeared without a trace. An AT&T van was found abandoned in a Wal-Mart parking lot in Arlington, Virginia. Information about both of the men was extracted from Thomas Kopf during extensive questioning by Federal agents. Warrants for their arrest remain outstanding.

FBI, ATF, and homeland security agents raided the large industrial complex of Balder Chemical Corporation outside Houston, Texas. Agents remarked that the site resembled the abandoned city of Chernobyl. The site had been hastily evacuated and stripped of any useful papers or computer data. Residues of the nerve agent Sarin were later discovered in several containers.

*****

Eighteen months later the Harrison family and a host of friends gathered at Faith Bible Church on the first Saturday evening in July. The occasion was the wedding of Greta Rose and Glen Harrison. The seed of the relationship had been planted as the family had waded through the river of grief after Jim died. Greta felt the loss of her friend was beyond what she could bear. But the love poured out on the family by their network of friends in Macon and around the country had carried them through. Greta had been the beneficiary of the spillover of that shared compassion.

At first, Greta and Glen spent time together just in the larger family setting — the visitation, the funeral, meals, and later in the spring, a family weekend at Lake Sinclair. As the months passed, however, Glen and Greta began to text and talk by phone. Glen made several trips back to Georgia, ostensibly to comfort and encourage his parents. Jean Harrison sensed, however, that their solace was not the only motivation for his return home. She began to see flickers of genuine joy in her son's face. But Jean was careful to caution Glen about nurturing a romantic bond with a woman who didn't yet share his faith.

What Jean didn't know was how very close Greta was to embracing Jesus Christ as her personal Savior and the Lord of her life. Greta's journey of faith had actually been accelerated by a sharp challenge thrown down by Washington on a visit to see the Harrisons over the first Easter weekend after Jim's death. Greta's mood was somber, her smiles forced. She rarely joined in the lively family conversations. The family, Greta, and Washington had gone to church together that Easter morning and gathered at the Harrisons afterward for dinner. All of the family had pitched in. Annette and Michelle had helped Jean cook ham, scalloped potatoes, green bean casserole, and Jell-O salad. Leigh brought pecan pie and chocolate cake for dessert.

Greta picked at her food and had seemed quite distant. After the meal, Washington asked Greta to join him outside on the back porch. She agreed, curious what he wanted.

Washington had Greta sit in one of the patio chairs. Standing facing the young woman, he got right to the point. "Miss Greta, I'm gonna be straight with you. Everybody else around here is kind and patient and gentle. But, lady, it's time to fish or cut bait. You're grieving over Jim. Well, we are to. But life goes on. Jim's in heaven. He would want to see you there too. It's been three months, and you're stuck in this great big swamp of despair. You're always down in the mouth. You hardly talk to anybody. You're here, but you're not really here. You're making everybody around you miserable. You have been comforted, cuddled, and encouraged by this loving family. They've put up with your whining and your long face. They've done everything possible to help you come to know the truth. Well, they can't do this for you, and neither can I. You can stay sad and hopeless and lost. Or you can come to Jesus and finally find forgiveness and meaning for your life. It's your choice. I'm tellin' you, you're missing out on livin'. The Harrisons won't push you because they're all too nice. Well, I'm pushin' you. It's time for you to put on your big girl pants and choose a new life. We've all been praying for you. And we're here for you." He paused looking at her.

Greta looked at the tall man. "Are you finished?"

"I am."

282 † The Jäger Journal

"Thank you." She abruptly got up, went inside, thanked Jean for dinner, and left.

Washington went back inside. Stuart spoke first, "Well, that went well."

"Maybe not. I just felt like it had to be said. Keep praying for the lady."

"We will," Stuart responded.

*****

Two weeks later, Jack and Jean were relaxing in the den, each quietly reading a book, when there was a light knock on the front door. Jack answered the door. It was Greta. He could tell she had been crying. "Greta! Good evening. Come in."

Greta entered and stood in the foyer uncomfortably, looking down at her feet. Jean came over, "Greta, are you ok?"

Greta burst into sobs as she reached out to Jean. Jean glanced over Greta's heaving shoulder and gave Jack a facial signal that it would be good for the two women to be alone. Jack excused himself to the kitchen.

That night Jean had the privilege of entering the secret place of Greta's heart and leading her to her Maker and Savior. For the first time in her life, Greta felt totally clean and new. Her understanding of the gospel was simple. But the solid certainty of the forgiveness that washed over her soul had changed her life ... forever.

*****

Pastor John Carmichael stood at the front of the overfilled church. To his left, Glen Harrison waited for his bride. Glen was flanked by four groomsmen: his brother Stuart, his brother-in-law Zach Black, and two friends from college. As music rose from the church's organ, one by one the bride's maids glided down the center aisle. Greta's little sister Marta came first. She was followed by Glen's two sisters, Michelle and Annette, and sister-in-law Leigh. Each lady took her station to the right of the pastor and waited for the coming of the bride.

With the first notes of "The Prince of Denmark's March," Jean Harrison and Greta's mother, Elena, both stood. The congregation followed and turned to watch a stunningly beautiful Greta, dressed in traditional white, start toward her groom. Escorting her in his immaculate military dress blues was Sergeant Gabriel Washington.

When Greta and Washington arrived at the altar, the pastor motioned for the congregation to be seated. Washington took Greta's right hand and placed it in Glen's left. The tall soldier took his seat, and the ceremony began.

Pastor Carmichael started by explaining the true meaning of the occasion. "Glen and Greta welcome each of you to share in this joyous occasion with them. The actual significance of marriage has been lost to much of our culture. Marriage is not an invention of man; it is a holy relationship established by God. It was designed to be the best picture on earth of Christ's relationship to his bride, the Church. Marriage is intended to provide great joy. It also demands great sacrifice. You see, that is the nature of true love, a word whose definition much of our culture has come to misunderstand. Marriage is the union of one man and one woman for life." At this declaration, spontaneous "amens" rose from the congregation.

"The husband is to lay down his life for his bride every day. He is to honor her, care for her, provide for her, lead her, and protect her. He is to put her good ahead of his own. He is to study her and learn her ways and her wishes." At this point, Pastor Carmichael looked at Glen and said, "Do your homework, son." This admonition elicited a chorus of chuckles from the audience.

"Glen, if you love Greta in this way, it will be easy for her to love and respect you." Glen nodded, soaking in the weight of the charge being placed upon him. "The task you are embracing is humanly impossible. Only as you listen to the Holy Spirit, are empowered by the grace of Christ, and follow the will of the Father can you fulfill your mission."

"In like manner, the wife is to love and cherish her husband. She must regularly express her admiration for him. She should encourage him, not nag him, in his daily walk with God. As he grows in his faith, the whole family will benefit. The wife is the heart of the home. She sets the emotional temperature. When she gets her joy from intimacy with the Lord, the marriage is energized. As we all know, 'When Mamma ain't happy, ain't nobody happy.'" More laughter. "The wife is to be patient and kind. She is to be faithful to her husband as the church must be faithful to Christ."

Looking at Greta, the pastor said, "Greta, love your man."

The congregation sensed the gravity of the commitments Greta and Glen were making as the rest of the ceremony unfolded. The service ended with the pastor instructing Glen, "Mr. Harrison, you may now kiss your bride." Glen willingly obliged. "Ladies and gentlemen, I would like to introduce, Mr. and Mrs. Glen Harrison."

*****

At the conclusion of the ceremony, Glen and Greta took their place in the reception line forming at the back of the sanctuary. They were all smiles as well wishers passed by, one by one. Next to them, Jean and Jack Harrison received the handoff of guests from Greta. Greta's mother came next.

The wedding guests advanced slowly from one happy face to another. After thirty minutes of handshakes, hugs, tears, and smiles, the end of the line neared. The next to the last person in line was a tall, attractive woman wearing a modest, but stylish blue dress. Her height was accentuated by an expensive pair of shiny black high heel shoes. The woman in blue stepped up to Glen and Greta and smiled, "Congratulations. I wish you a very happy life. You have an exceptional family."

Glen, assuming the woman was a friend of Greta's, responded with a handshake and, "Thanks. We will!"

Greta, discerning no connection between this stranger and Glen's family, simply said, "Hello."

"This came into my hands. I thought you might enjoy having it," the woman said as she handed Greta a wedding gift wrapped in silver paper with a white ribbon and bow.

"Thank you," Greta responded and placed the gift on a small table to the side. She then handed the woman off to Jack with a puzzled look. "This is, I'm sorry, what was your name?"

"Airica, a friend of the family."

"Thank you for coming," Jean said before Jack could speak. The shapely young woman grasped Jean's hand and looked straight into her eyes.

"Mrs. Harrison, you have a matchless husband. I just had to meet the woman who had captured his heart."

"He *is* the love of my life." Jean looked up curiously at her husband's face. She could tell he had no clue who this woman was. "How do you know him?"

"I met him in Atlanta once … a very long time ago."

Jack just nodded his head slowly, the gears in his mind whirling.

"All I can say is, hang on to him," the woman continued.

Jean put her arms around her good husband and then turned once again to speak to the woman in blue. But she was already gone.

*****

After the reception line, the church hosted a dinner for family and friends in the fellowship hall. Over-filled buffet tables bulged along one wall, the delicious food provided by the ladies of Faith Bible Church. Washington, the Harrisons, and the Roses sat at the head table enjoying the food and the blessings of the friends who came over to chat. At one point in the conversation, Jean asked Washington about his Army career. "So does military service run in your family, Gabriel?"

"Sorta. My father was a farmer in eastern Colorado. Raised wheat and chickens. But his father, my grandfather, was a scout in the Army in World War II. After the war he met and married my grandmother, an elegant black teacher from Memphis. Guess he came by the scouting skills honestly, a big plus in the Ardennes. He was full-blooded Cherokee Indian. Had a cool name, too-Shiloh. Shiloh Chadwell."

*****

One week later, Glen and Greta returned to Macon after their honeymoon cruise in the Caribbean. As the couple worked their way through the pile of wedding gifts they had received the day of the wedding, Greta came across a box shaped gift, wrapped in silver paper. She had forgotten the woman in blue until now. "Wonder what this might be?" she said to Glen who sat beside her, writing gift and giver in a small notebook.

"Don't have a clue," he said. "Guess you could just open it and end my suspense," he encouraged her as she read the card attached to the gift.

"Yeah, okay. The card says, 'Have a happy life! Sincerely, Airica.'"

Greta placed the gift on her lap and gently tore the paper off. She gasped as she recognized the dark gray cloth embossed with a diving eagle. "It can't be!" she said. Flipping open the cover, she ran her fingers over the familiar hand written lines. It was, indeed, *The Jäger Journal.*

Meet the Author

Dr. John A. Anderson III resides in middle Tennessee where he practices Family Medicine. Dr. Anderson is an avid reader and especially enjoys military history. He was raised in a military family, his father retiring as a colonel in the United States Air Force. Dr. Anderson and his wife Sandy have six sons and three daughters and have been blessed with two grandsons. He is grateful to his Lord and Savior Jesus Christ for his family and friends and for the opportunity to share his first piece of historical fiction.